ARMY GIRLS: BEHIND THE GUNS

FENELLA J. MILLER

B

Boldwood

First published in Great Britain in 2024 by Boldwood Books Ltd.

Copyright © Fenella J. Miller, 2024

Cover Design by Colin Thomas

Cover Photography: Colin Thomas and Alamy

Every effort has been made to obtain the necessary permissions with reference to copyright material, both illustrative and quoted. We apologise for any omissions in this respect and will be pleased to make the appropriate acknowledgements in any future edition.

A CIP catalogue record for this book is available from the British Library.

Paperback ISBN 978-1-80162-895-2

Large Print ISBN 978-1-80162-894-5

Hardback ISBN 978-1-80162-893-8

Ebook ISBN 978-1-80162-897-6

Kindle ISBN 978-1-80162-896-9

Audio CD ISBN 978-1-80162-888-4

MP3 CD ISBN 978-1-80162-889-1

Digital audio download ISBN 978-1-80162-890-7

Boldwood Books Ltd
23 Bowerdean Street
London SW6 3TN
www.boldwoodbooks.com

For my wonderful daughter-in-law, Karyn, who has read all my books and is still first to read a new one.

1

SEPTEMBER 1942

Ruth Cox was sad to leave Clacton, where she'd been working on the Royal Artillery practice site as a kinetheodolite operator, and especially her new friend Grace Sinclair, who was remaining and would be married to her handsome squadron leader in a few weeks.

Ruth was eager to begin this new adventure. She was going to be retrained to work on a mixed artillery site as a range finder or predictor, which sounded far more exciting than operating a kinetheodolite on a practice base as she'd been doing for the past few weeks.

As she'd arrived at the train station rather late, she had to walk the entire length of the platform looking for somewhere to sit on the already packed train. The guard was about to blow his whistle and wave his green flag, so she flung open the nearest door and scrambled in. Where had all these soldiers come from?

She found a corner in the train corridor and up-turned her large canvas kitbag so she could use it as a seat. The soldiers and ATS on this train would understand what she was going off to do but all a civilian needed to know was that she was going to be involved with firing the big guns that protected the RAF bases, naval dockyards, and other important strategic places.

A large sergeant stepped back and trod on her toes but didn't apologise. As she was only a lance corporal, she couldn't remonstrate with him. Instead, she drew attention to his rudeness. 'Oh, that hurt, someone trod on my foot.' She'd raised her voice so several heads turned, including that of the culprit.

'Then move your bloody feet, woman, there's a war on, you know,' he snarled at her.

What the war had to do with him being an oaf, she'd no idea but thought it better to remain silent and wished she'd not spoken in the first place. Ruth sank into the corner and looked at her boots.

'Don't mind him, love, he's a miserable sod,' a friendly private said to her.

She risked a glance up and smiled. 'Thank you,

I've been in the army long enough to know to keep my mouth shut.'

'Don't worry about it, I reckon he's pissed off about being posted away from his cushy billet here.'

Ruth didn't mind the bad language, but her friend Grace would have been shuddering. 'I asked for my new posting. What about you, where are you off to?'

'I'm not being posted, love, I've got a week's leave. Off to spend time with me missus and me nippers in Romford. Not seen them for three months, but some poor buggers haven't been home for bleeding years.'

'Smithers, shut your gob, a lady doesn't want to hear your foul language,' a young corporal spoke from further down the corridor.

'Beg your pardon, miss, I'll let me betters speak to you,' the soldier said cheerfully, unabashed by the reprimand from the NCO.

Ruth stood up, wanting to see properly the man who'd intervened. He was taller than her, almost six foot, had brown hair and regular features, but attractive, sparkling dark blue eyes. He was smiling at her in a way she'd come to recognise as appreciation. 'Thank you, Corp, but as I'm going to be working in a mixed artillery squad soon, I can't let a bit of swearing bother me.'

The NCO shouldered his way through the other

men and women squashed into the narrow space and ended up rather too close to her.

'I'm Sam Johnson, I'm artillery too.' He nodded towards the white lanyard on his shoulder. 'Are you going to tell me your name?'

Ruth had intended to remain aloof, not wanting to encourage this dangerously attractive man. Instead, she returned his flashing smile. 'I'm Ruth Cox, delighted to meet you.'

'Where are you headed?'

'Arborfield Barracks, I'm a kinetheodolite operator but am going to retrain as a range finder or predictor.'

'Interesting! I know there are already some mixed sections, but not seen one myself. Maybe we'll end up working together one day.'

'Where are you being posted to?' She thought it safer to ignore this last remark and not encourage him. She'd been out a few times with a couple of senior NCOs whilst at Clacton but neither of them had made her feel as flustered as he was doing.

'Can't tell you exactly but we're going to be protecting a bomber base.'

The train lurched and shuddered to a halt and if the passengers hadn't been so tightly packed, they would have gone flying. Sam braced his arms on either side of her and prevented her from falling but this brought him even closer. He didn't take advantage of the moment and immediately stepped away.

The other passengers recovered and began to moan, something soldiers were first class at. Someone near the door dropped the window down and leaned out. Then he turned and yelled down the corridor.

'Blimey, there's a herd of cows on the track. They ain't been hurt but they ain't budging. I reckon as we'll be here a long time.'

'I can shift them. I worked on a dairy farm one summer,' Ruth shouted back.

'My mum's dad was a tenant farmer and his farm has still got a small herd of cows,' Sam said. 'Let's give it a go.' They squeezed their way to the door followed by pats on the back and encouragement. Ruth wished she was wearing her battledress as herding cows would be much easier in trousers.

The train driver and stoker were already on the track, ineffectually waving at the cows who were milling about, as cows do, and mooing. The animals were clumped together and ignoring the men and Ruth thought she might know why they weren't shifting.

'Look over there, the fence is down, that's where they must have got out,' she said, and Sam nodded. Ruth dropped to her haunches and peered through the forest of legs. 'One of them has got a hoof jammed between the rails, we'll need to free the poor thing before any of the others will move.'

Sam called out to the two men making things worse. 'Hang on, mate, there's one stuck. Stop scaring the animals and we'll try and get her free. Have you called the signal box? Is there another train due down this line?'

It was a single line so as long as the signal stayed up, the down train wouldn't be a problem.

'There ain't another one for an hour. If we don't go past Thorpe le Soken then they'll not let the next one onto the line,' one of them said. 'Glad you can help, me and Dave ain't fond of cattle.'

Ruth pointed at the fence. 'Do you think you could check that? See if it can be repaired so they don't get up here again?'

'Fair enough. You get them off of the line and we'll do the rest.'

Sam was clearly enjoying himself. He was smiling, talking softly to the worried cows and they immediately turned to stare at him with their big, soulful brown eyes. 'You're right, I can see the problem. The leg's not broken, thank God, and doesn't appear to have any serious damage.'

'Shall I try and release her as you're doing a great job of calming the others?'

Ruth adopted his soothing tone as she approached the trapped animal and to her surprise, the cow stopped lowing and struggling and nudged her as if saying 'get on with it'.

She ran her hand down the trapped leg and received a second butt, almost tipping her over. 'Enough of that, silly girl, I've come to help you.'

Her highly polished shoes squelched in a cow pat and she heard Sam laugh. After a couple of attempts, the hoof came free but before she'd time to extricate herself from the centre of the small herd, they charged towards the field from which they'd escaped, taking her with them.

She caught a foot on a rail, lost her balance and would have fallen if Sam hadn't grabbed her around the waist. He put his bulk between her and the cows and, after a few seconds, the animals were gone and the drama was over.

* * *

Sam swore. Ruth laughed. He was back in control and let her go. 'That was close. Are you okay? Did any of them tread on you?'

'Apart from the manure on my lovely clean shoes, I'm tickety-boo. What about you?'

'Same here. Shall we try and get the worst off on the grass over there whilst the driver and engineer mend the fence?'

This lovely girl was from a higher class, she sounded different and he'd never met anyone like her. He reckoned not many girls from her posh background could handle a cow like she had. She was out of his league, that was for sure, but he wished she wasn't.

Sam was tempted to do her shoes for her, but Ruth didn't seem the sort of girl who'd appreciate the gesture. For a moment, he'd thought she was going to be trampled and had reacted instinctively. Why hadn't she thanked him for saving her from a nasty experience? As they were cleaning the muck off, he watched her. She'd made a point of choosing a different patch of grass and was making a complete balls of it.

'Here, let me do that. You're just smearing it everywhere.'

'I can do it. Please leave me alone, you make me nervous.'

His eyes widened and for a second he didn't understand. Then he did. Her cheeks were pink, her hands shaking and it wasn't a reaction to the almost accident. Ruth was finding him as attractive as he found her.

He moved nearer but not too close. 'Not half as nervous as you make me. I've never met anyone like you and am fair flummoxed, as my nan would say.'

Her smile did funny things to his insides and he wasn't sure he liked it.

'I've not heard that expression before, but I love it.' She giggled and this made her seem less sophisticated, less out of his league. 'Not a very romantic meeting with both of us smelling of cow pats.'

'I'm tempted to use my handkerchief but don't fancy having it in my pocket when I'm done.'

She tossed away a second handful of lush grass and straightened. 'There, that will have to do until I can use water.' She sniffed her fingers and pulled a face. 'Horrible! Not to worry, I shouldn't think anyone in the train will notice as there's already an overwhelming pong of unwashed bodies and cheap cigarettes.'

He sniffed under his armpit and shook his head. 'Sweet as a baby, no nasty whiffs here, but must agree about most of the others. Need a strong stomach to stand close to some of them.'

'Don't think that gives you permission to stand next to me, Corp, I've only your word about your fragrance. Anyway, as we both smell awful now, it's the others who'll be complaining, not us.'

There were dozens of men standing on the track, most smoking, some just chatting, but two were taking a leak. They had their backs turned but hadn't bothered to walk away from the train and the stream of piss was not only visible, it could be heard splattering on the ground. Ruth had spotted them and was unimpressed.

'I'll deal with those two cretins, they know better than to behave like that.'

'I suppose this sort of thing will be commonplace in a mixed section.'

'God, I hope not. Your sarge, or officer, will be pretty bloody useless if it is.'

She shrugged and climbed easily into the train, despite it being a couple of feet from the ground. As soon as she'd gone, Sam turned his attention to the two who were chatting away as they did up the buttons on their flies, unaware that the wrath of God was about to descend on their heads.

He didn't raise his voice, he spoke quietly so only they could hear. By the time he'd finished, they were ashen faced and terrified. They were also on a charge for conduct unbecoming and would be running around the parade ground in full kit for the next week.

Sam was travelling with his section to an RAF base in Lincolnshire and these men were under his command for the journey.

This wasn't the same as being on one of the big gun parks protecting a city. His section would work on one of the sites positioned close to the perimeter of the base. There would be a small camp for around a hundred or so men and women but only one section would be lucky enough to sleep there on a permanent basis. The other would be in tents when manning the guns and at the base when on general duties.

If he hadn't been flirting with Ruth, he'd have been aware of what was going on with his men and not allowed it to happen. Duty first always, and he'd concentrate on that and not on the lovely girl who'd turned his head so easily.

* * *

With the train corridor now briefly empty, Ruth was able to recover her bag easily and she grabbed it and headed back down the train, not wanting to continue the brief liaison with the charismatic Sam.

As half the passengers had taken the opportunity to exit the hot, stuffy train there were now seats to be had and she edged into the second one she spotted.

The two remaining soldiers inside scowled at her, but she ignored them.

'This seat's taken. Bugger off,' one of them said.

Ruth continued to heave her kitbag onto the overhead rack. She'd checked as she entered that neither of them had stripes, meaning she outranked them. She took a steadying breath and turned to face them. The one next to the speaker saw she was a lance corporal and tried to warn his friend by nudging him.

'I said clear off, you stupid tart. Get your bleeding bag and get out before I do it for you.'

The silent private shrank back into his seat and stared pointedly out of the window, making it clear he wasn't involved.

Ruth had memorised the foul-mouthed soldier's number so whatever happened he was going to be on a charge, even if she was evicted from the compartment.

'You must be blind as well as stupid, private. On your feet. Now.' She barked her order, satisfied she sounded fierce and not intimidated.

For a second, the man gawped at her, his face turned scarlet and he seemed to double in size. Her stomach somersaulted. If he attacked her, would his companion step in to stop him?

Then he launched himself, his fists flailing. One

caught her on the shoulder, knocking her off balance, the other missed. The second private remained in situ and did nothing to help.

Ruth tried to step aside, to avoid the next flurry of punches, but the enraged man, swearing horribly, stepped back, his lips curled in a triumphant snarl and prepared to deliver the coup de grace.

Then Sam was there. He snatched her up, tossed her out of the compartment and whilst she was recovering, he landed two massive punches to the snarling soldier, who flopped senseless in a heap.

The shouting had drawn a crowd and the bad-tempered sergeant shoved his way through the press of khaki and, to give him his due, he took in the situation in one glance. 'You three, take those two little sods and shove them in the guard's van. One of you remain on guard, the other find a redcap.'

'Yes, Sarge,' the men said and as Ruth leaned, breathing heavily, against the windows, the bully was manhandled to his feet and dragged off and the second man was pushed after him.

Sam's knuckles were split but he ignored this and spoke to the sergeant. 'I heard Corporal Cox give them a direct order as I was coming down the corridor and they ignored it. The one I floored attacked her, the other did nothing to help.'

'Bloody good job you were here. Disgraceful behaviour. Are you hurt, young lady?'

She'd recovered her breath by now and was able to speak. 'Just my shoulder and I think that's only bruised. If the corporal hadn't arrived when he did, I think that lunatic would have killed me. I don't think they wanted me to sit in here as these seats had been occupied by their friends.'

'Johnson, get your kit and sit in here with the lance corp. I'll stay here until you get back. Don't be long.'

Ruth needed to sit down but didn't like to step around the big sergeant, but he smiled and moved aside.

'Get settled, no one else will bother you. I'll get these bags shifted so you and Johnson will have the compartment to yourselves. Hope your toes didn't suffer earlier.' He gestured to two lurking privates, presumably the ones with their belongings on the racks above the seat.

'No, Sarge, thank you for asking.' This was the only apology she was going to get but after the way he'd dealt with the incident, she didn't care. She flopped gratefully onto the seat, trying not to wince as a nasty pain travelled from her damaged shoulder to her left wrist.

'You get yourself to a hospital as soon as you get to

London. Johnson's a capable bloke and can go with you. He can make his own way to our new posting once he knows that you're able to continue to yours.'

'Thank you, I'll do that. I'm right-handed but will need both arms fully functioning for my training.' Something occurred to her as he made way for the men to collect their kit. 'Will I have to give a statement?'

He waited until they had the compartment to themselves before answering. 'Give it to Johnson. He can read it out at their court martial.'

Ruth closed her eyes; the pain had become intense and was making her nauseous. It wasn't just a bruise. When she opened them again, Sam was sitting opposite, watching her anxiously and his sergeant had gone. The train was moving and every lurch and jolt made her bite her lip.

'You don't look too good, Ruth. I think you might have broken something.'

'I didn't break anything, that soldier did. Do you have any aspirins or water in your bag?'

He smiled, not the dangerous one he'd used before but one that made him look much younger, more approachable and less alarming.

'I've got some here and my flask's full. Fresh water in this morning.' He leaned across the narrow gap that separated the two rows of seats and dropped two tablets into her good hand. He waited until they were in her mouth before giving her his open flask. It was too heavy for her. He stood up, bracing himself on the rack, then held it to her lips and she was able to swallow enough water to wash the tablets down.

He then produced a folded triangle of khaki material. 'Let me put that arm in a sling. I've got a basic first-aid certificate, it was part of my corporal's course.'

He was professional and efficient and correct that the pain lessened as soon as her elbow was supported.

'I'm to give you a statement but, to be honest, I'm not up to it at the moment.'

'I can write it for you. I know roughly what happened. You can fill in the gaps when you feel better. I'll make things more comfortable for you then you can doze until we reach London.'

He removed her haversack and respirator and then propped them against the window wall and padded them out with his own jacket. He pulled the blinds down so none of the curious soldiers in the passageway could peer in. She smiled her thanks and with his assistance put her feet on the seat and carefully lowered herself back. It was uncomfortable but bearable.

'We're both improperly dressed, Sam, will we be put on a charge too?'

'Don't be daft, we're bloody heroes after saving that cow. Rest now, I'll wake you in time to get properly dressed.'

As she closed her eyes, her lips curved. He'd been quick to discipline that soldier for using bad language but seemed happy to use it himself. This wasn't how she'd thought her new adventure was going to start but it wasn't all bad. She'd dislocated her shoulder but met a very handsome young man. She'd dismissed all thoughts of romance when she joined the ATS, had believed herself immune to it, but there was something about Sam that made her feel he might be someone she wanted to get to know better.

2

Sam was conflicted as he watched Ruth resting on the opposite seat. He'd followed her, wanting to ask if he could write, maybe meet up if they were in the same place at the same time. When he'd seen that bastard about to seriously hurt her, his protective instincts had kicked in and all he could think of was removing the threat in the fastest way possible.

He wasn't a fighter, had never boxed, but from somewhere the necessary skill appeared and he'd knocked her attacker out. He sucked his knuckles and flexed his fingers, pretty sure nothing was broken. Firing one of the massive guns required both hands to function. Not that he actually handled the shells himself any more; his role was to keep his section working efficiently. He was about to go on a sergeants' cadre and when he returned it would be to take overall charge. He wasn't officer material but intended to work his way up the ranks of NCOs until he was a warrant officer.

As the blinds were down and the corridors tightly packed, no inspector would be banging on the compartment demanding that they take their feet off the seats, so he stretched out and tried to relax. He wasn't sure spending the next hour or so alone with Ruth was a good idea. She obviously wasn't as interested in him as he'd first thought or she wouldn't have run off as she had.

He smiled ruefully. She was above his touch anyway, came from the upper classes if her speech was anything to go by. Why would she want to get involved with someone like him? His dad was a builder, and it was his mum's family who were tenant farmers. Just a small place, more a smallholding than a farm, and it didn't make them posh.

Sam had left school at fourteen and worked for his grandad, who was knocking on a bit, until the war started and he immediately volunteered. He'd have liked to have been a Brylcreem boy, but you had to have a good education to join the RAF. He didn't like the sea, so the navy was out, which only left the army.

Ruth stirred and instantly he was sitting up, ready to offer his help. She opened her eyes and looked at him.

'Thank you for saving me, Sam, you're a real hero,' she said. He raised his eyebrows and she smiled. 'Don't look at me like that, I wasn't being facetious. Do you box for your regiment?'

'No, that was the first time I've ever punched anyone. I prefer words to fists.'

She nodded. 'Why did that soldier react so violently? Is he unbalanced?'

'To be honest, I don't know him very well as he only joined the section a few weeks ago. He was transferred.'

'What will happen to him now?'

'He'll have the book thrown at him. If you're feeling well enough, shall we get your statement done now?'

Ruth gave a clear and brief account of what had happened and as she dictated, he wrote it down. He'd always had a flair for English and had won a school prize for his handwriting.

'That's perfect, Ruth, and I can confirm your statement as I heard most of what happened from outside. It will make it simpler for the panel.'

She frowned. 'Simpler? Are you saying my word isn't good enough?'

'Of course not. You're a lance corp, anything you say trumps whatever version those two might come up with. I'm going to dig out their service records and see if there's anything there of interest.'

She sighed and closed her eyes again and he studied her, trying to fathom why this girl had had such an impact on him. She was about average height, had ordinary brown hair, a pretty smile and astonishing blue eyes. He'd met far more attractive girls before but had never felt an instant connection like this.

'Do you like what you see, Sam?'

He laughed. 'Ruth the Remarkable. Not only able to wrangle cows but also can see with her eyes shut. You'd make a fortune in the circus.'

'My eyes aren't quite shut. You didn't answer my question.'

'Yes, I do like what I see, in fact I like it far too much. Isn't there a French phrase for what's happened?'

'*Coup de foudre* is what you're searching for.' Her eyes flickered open and she stared straight at him. 'I find you attractive too, but I'd not go as far as saying I'd been stuck by the lightning bolt of love.'

He clutched his chest and widened his eyes. 'I'm

devastated that you don't return my undying affection. I shall wither away, drowned by my unrequited love.'

Ruth giggled. 'You can't wither and drown, but I'm touched by your sentiments, misplaced though they are. Be quiet and let me suffer in silence.'

'As long as there are no more delays, we'll be in London in an hour. I'll organise transport for us to the nearest hospital.'

She didn't answer but raised a hand to acknowledge that she'd heard. It was strange how it was as if they'd been friends for weeks, not an hour. Was it because they'd already shared more excitement than most couples do in a year?

He was still pondering on the mysteries of love when there was a kerfuffle in the corridor and he just had time to sit up and drop his boots to the floor when the door slid open.

He jumped to his feet and saluted. Ruth tried to move, but the pain made her yelp.

'At ease, both of you. I've just heard what happened. Bloody bad show.'

The officer, a major, was a senior medic, but Sam didn't know his name.

'Right, you clear off, Corp, I'm going to examine my patient.'

Sam was at the door when Ruth stopped him.

'Please stay, Sam.'

She should have asked the doc but he nodded and then ignored him.

The medic deftly unbuttoned Ruth's jacket and shirt. He muttered under his breath.

'Make yourself useful, Bombardier, get over here and give me a hand.' He then spoke to Ruth, who was gritting her teeth and ghostly pale. 'You've partially dislocated your shoulder, young lady, I'm going to put it back in place. It will be bloody painful for a few seconds but then you'll be fine.'

Sam had seen this done once before and knew why he was needed. His job was to hold her still whilst the shoulder was put back in place. Ruth was now sitting up, her feet on the floor, and he knelt on the seat to her right and then put his arm firmly around her.

He nodded and gripped tight. The doctor held her left elbow at right angles to her body and slowly rotated her arm. Ruth was magnificent and didn't move, even though the procedure must have been agony.

'There, all done. Good girl, you made less fuss than many men I've treated.'

She slowly relaxed and then opened her eyes. 'That was horrible but it's so much better now, thank you, sir. Does that mean I don't have to go to hospital?'

'Keep it in the sling for a few days to give the muscles and ligaments time to heal. You were lucky, if it had come right out you might have been on sick leave for a fortnight. I'll give you a note for your CO.'

Fifteen minutes after his arrival, the medic was gone, no doubt back to first class. The lowly rank and file travelled in third.

'You look much better, Ruth. Are you okay now?'

'Tickety-boo, thanks. Just a bit sore and stiff. Hefting my kit about one-armed isn't going to be fun, but I'll manage.'

'I'll escort you to your train and carry it for you.'

'You could put up the blinds and let some of those who are standing come in.'

'No, I want to get to know you a bit better first. We've still got half an hour before we arrive at Liverpool Street so we can tell each other our life stories.'

* * *

Ruth wasn't sure she wanted to know Sam's life story as the more time she spent with him, the better she liked him, and she didn't want to be involved with anyone right now. She was determined to do her duty to king and country and falling in love with a stranger wasn't part of her plan.

'It's not fair to hog this compartment when our men have to stand. I'm letting them in.'

She didn't wait for him to disagree, or even worse, to give her a direct order to sit down, and she was about to release the blind on her side and had her hand on the door before he reacted.

'Stop, don't try and open it. You've got to be careful with your shoulder for a week at least. Let me do it.'

'I was going to use my good hand. I didn't realise doing that wasn't allowed.'

He smiled. 'I understand if you're not keen on being alone with me, after all, you don't know me. However, would you really rather spend the remainder of the journey squashed in with the great unwashed? They'll want to smoke.'

'If you put it like that, then probably not. Do you smoke?'

'I used to but gave it up, I don't like the taste of tobacco in my mouth first thing. Same with beer. I like one or two but don't like spirits, not that you can get any nowadays unless you're an officer.'

They resumed their seats and after a few minutes her reservations about Sam began to fade. He was charming and excellent company. She told him about being brought up by a maiden aunt and how she'd met her best friend, Grace Sinclair, whilst training to be a kinetheodolite operator.

'A skilled and necessary trade but taking photographs of incoming aircraft and then analysing the photos later isn't the same as actually working on a live site,' he said. 'I'm not surprised you want to train to be a range finder or predictor. Would you be happy on the searchlights?'

'Absolutely, I applied for all three but this course came up first. I'm going to go on the cadre to become a corporal as soon as I've passed.'

'I'm off on a similar course to be a sergeant. I've got to settle my men in and then will be posted but not sure where. Like you, I couldn't wait to leave Clacton, firing at an aircraft towing a banner isn't the same as shooting down a German.'

'I don't suppose all your section are as eager as you to leave what's basically a cushy posting. No danger, often no work on weekends and plenty of things to do in your free time.'

'Only a few are fed up about the move, most of them want to do more than practise just so the engineers and technicians can improve our accuracy.'

The engine driver was applying the brakes for the final time. In a few minutes, they'd be steaming into Liverpool Street. Her injured shoulder was sore but nothing to worry about, but she was glad Sam would be there to heft her heavy kitbag on and off the bus that would be waiting for them outside the station.

'Let's wait until the train's empty, Ruth, that way you won't be jostled. We're not in a hurry, in fact as you've now got three days' sick leave, why don't we skive off and find a Lyons Corner House and grab a cuppa?'

'You don't have leave and I don't want to get you into trouble.' He looked disappointed so she compromised. 'Why don't we find something at Paddington? There's usually a decent cafe, isn't there?'

The train rocked to a standstill whilst they were talking. The noisy soldiers had gone and the passageway would be clear now.

'Not just beauty but brains too. Much better plan. Come on, we can venture out now.'

He released all three blinds before opening the door. Then he tossed his own bag over his left shoulder and grabbed the handles of hers.

As he'd used his left hand, this meant he had his right one free so he could assist Ruth if she needed it. The carriage door was swinging open and she stepped out carefully, not sure if the jar of her foot hitting the platform would aggravate her shoulder. It did and she winced.

'I'd offer to give you a piggyback but there's no room, sorry.'

'Golly, that would have been fun. I'm sure I could hop aboard if you weren't so feeble that just two kit-bags are too much for you.'

He laughed and so did she. Saying goodbye to him was going to be hard and that was silly as they'd only been friends for an hour or so. There was an empty bus just pulling up but there was still a long queue of soldiers waiting to get on.

'We'll catch the next one, Ruth, they come round every five minutes or so at busy times like this,' Sam said.

'It's a terrific system, isn't it? Free transport to all the mainline stations for all service people. It must have been more difficult during the Blitz last year.'

'Still is where there's been a lot of bomb damage.'

They didn't have to wait long but as the next bus was full too, Sam stood and Ruth took one of the few free seats. He stood the bags on end, on one on top of the other, and gripped them with his knees.

'What are you going to do if someone wants to get off before us?'

'I'll put one on your lap, if that's okay.'

Their luck held and Sam didn't have to move until it was their turn to disembark. Ruth's shoulder was suffering from the jolting and jerking and she wasn't looking forward to the long train journey, possibly crammed into the corridor.

Paddington had a small restaurant and they found an empty table. She was conscious of the sympathetic looks she was getting because of her sling.

'Do you think I could ask to sit in a ladies-only compartment because of my injury?'

'I'm going to insist that they allow it. Might even be able wangle first class.'

Ruth wasn't sure how he'd be able to achieve this as he might be an imposing figure, but he wasn't an officer, and she doubted a lowly corporal would have much influence over a ticket inspector.

'I should have checked when my train leaves before coming in here.'

'I don't mind what I eat, so will you order something for me whilst I go and find out? I'll also speak to someone about your upgrade.'

He stacked the two bags against the wall and was about to leave when he hesitated. 'I'm rather taking over, aren't I? Do you mind? I don't want to seem overbearing. I'll stay here and order if you would prefer to organise things for yourself?'

A rush of something she didn't recognise enveloped Ruth. He was so kind, so empathetic, and she nodded. 'Thank you so much for asking. Yes, please do it all for me, I've looked after myself for the past two years and I'm rather enjoying being taken care of.'

His smile was blinding. 'Yes, ma'am, Bombardier Johnson, soon to be Sergeant Johnson, at your service.'

'Before you dash off, I'm happy to pay the extra if you can't arrange an upgrade for free.'

'Understood. I'm going to try and persuade whoever's in charge at the ticket office that you deserve to be travelling comfortably, but if that fails I'll buy a ticket and you can reimburse me.'

A tiny waitress who looked about ten, in a uniform that swamped her, hovered by the table, her order pad at the ready.

'I'd like a pot of tea for two and whatever sandwiches and cakes are available. We really don't mind as long as there's plenty.'

The diminutive girl beamed. 'That's easy then. How'd you hurt your arm?'

'I was knocked over by a herd of cows whilst saving one from an oncoming train.' Not true but it made a good story and made the waitress laugh.

'Blimey, that's a turn-up for the books. I never heard the like. Did the cow get free all right?'

'It did. I dislocated my shoulder but an army doctor put it back on the train, hence the sling.'

'Is that handsome bloke your fella? Wish he was mine.'

Ruth thought the girl was far too young to be interested in boys but smiled and shook her head. 'No, his commanding officer ordered him to accompany me and see me safely onto my next train.'

The girl smiled sympathetically. 'Shame that, he's a smasher.'

Ruth smiled. She didn't think being handsome was important, but it certainly helped.

When Sam returned, Ruth told him how her friend had rescued four horses at Romford market and he laughed.

'We're exactly the same age and hit it off from the start,' she said. 'Grace is tall, blonde and beautiful, whereas I'm average in every way.'

'Average? If you're average then I'm the Queen of Sheba,' he said as he picked up a fourth sandwich. 'You're stunning, intelligent and funny.'

'Goodness, how kind of you to say so, thank you. I wasn't fishing for compliments. I really do think I'm nothing out of the ordinary.'

'Then it's my pleasure to inform you that you're nothing of the kind. Now, eat up, there's plenty left.'

'I couldn't eat another morsel. I'm hoping our little waitress will pack it up for us so we can eat it later. I have to get transport to the barracks at Arborfield from Reading station. I might have a long wait as they won't send a lorry until all the trainees have arrived. Having the remains of our lunch to keep me going would be helpful.'

The remaining sandwiches and pastries were packed in two greaseproof paper parcels neatly tied with string and returned by the smiling girl who'd served them so well.

'There you are, they'll stay nice and fresh for your journey now,' she said.

Sam slipped his into the top of his bag and then did the same for hers. He then gave the girl half a crown and asked for the bill.

The waitress skipped away clutching her tip. 'That was far too much, Sam, it's more than she's likely to earn in a day,' Ruth said.

'I'm flush at the moment, and she deserved it. I'm also paying for the food and want no argument from you, Lance Corporal. Is that clear?'

'I'm not going to argue. Thank you, but next time I'm paying or there won't be a next time. Do I make myself clear, Bombardier?'

* * *

The time passed too quickly and they were both unwilling to end the meeting. In silence they walked the length of the station and onto the platform where her train was waiting. Ruth was thrilled that Sam had a first-class ticket for her and it hadn't cost her a thing.

'You could go to the dining car for a meal if you wanted to. Only the wealthy have that luxury.'

'I might ask the attendant to bring me a coffee, but I won't venture there myself.'

He turned suddenly and his expression was serious. 'Will you write to me, Ruth? You've got my number.'

She didn't hesitate. 'Yes, of course I will. I'll write as soon as I'm settled. Will you do the same? I've enjoyed meeting you. You're the nicest soldier I've met.'

'And you're the best ATS I've met. I can't tell you how happy I am that I was on that train.'

'Cows and punches, what a start to our friendship.'

They exchanged a friendly smile.

3

Sam hoped he'd hidden his pleasure that Ruth had agreed to meet him again. 'You've got my name and number and I've got yours so writing to each other will be easy. You won't get any leave whilst you're training but you should get at least a week before your permanent posting. If we're lucky, my leave will coincide with yours and we could meet up in the Smoke.'

'I'm going on the corporal cadre as soon as I'm qualified to do whatever I'm going to be doing in the future. I don't think there's any restriction to NCOs going out with each other.'

'There certainly isn't, so unless you become an officer, which I think's quite likely…'

She shook her head. 'I've absolutely no intention of doing that. My friend Grace is going to become an officer but I decided a long time ago I didn't want to be one.'

'I'll say goodbye now as I don't have to come into the train with you,' he said, not sure if he would risk a small kiss before he left. He handed her bag to the waiting porter and she showed him her ticket.

'This way, madam, I'll take you to your designated seat.'

'Thank you, I'm just going to say goodbye to my friend.'

She closed the few inches between them and hugged him. He held her close for a few seconds and stepped away.

'Today is the best day of my life, Ruth, I think this might be the start of something really special, don't you?'

Her eyes shone and she smiled. 'I keep talking about my best friend, Grace, but it's quite extraordinary, really. She met her future husband, Squadron Leader Christopher Holloway, and within hours they were inextricably linked. She's only known him a few weeks and already they're planning to get married.'

He clapped his hand to his forehead and made a

pretence of staggering back in shock. 'Married? I only asked you to write to me.'

She giggled and he grinned. 'You never know your luck, Bombardier Johnson. Maybe in a decade I might have decided I do want to get married and possibly to you.'

The porter had appeared at the door and was looking impatient. 'You'd better go, Ruth, and so had I. Thank you for an exciting and possibly life-changing few hours.'

She squeezed his hand, smiled and jumped into the train. He wasn't going to hang about and wave, that wasn't his style, so he slung his bag over his shoulder and marched out of the station.

Sam made his way into the forecourt, where he was fortunate to find a bus just pulling up. He climbed on board and settled back, not sure exactly how far King's Cross was from Paddington. He didn't notice the landmarks, nor was he aware of the time, he was lost in thought. Why had he fallen so hard and so fast for a girl he scarcely knew?

'King's Cross, next stop,' the conductor yelled from the front of the bus, disturbing his musing. Sam grabbed his bag and was ready to jump out as it rattled to a halt.

On entering the noisy station, he immediately

spotted four men who were directly under his command. Surely there'd been a train earlier than this? He recognised them as men he'd had to caution, cajole, and bawl out on many occasions. He strode across to confront them.

'What the hell are you shower doing here? Why aren't you halfway to Lincolnshire by now?'

The leader of the group, a slimy bastard with an unsavoury reputation, smirked and Sam almost lost his temper.

'Well, I'm waiting? Benson, you seem to find the situation amusing. Do you want to share the joke?'

Benson took a final drag on his fag, pinched it out and pushed the stub into his top pocket before answering. Sam clenched his fists – punching another private wouldn't be a good idea.

'It's like this, Corp, we had to go to the bog, got caught short we did. When we got to the platform, the bleeding train had gone. Ain't another one until four o'clock.'

Sam glanced at the large station clock. It was two thirty and he knew for a fact there was a train that left in five minutes. 'I don't believe a word, but I'll deal with you when we get to the base. We'll travel together. Fall in. Shun.'

He barked the last command and obedience was

so ingrained into the four of them that they jumped to attention. 'Pick up bags.' He waited a few seconds for them to comply. 'Quick march, left, right, left, right.'

They had no option but to obey and he marched them in reasonable order to the train and they clambered into the carriage he indicated and shuffled along the narrow corridor, looking into the doors in the hope there might be a free seat. For once it wasn't standing room only.

The guard slammed the door behind him, the whistle shrilled, and the train lurched forward. The four men stopped at a door further down and vanished. There were a couple of empty seats in the compartment nearest to Sam and he edged his way in. There was an ATS corporal, a couple of privates, a harassed-looking young woman with two small grizzling children and a Brylcreem boy. He thought that RAF aircrew travelled by plane, not in a train.

'Excuse me, folks, I'll put my kitbag on the rack and sit down.' Only the pilot responded.

'Teddy Atkinson, are you heading my way?'

'Sam Johnson, I think I probably am.'

Neither of them mentioned the name of the base as there were civilians present. The mother became exasperated with the older child and slapped him hard on the back of his legs, which just made him howl even louder.

'Do you want me to have him over here for a bit?' Sam smiled at the woman and held his hand out to the boy. The still-crying child didn't hesitate and rushed across and clambered into the space in the seat between Sam and the airman.

'Here, son, use my hanky. I don't want you to wipe your nose on my jacket.'

Teddy, who was sitting next to him, dipped into his pocket and pulled out a bag of humbugs. God knows where he'd got those. 'If you stop making that racket, you can have one of these. What's your name?'

The boy gulped and sniffed and blew his nose before answering. 'I'm Alfie Smith, mister, and that's me sister Mary. That ain't me ma – that's me auntie. Me ma's dead, me pa's in the army and we've got to go and live with me auntie and me grandma in the *country*.'

Sam and Teddy changed an astonished glance. The little boy couldn't be more than four or five years old and yet spoke like a child twice his age. He emphasised the word country as if he was being sent to a prisoner of war camp. He then held out a grubby hand for his promised treat.

'Here you are, Alfie. Is your sister old enough to have one of these without choking?' Teddy asked.

The auntie nodded vigorously. 'Yes, please, sir. Might I have one too?'

Again, Sam was surprised that the young woman spoke so well – no sign of the East End in her diction.

'Of course, there's plenty here, I was fortunate enough to go to the PX – the American equivalent of the NAAFI, in case you're wondering – and was given these.'

The other three in khaki were now looking hopeful and everybody in the carriage was soon sucking away happily, the atmosphere changed and there was a pleasant aroma of mint. By the time they arrived at Lincoln, they were all the best of friends and Flying Officer Teddy Atkinson had already got the name and address of the harassed young woman escorting her niece and nephew from London to their new home.

Sam was smiling as he rounded up his errant men and herded them to the exit. He wasn't going to hang about and if there wasn't transport waiting then they'd have to march to the base, which would serve them right for trying to waste time in London.

* * *

Ruth decided that travelling first class for so short a journey wasn't really worth the expense. Scarcely an hour after leaving Paddington, she was told discreetly that the next stop was Reading. There was no need for her to struggle with her belongings as, being a first-class passenger, this was taken care of for her.

A porter was waiting to assist her from the train and he shouldered her large bag and her haversack and she followed him through the quiet rural station to the exit.

'There aren't any taxis any more, miss, so I hope someone from Arborfield is coming to collect you.' The porter dropped her kitbag beside her feet and waited expectantly for his tip. She had a silver six-pence ready and he seemed satisfied with that.

She'd no idea where the barracks were but assumed there must be a regular bus service which would run from somewhere close to the station. As she couldn't carry her kitbag, she was stumped as to how to proceed.

'You must be going to Arborfield too,' a tall, slim, bespectacled girl said as she dumped her bag next to Ruth's.

'I am, were there any more of us on the train, do you know?'

'I didn't see anybody, but I expect they caught the

earlier train as we were supposed to be there an hour ago. I can see that you've got a really good excuse for being late, I wish that I had.'

Ruth didn't hesitate. 'I'm Ruth Cox, I'll say that you stayed behind to help me. That should be sufficient.'

The girl flushed and seemed unsure whether to accept this offer. 'I'm Jill Fisher, thank you ever so, but I don't think that will work as we didn't travel together.'

'Well, there was nobody there to confirm or deny this and I'm sure nobody will bother to investigate. We just need to get our story straight. I came from Liverpool Street – where did you come from?'

Jill shook her head. 'Good grief, so did I. You must be the heroine who saved the day and moved the cows from the line. I suppose I'd better explain why I am actually late. My fiancé managed to wangle a few hours off – he's something at the War Office and we spent a few precious hours together.'

'Good for you, I ate a leisurely lunch at the restaurant at Paddington with a friend, so we can help each other out.' Ruth smiled encouragingly. 'Sam's assistance can be replaced by yours and nobody will be any the wiser.'

The girl nodded. 'All right then, thanks! I heard the porter say there aren't any taxis. How on earth are we going to get to the barracks as they're hardly going to send transport for two tardy arrivals?'

Ruth had been watching the road that ran past the station and saw a camouflaged staff car turning in. 'You're wrong – I think this car's for us.'

She was right and the ATS driver greeted them cheerfully. 'Good show, I was wondering how you managed to get here with only one arm in use. I'll put your bags in, you hop in.'

The bags were stowed in the front passenger seat and the chatty girl driving them gave them some invaluable information.

'The others went to Wokingham station and arrived ages ago. Your sergeant said you must have come here instead and sent me to find you. Did the cows hurt you?'

'No, I was attacked by a private on the train who didn't want me to sit in the same compartment as him.'

'Crikey, how shocking! It's not far so don't get comfortable. I'm to drop you at the medical centre, Lance Corporal Cox, the doctor wants to check you out himself.'

'What about me? Do you know where I'm to report?' Jill asked anxiously.

'I expect there'll be someone there you can ask.

The new intake of trainees are all in the same hut, so you might as well go straight there.'

The car was comfortable but Ruth was glad to get out, even if it did mean being prodded and poked by another medic.

'Jill, would you please take my bag and find me a bed?'

'I'd be happy to. I'll unpack for you as well if you'd like me to.'

'That would be so kind. I hope I won't be long.'

Ruth had expected to be examined by a junior doctor but was ushered into a room where a grey-haired man was waiting to examine her. He was obviously somebody senior – from his insignia, she could see he had the rank of major.

'Where the devil have you been? I've been hanging about here for an hour and I've got better things to do than look after an ATS girl,' he snapped.

She couldn't salute so didn't try. 'I apologise, sir. Travelling with a recently dislocated shoulder isn't pleasant and it wasn't possible to get here any sooner. Without the help of Private Fisher, I'd still be at Liverpool Street station now.'

He raised a bushy eyebrow and for a second she thought she was in big trouble. It wasn't a wise move to contradict an officer.

'Hmm, fair enough. Now, let me have a look.'

Despite being grumpy, he was gentle and hardly hurt her at all. 'Right, there's inflammation and bruising which is only to be expected. You can attend the lectures and observe the practical stuff but you can't participate until I've given you the all-clear.'

This was the best possible news as Ruth had expected to be sidelined for the next few days. 'Thank you, I don't want to miss a thing. How long will it be, sir, before my shoulder's fully functioning?'

'Not as soon as you were hoping. If you use it before it's fully recovered, you'll have problems with it for the rest of your life. Don't look so dispirited, young lady, you're an intelligent girl and will learn everything you need to whilst you're here.'

He moved the screen back in front of her so she could dress and then handed her a slip of paper. She glanced down and saw that it excused her from any physical activities for the next two weeks.

'Off you go. No rush – your course doesn't start until tomorrow morning.'

Ruth didn't like to ask him where her billet was but she found a helpful male private who gave her excellent directions. As she arrived, a dozen girls came out and they seemed a friendly enough bunch.

Her home for the next few weeks was a large

wooden hut, spacious, but the sleeping arrangements were alarming. Rickety metal bunk beds that swayed when anyone got on or off weren't ideal for her injured shoulder.

Jill was apologetic about the sleeping arrangements. 'This was the only one left, all the others were occupied. I've taken the top as obviously you can't scramble onto that at the moment.' She pointed to the hooks and the locker on the adjacent wall. 'I've put everything away for you – at least I knew how to do that properly as everybody has to do it exactly the same way.'

'It's a relief to be on the bottom bed. Thank you for unpacking, I really do appreciate your help.'

Jill glanced over her shoulder nervously and didn't answer until she was sure nobody could overhear them. There were only half a dozen girls in the large room and they were at the far end.

'I should be thanking you. I was terrified I was going to be put on a charge and have to clean the lavatories for a week or march around the parade ground in full kit every evening for being AWOL.'

'Good heavens, Jill, you were hardly absent without leave. You'd only been missing a couple of hours. I think we're more than even.'

Ruth quickly explained what the medic had said

and they both agreed this was the most practical solution. 'We've missed tea, but you must have seen the slightly squashed selection of sandwiches and pastries I had in my bag. If we can scrounge a mug of tea, there's more than enough for the two of us.'

'I've put the food in your locker – it looks and smells very appetising. Mind you, I've not eaten since I left Clacton this morning and am absolutely ravenous.'

Ruth looked around her temporary home and was satisfied that she'd be comfortable here. She was used to sleeping on uncomfortable beds and at least these beds had an actual mattress, so they didn't have to assemble the three biscuits into a lumpy bed.

'If you go in search of the tea then I'll put things out on the table at the far end of the room. It's nice that we've got somewhere to sit and that we don't have to stack the beds every morning as we usually do.'

'I won't be long. I've just got to post a letter to my Arthur letting him know that I've arrived safely and won't be put on a charge.' Jill smiled as she spoke, her eyes alight with love, and she changed from plain to beautiful.

Ruth really liked Jill and hoped they were going to be good friends.

Over the impromptu shared tea, Ruth learnt all

about her new friend and her fiancé. Arthur sounded as if he was some sort of intelligence officer, but she didn't like to press for further information. They planned to get married as soon as they could after Jill finished this training.

Ruth didn't contradict Jill, who just assumed that she and Sam had already been going out together before the incidents on the railway track and in the train. She didn't want to shock her new friend by revealing the true circumstances.

'I'm going to enjoy working in a mixed section, aren't you?'

'Actually, I rather liked being just with women. I find men rather intimidating – apart from my Arthur. He's a lamb in wolf's clothing if you get what I mean.' Her happy smile slipped a little. 'At least he is with me.'

Ruth wondered what Jill meant but smiled anyway. 'I certainly do. I have friend who is also engaged but to a squadron leader and she hopes to get married fairly soon too. Imagine that – I might be invited to two weddings, and I've never even been to one.'

'Perhaps the third wedding will be your own.'

'Good heavens, I shouldn't think so. We're not at that point yet.'

4

Sam delivered the men in his charge to the redcaps and gave the army military police a full account of what he'd encountered. 'This shower need a wake-up call. I think a week's fatigues and doubling round the parade ground in full kit should do the trick.'

'Righto, Corp,' the MP said.

Sam completed his written statement and then went in search of his billet. Sometimes a Bombardier had to share a small, curtained cubicle, which gave him limited privacy, in the same hut that the men lived in. They had their own mess, that was the only privilege.

However, as he was about to be promoted to sergeant, he was given separate accommodation – not quite his own room, as he had to share with another senior NCO, but better than sleeping with the privates.

If he was an officer, he'd have an orderly to take care of him but he was happy with his lot. He was used to taking care of himself. The room was a decent size with two wardrobes and two chests of drawers, as well as hooks on either side of the door. No sink, so he'd have to use the ablutions like everyone else. The bloke he was sharing with was obviously like him and preferred his personal space tidy.

It might be a bit tricky sharing with a sergeant until he was actually at the same rank, but Sam was sure he'd have no difficulty as he considered himself an easy-going sort of bloke. He came across the grease-proof paper-wrapped parcel of food and tucked it into his pocket. All he needed was a cup of char to go with it and he'd be tickety-boo.

He was singing a Glen Miller favourite of his, 'Chattanooga Choo Choo', but not loudly as he knew there could be people on nights trying to get some kip. He was a decent tenor and was always in demand when there was a sing-song in the local pub. He could also play any tune on the piano that he heard on the wireless. He was interrupted by the door bursting open without the courtesy of a knock first.

'Bloody hell, you're just the man I'm looking for.

I'm Charlie Green, ENSA, the Entertainments National Service Association. We're doing a show tonight at the officers' mess and my lead singer has got the squits.'

Sam laughed. The men he'd met who travelled around the place entertaining service people were a law unto themselves. 'Okay, I'm happy to help. I've only just arrived, as you can see, so I need to report before I can do anything else.'

'Fair enough, I'll come with you so you can't escape. The Brylcreem boys will appreciate your sacrifice, although I doubt that your commanding officer will be as pleased.' He beamed. 'This is our last performance before we head out to entertain the troops overseas. We want it to be memorable for the audience and for us.'

Until Charlie had mentioned the RAF, Sam hadn't grasped the fact that he was going to have to ask his new commanding officer for permission to leave the barracks when he'd only just arrived – even if the reason was a good one. There was intense rivalry between those in khaki and those in air-force blue and somehow, he doubted he'd be allowed to go and sing with the troupe when he'd just arrived.

'How did you come to be prowling around my billet, Charlie?'

'Good question, I was on my way to break the bad news to our troupe when I heard your dulcet tones through the open window and came at once to find you.' He smiled hopefully. 'I don't suppose you play the Joanna as well.'

'I do, but I don't read music so unless I know the tunes or can hear them first, I won't be any good to you.'

'That's the ticket – we're rehearsing in your rec room. You go ahead and tell them you're joining us for today and I'll beetle off to speak to your CO.'

'Good luck with that, my friend, I don't envy you. I'm supposed to be getting my lads into shape, not gallivanting about the place singing songs to the boys in blue.'

Charlie rushed off and Sam wandered into the room that was usually peopled by off-duty NCOs and officers who didn't want to spend time in the bar. He was surprised to find it empty of these NCOs and officers but brimming with members of ENSA. He quickly explained why he was there and they greeted him like a hero.

He didn't want to tell them that their enthusiasm was misplaced as it was unlikely he'd get permission to join them even for an evening, but to his surprise and their delight, he was proved wrong.

'Major Silverton's going to be at the performance at the invitation of Wing Commander Reynolds and is only too happy to have one of his men make the performance viable.'

'What about my duties here? Did he say anything about that?'

'He said you can be spared from those but not from being part of our performance. Now – I'd better fill you in on the programme.'

* * *

At the end of the afternoon, Sam was fully integrated into the ENSA party. He'd drawn the line at dressing up in silly clothes but was quite happy to accompany those that did and sing lustily when required. The fact that he had two solos didn't faze him and he was looking forward to the evening.

'Okay, Charlie, I'm going to eat my scoff and find something hot and wet to wash it down with. Where's the NAAFI?'

Sam found it easily and with a mug of strong stewed tea, he retreated to the far side of the noisy room, where there were a few empty tables. He nodded at the men and they nodded back. Only privates over here, the officers and senior NCOs seemed to sit on the other side of the NAAFI. He wasn't sure about the etiquette of eating your own food but there was a war on, nothing must be wasted, even if it meant breaking some rule or other.

He was happily munching a squashed sausage roll when a grey-haired sergeant, with an impressive moustache, stomped over to his table.

'I'm Tommy Hart. You've just moved into my room.'

The bloke didn't seem too happy about this. Sam swallowed his mouthful and tried to look enthusiastic, although the prospect of sharing with this old bloke didn't appeal.

'I'm Sam Johnson, but I'm assuming you already know that. Pleased to meet you, Sarge.'

'I'm having you relocated. Being asked to share with a new sergeant was bad enough but I'm certainly not sharing with a yet-to-be-promoted whipper-snapper like you.'

'Hardly worth the effort, Sarge, as I'm only going to be here a few days before I go on the sergeant's cadre. I should think you'll probably have retired by the time I return as your equal.' This was hardly conciliatory, but he wasn't going to be pushed about by anyone and certainly not going to allow Hart to turf him out of his room.

Sam was waiting for the outburst, for the direct order to move his stuff, but to his astonishment the old codger smirked and pulled out a chair.

'Well said, my boy, I'm not prepared to share with any mealy-mouthed little bugger. We'll get along famously. What's this I hear about you cosying up with those ENSA poofters? Hope you're not a shirt-lifter yourself?'

Sam choked on his tea. He spluttered for a few moments before he was able to reply to this outrageous remark. 'The lads in ENSA are decent chaps. I don't appreciate your crudeness, Sarge, and if you don't mind, I'd prefer to finish my meal in peace.'

This time he'd really offended his roommate, but it couldn't be helped. Prejudice of any kind wasn't acceptable.

The remark didn't go down well. Hart slammed back his chair with such force it clattered over and attracted unwanted attention. 'You'll regret talking to me like that, Johnson. I'm going to make your life a misery. You'll be begging for a transfer by the time I've finished with you.'

Sam ignored this outburst, didn't look up and continued to eat his crumpled sandwiches and drink his tea as if Sergeant Hart was invisible. He waited until he was alone before calmly getting up and replacing the chair. He looked up and nodded at those staring in his direction. He wasn't reassured when they all looked away.

He had a nasty suspicion he'd poked the hornet's nest and was going to regret this incident. There was nothing he could do about it and he wasn't a man to worry about things he couldn't change – if the old bastard wanted to make his life difficult then so be it. He'd had worse when he was in basic training and survived.

* * *

Ruth enjoyed Jill's company and knew she'd be a good friend, but perhaps not as close as Grace was. After their impromptu tea, Jill kindly washed their irons – which was what they called their cutlery and mug – whilst she wrote her first letter of what she hoped would be many to Sam.

There wasn't a lot to tell him apart from having met a new friend and having to sleep on an unstable ancient bunk bed. She was surprised that some of the girls had left the base and didn't return until curfew. One of them told her that they'd found a dance hall about three miles away and had walked there and back as well as dancing every dance.

'I suppose I can't really go off base until I'm given

the all-clear. If I'm fit enough to walk six miles and whirl around a dancefloor then really I should be participating in the physical aspects of our course.'

'While I'm quite happy to give it a miss, I don't want to dance with anyone but my fiancé. We can play cards and board games as well as write letters – we won't be bored and will certainly be less exhausted than those that have just got back,' Jill said as she collected her wash bag and prepared to go to the ablutions and latrines before turning in.

'At least my arm's not in plaster so I can take it out of the sling to wash and so on.'

They'd left it late to avoid the rush and when they went out in the dark, glad they'd remembered their torches, they realised they didn't know exactly where these blocks were.

It was much further than they'd expected and when they eventually discovered what they were looking for it was the men's block.

Luckily, they hadn't approached near enough to be seen.

They were met by a flustered corporal. 'My word, I should have explained to you that these are the men's blocks – ours are directly behind our hut.'

The poor woman was so upset that Ruth took pity on her. 'It was our fault, Corp, we could have asked one of the other girls but most of them are now safely in bed.'

'Did the girls who left the base get back?'

'Yes, all six of them are fast asleep.'

Having the necessary washrooms and lavatories so close was a bonus and as Ruth climbed gingerly into her bed, she decided that all in all it had been a highly satisfactory day.

* * *

After breakfast – not served in mess tins as it had been at the other barracks where she'd trained – they paraded, their names were called out and the men and girls were formed into sections and then marched away in different directions.

Ruth was shocked that they had to drill at the same time as the three other squads. Each one was being drilled by a regular army sergeant who for some reason stood a considerable distance from his men or women. This caused a lot of yelling and swearing by those calling instructions as more often than not, one or other squad followed the orders from the wrong instructor.

While the other groups were on the gun park, Ruth's was going to be in a lecture room. There were going to be lectures on discipline, security, defence and aircraft recognition.

'Goodness, it's like being back at school,' Jill said as she looked around the large room. 'Blackboards, and rows of tables and chairs.'

The men naturally wore battledress and had heavy boots on and they looked quite old – possibly in their thirties and she hoped that wouldn't be a problem. The men avoided looking directly at the girls but were taking surreptitious glances whenever they could. She wondered if they were surprised at how young the ATS girls were. Certainly, too young to be the girl-friends of the men who could almost be their fathers.

A young lieutenant and an older sergeant strode in, and they were called to attention. It sounded like machine-gun fire as the men's metal-studded boots clattered on the boards. It became clear immediately that their officer wasn't happy about having a mixed section, but he told them he'd had no option and was going to make the best of it and so should they. This was hardly encouraging and Ruth vowed to prove him wrong.

'You're C section 453 – Heavy Anti-Aircraft Battery of the Royal Artillery. There are four sections in a battery and these man two gunsites. One of the sites will be your HQ – your headquarters. When you finish your training, you'll be posted to defend an airfield, dockyard or an arms depot.'

He stared around the room to make sure every eye was fixed on him and taking in his every word. Ruth certainly was.

'Each site has 43.7 guns with possibly smaller Lewis guns or Bofors as well. No doubt you ATS are not familiar with any of those, but I can assure you by the end of your training you will be.'

As he talked, he tapped his cane to emphasise a point but there was no need to do that as he was a riveting speaker.

'Gunners are to treat the ATS as equals in everything. Regardless of sex, you have a job to do and that's to win the war and to defend Britain from the air. You will have to work together, live together and quite possibly die together.'

A ripple of what could have been fear, but Ruth thought was excitement, went around the room. She exchanged a glance with Jill and her new friend nodded. This was more like it – once she'd completed this training, she would be on an active site doing something tangible for the war effort. The fact that she was the only girl, as far as she knew, who was already trained in another skill didn't matter. She was just thrilled to be there.

As they left the lecture, the ATS were inspired by the talk and especially the fact that this young lieutenant had given them equal status with the men. A different corporal, less flustered and more efficient, marched them all, men included, to the gun park.

'I expect the men will have seen the guns before,' Ruth said to Jill as they marched side by side. Unlike during basic training, they didn't have to sort themselves into alphabetical order before they went anywhere, which made things simpler.

'I've seen them; don't forget I've been working on a practice gunsite for the past few weeks,' Ruth replied.

'As have I, you can't fail to miss them if you spend time in London.'

They spent an hour examining these massive weapons of war and Ruth was aware that one or two of the girls looked less than enthusiastic. They all had to pass every aspect of the course or they'd be sent back to be retrained for something else. If anyone was going to fail, it would be the nervous ones, but at least if she didn't pass muster she could go back to her original job.

* * *

Over the next two weeks, C section shaped up and became a force to be reckoned with – in Ruth's opinion the best of the four groups that were being trained. Lieutenant Rush was, according to those that knew him, the best officer in the battery and they were lucky to have him knocking them into shape.

There were lectures, practical demonstrations, and every day they trained as a team. The fact that Ruth couldn't participate in a lot of the physical work was a serious disadvantage, but she excelled at the things she could do and prayed that would be enough for her to pass the course.

The first letter from Sam arrived on the day that she was due to find out if she would be declared fit for duty. She also received a letter from Grace, which she read immediately, inviting her to the blessing of her wedding and a memorial for her brother who'd been shot down in France. Ruth hadn't even known her friend had got married so suddenly and was sad it wouldn't be possible to attend as she would be in the middle of her cadre to be promoted to bombardier. This would finish on 15 October and the memorial and wedding blessing would be on the 9th.

She arrived at the medical centre nervous, expecting to be snarled at, but the grumpy doctor was charming this time and greeted her with a friendly smile.

'You've done well, Lance Corporal, I've been hearing good things about you. I don't think the fact that you've been unable to participate in everything will make the slightest difference. If you weren't already marked for promotion, you would be now. I expect you to be a sergeant before the new year.'

'Thank you, sir, that's wonderful news. I just wish I'd chosen this trade first as it's exactly what I wanted.'

'Don't overdo things with this arm, but you don't need to have it in the sling. Your officer's aware of the circumstances and won't ask you to lift anything heavy.'

She saluted smartly and almost skipped out. She headed for the hut, knowing it would be more or less empty, as half the girls had trekked to the dance hall and the rest would be in the rec room.

Jill was writing a letter at the table and Ruth joined her. 'I'm pronounced fit and can now do everything. Thank goodness I've been able to do what the spotters have to do with the binoculars and the small telescope. I now have to get proficient on the predictor and height finder.'

'After what you had been doing previously, I'm sure you'll pick it up first time.' Jill gestured with her pen at the letter Ruth was holding. 'Is that from your Sam? I've got one too and I'm just replying.'

'It's the first and I was beginning to think he wasn't going to answer as I sent mine two weeks ago. I'm a bit nervous about opening it.'

'It looks as if it's got more than one sheet of paper so he's not brushing you off – that would only require a single piece, wouldn't it?'

Ruth carefully opened the letter. Jill was right. It was a two-page letter. It had seemed bulkier because he'd included a snapshot of himself. She took out the photograph, happy to have it – she must send him one as soon as she was able to. With a smile, she sat down and prepared to learn what had delayed his response.

5

Dear Ruth,

I apologise for not replying sooner but when you read this letter and see what's been going on, I'm sure you'll understand and forgive me.

I've been forced to share my billet with a nasty bit of work, a bullying sergeant who has been making my life as difficult as he could.

I survived – obviously – and the horrible little man has now been posted elsewhere, much to everybody's relief.

I'm about to leave for my course and will get a few days' leave when I've finished and before I get my next posting, which is probably going to be back where I am now. My reckoning is that *you'll have finished your training and will also be a gunner by then.*

I'm pretty sure you should get at least a forty-eight-hour pass so can we coordinate and meet up in London? It doesn't have to be London, I'll come wherever you are. My family live near St Albans and I'd love to take you to meet them but I suppose it could be too early for that.

If I've got my calculations correct you ought to be on leave around the 15th and I'll have finished and be promoted – God willing – on the 16th.

I promise I'll not leave it so long to reply next time. I hope you don't mind me sending you the photograph. If you've got a snap of yourself, I'd love to have it.

I've thought about you every day. I should have asked immediately if your shoulder's better, if you're enjoying your course, but you can tell me in your next letter.

Take care,

fondest wishes

He'd scrawled his name underneath and she couldn't stop smiling as she read it a second time. She'd never had a serious boyfriend. In fact, she wasn't really sure that Sam qualified as one as they'd not even been out on a date. Her thoughts at night were filled with images of him and she knew she found him very attractive but didn't know him well enough to say he was her actual boyfriend.

She lifted the paper and sniffed it, not sure why she'd done it, and Jill laughed. 'I know, I always do that hoping I'll be able to smell Arthur somehow on the paper but I never can.'

'I've never had a letter from someone I'm going out with – I've had a few boyfriends but no one I wanted to write to.' Ruth carefully folded the paper and pushed them back into the envelope. 'He's leaving today to do his promotion course and when I see him again, he'll be a sergeant. I'm going to be a bombardier so we'll both have something to celebrate.'

She frowned. 'Bother, I'll be on my cadre when he wants us to meet. What a shame.'

'That's a pity but don't tell him that in your letter, things might work out and you don't want to upset him,' Jill said.

Ruth agreed and continued with her letter without mentioning she probably wouldn't be there. 'Sam thinks that I'll be free on the same day that I finish. He wants us to meet somewhere in London as he's in Lincolnshire and we're here. He did suggest I might want to meet his parents but it's far too early for that.'

'If it's just a convenient place for you to spend time then I don't think it matters. It doesn't always mean that you're about to get engaged or something like that.'

Ruth nodded and then told her friend about Grace. 'It's a shame I won't be able to go but I expect the others will be there and I've yet to meet the three girls she became pals with at basic training and I'd really like to.'

'Are you going to finish your reply as I'm halfway through my letter to Arthur and we could go and post them together?'

Ruth wrote a quick note to Grace, congratulating her and saying that unfortunately she wouldn't be able to attend the ceremony in Romford. She had now completed her reply to Sam, omitting the fact that she couldn't actually meet him, blotted the paper, addressed the envelope and was ready to take an early-evening stroll to the postal office.

* * *

The following day, she used the range finder and predictor for the first time and could sense that their sergeant and lieutenant were watching her closely. For some reason, this made her more confident, not nervous at all, and she completed both tasks perfectly.

As she'd done well, she wasn't worried about being summoned after they'd finished for the day. There was going to be a dance at the barracks tonight, which meant both she and Jill had no excuse not to go. But first, she had to march to the lieutenant's office to hopefully hear some good news.

After saluting smartly, she stood at ease. 'Lance Bombardier Cox, I'm having you made up to Bombardier immediately. You don't need to go on a cadre as you've already got more than enough experience. Well done – I'm looking forward to working with you on a live site very soon.'

Ruth saluted again, having not said a word and about turned and marched out. All gunners were known as bombardiers not privates. Once safe from view, she leaned against the nearest wall and forced her fingers to unclench. Even though she'd known she wasn't being called for any disciplinary reason, she'd still been apprehensive. Officers were fine when you were working but quite terrifying sitting behind a desk.

It only took a few deep breaths for her to feel calm. As she was walking briskly back to the billet, it occurred to her that she should have gone to collect her second stripe, but she wasn't exactly sure whether she should go to the stores or somewhere else.

She seemed to recall that if you went on the course then you had the stripe presented to you when you completed it successfully. What was she going to do? She saw the nervous corporal, the one who'd been so upset about them almost wandering into the men's ablutions, who hadn't been around much lately.

'Excuse me, Corp, I've just been made up and was wondering where I should go to collect my stripe.'

'Jolly good, I could see that was on the cards. Come with me and I'll find them for you. You can sew it on before the dance and then everyone will know. It's not often a girl gets made up without having to go on the cadre.'

Ruth returned immediately to her billet and got out her hussif – her housewife – which was an excellent small sewing kit that had been invaluable over the past few months, and attached the second stripe to her uniform jacket. She had two extra stripes for her number one uniform and her battledress jacket.

Feeling proud and excited, she marched into the canteen, half-hoping that everybody could see she was now a bombardier. They noticed, and she was universally congratulated.

Jill was on her feet and hugged her enthusiastically. 'How absolutely super – you're not the only one with a new stripe.' She showed her single stripe, indicating she was now a lance bombardier.

'Absolutely spiffing! Now we've really got something to celebrate. I wasn't looking forward to this dance, but I am now. I wish I'd waited to post the letter so I could have told Sam that I could meet him and not just avoided the subject, but I'll do it in the next letter.'

She joined the mixed group at the table, knowing things would be different. The privates – both male and female – would now have to take orders from her and she was half looking forward to being in that situation and half dreading it. Most of the men were now good friends but there were one or two she didn't quite trust and was worried that they might make things difficult for her. But tonight, she was going to enjoy her promotion and leave the worries for another time.

* * *

Sam had left it far longer than he'd intended to answer Ruth's letter but the bully he'd had to share his billet with had been making his life difficult. Vital pieces of his kit had vanished and he been forced to purchase new items from the stores. He'd been sent on unnecessary errands at mealtimes and missed more scoff than he'd eaten.

The wretched man hadn't gone as far as to put him on a bogus charge but had done whatever he could to try and push Sam into retaliating. If he either physically or verbally attacked a sergeant, he'd be demoted and his chances of future promotion would vanish.

Eventually an eagle-eyed lieutenant had picked up on what was going on and Sam's tormentor had been immediately transferred. Nothing was said openly, but a collective sigh of relief went around camp when this bully had gone.

His section was now settled and tomorrow he was leaving to attend the sergeants' cadre. He'd be leaving this posting first thing and had to take his full kit with him as when you'd finished and got your extra stripes, you received a fresh posting. Although it was quite likely he'd return here. The wide skies of Lincolnshire were ideal for bombers to take off and land, but Sam found it too flat and too windy.

As a sergeant had been removed from their battery then it probably made sense for Sam to replace him. If this proved to be the case then it was a bloody nuisance having to take his kit when he could just have left it where it was, but that was the army for you.

He'd managed to buy a pad of Basildon Bond writing paper and half a dozen matching envelopes at the NAAFI. He had a fountain pen that his mother had given him when he'd enlisted and he'd already filled the reservoir so was ready to write.

Pleased with his effort, he dashed off to the postal department and dropped his letter into the bag. With any luck, Ruth would get it within twenty-four hours as the BFPO – British Forces Postal Office – was often quicker than the national service. Mail for service personnel was prioritised over that of civilians.

With his kitbag packed, all he had to do in the morning was put in his wash bag and shaving kit. He didn't fancy an evening in the bar, he wanted a clear head when he left, but he liked the majority of the blokes in his section and he'd be sorry not to see them again.

The Lancasters were magnificent; four-engined beasts taking off one after the other into the night to bomb the poor sods over the Channel. He didn't envy the aircrew, though, as the loss of life in Bomber Command was heinous.

He'd enjoyed his late-evening stroll and was somewhat surprised to be called over by his officer on his return.

'Right, don't bother to take your full kit as I've managed to wangle you a permanent posting here. I need a competent and intelligent sergeant and you're just the man for the job.'

Sam had jumped to attention and saluted after being hailed and now smiled. 'Thank you, sir, I appreciate your faith in me. And I'm even more grateful that you've told me before I leave so I don't have to lug everything there and back.' Then something less positive about this news occurred to him.

'Do I still get my leave even though I'm returning here? I'm hoping to meet my girlfriend in London as she'll have also completed her training.'

'Don't worry, you get a four-day pass – I can't spare you for any longer than that. You never know, your young lady might end up working in this neck of the woods. I've heard that there's going to be a few mixed batteries on several of the bases in Lincolnshire.'

'Now that would be just the ticket.' He nodded, didn't salute a second time as that seemed unnecessary, and was about to hurry back to his billet when Lieutenant Culley called him back.

'You'll remain in the same billet, obviously, and at

the moment you won't have anyone sharing with you. Make the most of it – not many sergeants are so lucky.'

'Yes, sir, thank you again.'

* * *

The course was interesting and informative – he passed every section top of the class and was inordinately proud to be handed the neat parcel containing his third stripes. He'd arranged to meet Ruth at King's Cross tomorrow and couldn't wait. She was now Bombardier Cox and he was Sergeant Johnson. Life couldn't be better for both of them.

He shook hands with the other newly promoted sergeants and then collected his overnight bag – everybody apart from him was being posted somewhere new.

There was transport laid on for them and he scrambled into the rear of the ancient, camouflaged lorry, glad the distance to the station was short. From the racket the engine was making, he doubted it would even make the return journey without breaking down.

He'd taken longer to shave than usual, had on a clean collar and was looking smart, if he did say so himself. His boots were shiny, his buttons gleamed and he was proud of his three stripes and the white Royal Artillery lanyard that he wore proudly on his right shoulder. Ruth would now be entitled to wear one, but she'd have to purchase it as it wouldn't be included with her uniform.

This time he didn't take the service bus but travelled on the underground. This was quicker and he didn't want to be late. They'd agreed to meet under the station clock but as neither of them had been entirely sure when they'd arrive, he was worried she might be standing alone and be bothered by other servicemen. He'd flatten any man who upset his girl.

He shouldered his way through the press of people, took the stairs at the double and emerged into the noisy, smoke-filled station and headed for the clock. He wasn't late – he was first so could relax and keep an eye out for her.

* * *

Ruth had travelled up to London with Jill, who was staying in a B & B somewhere near the War Office. Their section was being posted to a bomber base in Lincolnshire – she couldn't be happier as at least there was some chance of seeing Sam if they both got time off together once she was at her permanent posting.

As soon they'd disembarked, they rushed to the left luggage office and deposited their bags. No point in carrying them about the place when they had everything they needed in their haversacks.

'We'll meet here in two days. Good luck with Arthur, I hope you get to spend some quality time with him,' Ruth said as she hugged her friend.

'Thank you, it's not nearly long enough but there's a war on so we mustn't grumble.' Jill stopped and pointed. 'Is that your young man striding towards us? My word, you never said he looks like a film star.'

'It is. Don't rush off, I want you to meet him.'

'I need to spend a penny. I'll be back in a tick.'

Ruth's eyes were wide. Until Jill had spoken, she'd not really thought much about just how handsome Sam was. He was certainly getting a lot of appreciative glances from the women he strode past. Then she forgot all about his looks and ran into his arms.

A highly satisfactory and quite wonderful few minutes later, she was breathless, her cheeks pink and her lips tingling. She rested her head against his shoulder for a few seconds to recover.

'You look absolutely stunning, Ruth, those stripes suit you. I can't tell you how happy I am to see you.'

'Not nearly as happy as I am to be here. My friend

said you could be a film star – I hadn't realised how good-looking you are until she mentioned it.'

'Thank you for the compliment. Now I've finally got a girlfriend who lives up to those high standards.' He looked around for her kitbag. 'Even better, have you already dumped it?'

'I have – what about you?'

'I'm going back to Lincolnshire...'

'That's where I'm going, so we'll be able to meet up occasionally. We're going to be at Binbrook. Is that near you? You've never actually told me the name of your base.'

He was staring at her and shaking his head. 'I'm based at Skellingthorpe. It's no more than thirty miles from Binbrook. I don't believe this. It couldn't be better. We can meet in Lincoln, which is only three miles from me.'

'That's incredible. What a good start to our leave. Have you booked anywhere or are we going to wander around looking for a guest house or B & B?' Ruth looked at him seriously. 'We're not sharing a room or a bed, in case you thought we were.'

'Of course we're not. Your friend who dashed off without waiting to be introduced could perhaps have advised us.'

'She's coming back, in fact I can see her,' Ruth said

and turned to face Jill with Sam's arm still around her waist. After introducing them, Jill was able to give them exactly the information they wanted.

'We stay at a lovely inexpensive guest house just off the Strand, it's perfect for cinemas, theatres and restaurants. I've got their telephone number and there's a kiosk over there. Would you like me to see if they've any rooms?'

'Oh, please do that, I hate not knowing where I'm going to be sleeping,' Ruth said.

They followed Jill and waited outside the telephone box whilst she was connected by the operator. She pushed button A and was immediately in conversation with someone. She put the receiver down and pushed open the door.

'There are no spare rooms, but Mrs Fredericks suggested that Ruth and I share and Arthur and Sam do. Both rooms have twin beds. Will that be suitable for you?'

'Fine for us, Ruth, but what about your Arthur? He won't be used to sharing.'

Jill laughed. 'Heavens, he's in rotten digs, sleeps in an attic room with three others from the same department. Sharing with just one will be luxury for him. Also, it will be so much cheaper to split the cost.'

She vanished back into the telephone box and completed the call and then came out smiling.

'Arthur's a junior member of his department and I can assure you that they're not well paid.' She looked a little uncomfortable. 'He does have a private income but that doesn't go far. He earns more than we do but then I think just about anybody in full employment does. It's always a struggle for us to meet the cost of two rooms even at this modest guest house.'

'It certainly will make things easier for me,' Sam said happily. 'Are we catching a bus down Gray's Inn Road or going on the underground?'

'I'd prefer to walk and it'll probably be quicker,' Jill answered. 'It's not much more than a mile. The guest-house is in Adam Street and has pretty gardens at the back, perfect for afternoon tea. You can also exit through them onto the Embankment.'

'That sounds perfect. As we don't have heavy bags to carry, I'm happy to walk. When are we meeting up with Arthur?'

'He's free from four o'clock and will meet us at the guest house – not that he knows it's an "us", but he'll be pleased, I can assure you.'

* * *

It seemed rude to walk hand in hand with Sam when Jill was on her own, but Ruth didn't want to miss a minute of being close to him. As they walked, she stole surreptitious glances at him, hardly able to take in that somehow, after just one meeting, they seemed to be in a serious relationship.

He turned his head and caught her looking and his eyes flashed. Before she could protest, he'd gathered her close and kissed her with a passion that made her toes curl. For a few blissful minutes, she forgot there was a war on, that they were blocking the pavement with unseemly behaviour, and just revelled in the sensation.

He was the one to break the embrace and she regained her composure and looked for her friend. Jill was unaware that they'd stopped and was happily chatting to a complete stranger walking behind her.

'Oh dear, we'd better catch up with her. She's going to be so embarrassed,' Ruth said and they dodged through the pedestrians and slipped in behind Jill.

Her friend stopped and put her hands on her hips as if annoyed. 'About time – I think I've told two sailors intimate details about my relationship with my fiancé. I hope you're ashamed of yourselves.'

There was no need to apologise – they laughed

and continued their stroll down Gray's Inn Road, across Holborn and then along Chancery Lane to the Strand. They walked for half a mile towards Trafalgar Square before turning into the road they needed.

The guest house was in a row of Georgian terraced three-storey houses, nothing to indicate it was anything other than an expensive residence. Jill saw Ruth's expression.

'I know, it's word of mouth only. Mrs Fredericks isn't really supposed to have a business here but as it's so discreet no one has complained. We were told about it by someone at the War Office.'

'Then it's not as expensive as it looks, that's a relief.'

6

Sam was impressed with the place where he would be spending the next two evenings with the girl he was already completely in love with. They might only have spent a few hours together a month ago but each letter they'd exchanged had confirmed his initial reaction.

Their hostess – it seemed impolite to think of her as their landlady – welcomed them with a charming smile.

'I'm so glad you've brought two of your friends, Jill, I love to see new faces here. Follow me, Sergeant Johnson and Corporal Cox, and I'll show you around.'

The handsome staircase in the centre of the entrance hall led up to a wide gallery and facing them were half a dozen doors. Ruth was looking around as excited as he to be here.

'Jill will show you the room that you'll be sharing with her, Bombardier, and I'll take your sergeant to his room.'

The girls went to the left and he was taken to the room at the far right – Mrs Fredericks might be relaxed and using Jill's first name, but she was making very sure there'd be no nocturnal visits. The room he and Arthur would be sharing was as far away from Ruth's as it could be.

She stepped aside and gestured expansively. The room was huge – elegantly furnished and had a view of the river. The distance between the beds was equal to the entire width of his billet.

'This is a beautiful room, ma'am, I feel as if I'm stepping into a Jane Austen novel.'

His response made her smile genuine. 'Exactly the ambience I intended. Through the door on the right is a small washroom – I'm afraid that the WC and bathroom are shared by all the rooms.'

He beamed. 'At the moment I share with thirty blokes so there's no need to apologise.' He walked across and put his bag on the bed on the left. 'Are there any house rules we need to know?'

She smiled again. 'I'm sure that Jill and Arthur will

tell you everything. I don't provide luncheon or dinner, but I do a sumptuous breakfast.'

'That sounds excellent, thank you so much for allowing us to come.'

She nodded regally and glided out. He smiled, presumably being told where the ablutions were was going to be Jill's job. He was about to go in search of the girls when he heard the front door open and shut and a male voice. This might well be Arthur arriving.

He decided to remain where he was and allow Jill to greet her fiancé without him rubbernecking. The bedroom door stood open and a tall, slender young man with horn-rimmed glasses rushed in, his hand extended.

'How do you do? I'm Arthur Humfrey, Jill's chap. You must be Sam, Ruth's chap.'

They shook hands and he liked him immediately. The glasses might explain why Arthur wasn't in the services, but Sam thought it more likely the bloke was at the War Office because he was one of the elite – a top graduate from Oxford or Cambridge. He certainly looked intelligent.

There was no time for them to talk as the girls joined them. After a flurry of introductions, they agreed to go out for an early-evening meal and then maybe find a cinema. None of them wanted to go to a nightclub.

Arthur had his arm around Jill's shoulders and Sam did the same with Ruth. He hung back, letting the others go ahead so he could talk privately to her. 'I like him, in fact I like both of them, I'm glad you've made such a good friend. There's something about him I can't quite put my finger on – if he's a junior in the War Office then I'm the Queen of Sheba.'

'I agree. He's constantly watching, you can almost see his brain analysing everything. I think he's a spook – he's in the intelligence service.'

'It's not something we can ask him, but I like the idea that there are men like him keeping an eye on things for us ordinary folk.'

'I don't know why he's on such high alert – do you think he believes that we might be undercover agents for Hitler?' Ruth said behind her hand.

'Good God, I hope not. I'm surprised that Jill didn't hint that Arthur's not what he appears,' Sam replied. 'He looks inoffensive, but I'm sure he isn't.'

The couple stopped and Jill waited for them to catch up. 'Come on, you two laggards, if you don't keep up you won't see where we're going. The pavements are getting busier and we could easily be separated if we don't stay together.'

'There's a British restaurant not far from here – I've eaten there a couple of times. Nothing fancy, but always tasty and good value.' Sam looked particularly at Arthur, who was watching him closely. 'Unless you had something grander in mind.'

'I know exactly the place you're referring to. It's where we're heading. I don't suppose by any chance that either of you play bridge or any sort of card games?'

Sam laughed at the absurdity of the idea that he played bridge, but Ruth nodded. 'I do, I used to partner my great-aunt and we usually won.' She smiled up at him. 'I take it from your reaction that you don't.'

'I play poker, brag, pontoon and whist. Bridge is something officers play, not lowly NCOs like me.'

'Poppycock! If you can play whist, old boy, you can play bridge – we can explain the basics of bidding over dinner,' Arthur said.

* * *

Sam didn't need to be told how to play bridge but over their meal Jill explained in minute detail what was involved in the bidding process – this was where the players used a recognised code to indicate what cards they had in their hand.

He thought it significant that Arthur didn't join in – he couldn't quite make up his mind about this bloke. His initial impressions had been favourable but now he wasn't so sure. His intensity when discussing playing cards had seemed a bit odd.

He dropped his pudding spoon in the empty dish and raised both hands in surrender. 'Right, girls, I give in. I'll try bridge but I don't promise that I'll enjoy it or be any good at it.'

'Fair enough, Sam, if we play a few hands and it's not working we can change to one of the games that you're familiar with,' Jill said.

He looked at Ruth and she reached out and took his hand. 'I'm so sorry, you've been rather bombarded with information you didn't really want to know. I'm quite happy to play whist or cribbage but I'm not familiar with poker or pontoon as my aunt didn't approve of gambling.'

Arthur snorted. 'I bet money was put on every rubber even if you weren't aware of it.'

'Rubber? What's that? Surely there aren't more things I've got to know before I play this complicated game.' He dropped his head dramatically into his hands and sighed loudly.

Ruth giggled, which was his intention. 'You poor old thing – we've overloaded your pea-sized brain. You're going to be my partner and I am an absolute whiz, so your imagined inadequacies won't matter.'

'Don't put money on it, love, if I make up my mind I can't do something then I'll move heaven and earth not to be good at it.'

This ridiculous statement made everybody smile and they left the restaurant in good spirits. This time he and Ruth walked ahead; he had his arm around her waist holding her close. He didn't give a bugger about bridge; as long as she was happy then he'd happily play tiddlywinks all night.

There was a table with four chairs in the room he was sharing with Arthur and they made their way there. He drew Ruth to one side for a moment, allowing Arthur and Jill to enter first.

'I've slightly misled you, love, I've not actually played bridge, but I've watched others in the mess do so. I was feigning complete ignorance in the hope it might give us the upper hand.'

She stood on tiptoe and kissed him. 'I guessed that when you winked at me whilst Jill was explaining so authoritatively, and you were nodding like a village idiot. If Arthur is as intelligent as we both think then I'm sure he's seen through your nonsense.'

'I'm actually looking forward to playing, it's complicated but fascinating. The only drawback being it tends to drag on rather.'

Jill overheard this remark and laughed. 'You're right, but not as bad as Monopoly. That's been known to go on for more than a day.'

Arthur had set out the table and produced two packs of cards. He was seated and shuffling the blue pack like a croupier. This rang a warning bell. In Sam's experience only those who played cards for money could shuffle like that. There was something definitely odd about this bloke – he was a contradiction.

'You play cards a lot, Arthur?' Sam's question was innocuous but Arthur's eyes flashed and for a second he looked quite different.

'Why do you ask that? Can't a fellow shuffle efficiently without being accused of being a gambler?' Arthur's tone was unpleasant, not at all friendly.

Ruth recoiled, Jill looked upset and Sam was shocked.

'I just asked if you played cards, no need to be offended.'

'Get on with it, man, we haven't got all night,' Arthur snapped.

* * *

Ruth frowned as she recovered from this unexpected outburst; Arthur was obviously no amateur but an expert card player. Would his next request be to play for money? From Jill's worried look, there was obviously more to this than she and Sam had realised. There was something about the intensity of his expression that made the hair on the back of her neck stand up. This man wasn't who he appeared to be and it made her wonder if Jill was covering for her fiancé.

She exchanged a worried glance with Sam and he nodded.

'Shall we play? Do you want to shuffle again, Sam? It's your deal,' Arthur said.

Instead of answering, Sam nodded, ignored the blue pack that Arthur had been handling, picked up the one with the red backs, and then shuffled the cards but not expertly as Arthur had. This was going to be an interesting evening.

He winked at her and she understood. Sam knew more than he was admitting and Arthur's attitude had annoyed him. It had upset her too but she wasn't quite sure whatever Sam was planning was a good idea. She didn't want the evening to end on a sour note.

Jill looked around and smiled a little nervously. 'I know you don't like to gamble, Ruth, but we always play for a penny a point. It just makes it more fun and however badly any couple might lose over an evening, they never owe much more than a few shillings.'

Ruth was about to refuse but Sam spoke first. 'Fine by me – it just adds an edge to the proceedings. Don't worry, love, I'll pick up the tab so you can consider yourself not involved in any gambling.'

'Very well, I don't want to be a wet blanket. If the rest of you want to play for pennies, then so be it.'

Arthur's concentration was unnerving. His knuckles were white as he gripped the cards he'd shuffled. What was going on?

Sam dealt and she flicked open her hand. She had a lot of hearts, but no picture cards in that suit, but did hold the ace of spades and clubs. To her astonishment, Sam opened with one heart and when it was her turn to bid, she replied with three no trumps.

Sam understood and went for a slam, which meant he had to take every trick. She was glad she wasn't playing but just had to put down her hand and let him do it. How had he managed to understand so easily how this game worked?

He won the game, and she wasn't the only one surprised by his skill. Arthur stared at him through narrowed eyes.

'I thought you said you'd never played. No complete beginner could start with a grand slam the way you did.' Arthur spoke softly but there was an aggression to his tone. 'That's tantamount to cheating.'

'I've never played but I've observed others. Should I have mentioned that? Sorry, old boy, I thought it would be a bit of a lark letting you both think I knew nothing about the game.' Sam was mimicking Arthur and that didn't go down well either.

The evening wasn't turning out as she'd expected and even her friend was looking decidedly put out by having lost the first hand, or maybe it was because of Sam's remarks? Jill was whispering to Arthur but he was sitting rigid in his chair.

'Shall we just play the one rubber? If Sam and I win the next game, then we take it. Do you think Mrs Fredericks provides cocoa for her guests?' Ruth smiled gaily around the table and Sam responded but the other two remained silent.

'I don't play with cheats,' Arthur snarled and tossed the cards across the table.

Sam stood up. 'Neither do I. This was a mistake.'

Jill glanced at Arthur before hurrying across to speak quietly to them. 'He promised me he wouldn't play cards. He gets too intense when he does, not like himself at all.'

'It was only bridge. I can't see why losing a hand of that would make him so cross,' Ruth said.

'He doesn't like to lose at anything.'

Ruth began to understand. Sam nodded.

'Shall we go for a walk, love? Let him calm down for a bit?'

'Yes, please go. He'll be fine in a bit,' Jill told them.

Ruth followed Sam onto the gallery, glad to get away from the nasty atmosphere in the room. 'He shouldn't have called you a cheat but what you did wasn't good either. Why don't you apologise and smooth things over?'

'I don't want to, but you're right, I started this. I'm not playing cards with him again, though.'

They turned back and walked into the room. Jill looked worried and Arthur angry.

'Look, I'm sorry I didn't tell you I knew more about the game than you thought. It wasn't a good idea,' Sam said.

'It was cheating. I don't accept your apology.' Arthur turned his back on them and Ruth felt Sam tense. Jill looked at her with tear-filled eyes.

'Come on, Sam, let's go.' Ruth tugged gently on his arm and to her relief he responded. Once outside in the passageway, he said what she'd been thinking.

'I'm sorry, I know this place is inexpensive and in the centre of Town, but I'm not comfortable sharing a room with that bloke after what just happened.'

'I think we might have to stay here tonight as it's probably too late to find anywhere else.' She smiled. 'There's a good hotel in Chelmsford we could go to tomorrow.'

'Seems a long way to go when there are hundreds of other B & Bs in London we can use. Let's go for a walk along the river and see if we can find somewhere to have a drink – I could do with a beer.'

They were halfway down the stairs when Arthur appeared and leaned over the balustrade. 'You two, come back. I need to speak to you.'

Ruth was tempted to ignore him, but Sam turned, taking her hand and making it hard for her to do anything but retrace her steps.

'Let's hear him out. Might make things a lot easier if we do.'

They were talking in whispers but she was pretty sure they wouldn't have been overheard.

She couldn't refuse – he was quite irresistible when he smiled at her like that.

Jill was sitting on the bed looking miserable and Arthur was pacing up and down.

'Well, we're back, what do you want to say to us?' Ruth said and Sam raised an eyebrow, which made her want to giggle. He really wasn't an eyebrow-raising sort of man – men like Arthur were better suited to this.

The pacing stopped and Arthur faced them. He looked contrite, wretched even, the way he had when they'd first met.

'I shouldn't play cards as it brings out the worst in me and it was silly of me to suggest we did so. I apologise wholeheartedly and hope that you can forgive me for ruining your evening.'

'Oh, I see. Thank you for explaining.' Ruth was unsettled, this strange young man unnerved her.

Jill was now standing. 'If you're going for a walk, would you mind very much if I came with you? I need the fresh air.'

Arthur remained silent. Sam was staring at him.

'Yes, please come with us, Jill. We're going to try and find somewhere to get a drink.'

She grabbed Sam's elbow and he had to come with her. There was no conversation between the three of them as they hurried down the stairs and out of the building. Ruth realised she'd been holding her breath until she was on the pavement.

'Jill, Arthur frightened me. Does he lose control often?' Ruth asked.

'I'm sorry.' She hesitated and then blurted out some extraordinary information. 'He's a gambling addict. I don't understand what possessed him to suggest we played cards. If the War Office was aware of how serious his addiction is, he'd be moved somewhere far away from any secrets.'

Sam no longer looked so fierce. 'And so he should be. Don't you realise, Jill, that his weakness makes him a possible target for German intelligence.'

Jill glared at him. 'I'm not a moron, thank you, Sergeant Johnson. I'm well aware how vulnerable he is and so is he. That's why he's so upset about what happened.'

Sam nodded. 'If he doesn't resign his position then I'm going to do it for him. I'm sorry, I know you love him, but better to remove him from the possibility of turning into a traitor than ending up on the end of a rope.'

Ruth gasped and moved closer to her friend. She was seeing a different side to Sam and it wasn't one that she particularly admired. She didn't actually know him at all.

'Thank you for pointing out the blindingly obvious, Sergeant, if you'll excuse us, we're going to walk on our own,' Jill said icily and Ruth didn't blame her for being so angry.

They linked arms and dashed down the narrow street towards the Embankment. The sun was only just setting – British Double Summer Time meant it stayed light until much later.

'What a ghastly evening this has turned out to be, Ruth. I hope what's happened won't come between us,' Jill said.

'Absolutely not – to be honest, I know you much better than I do Sam. It was quite a shock hearing what he said. Do you think he'll actually report Arthur?'

'I'm sure he will, and you mustn't blame him. It's the right thing to do and even though it will mean Arthur won't be able to continue to do the work he's so good at then at least I'll know that he's safe. If it's any consolation to you, I wish I'd had the strength to do it myself.'

'Has he got himself horribly in debt gambling? How did you find out about his problem?'

Jill pointed towards a bench and they sat down. Ruth's legs were a bit wobbly after all the excitement.

'He told me that he was almost caught more than once when he was at Westminster School but being so clever, he managed to avoid it. Then at Oxford he did get into a frightful muddle financially but again, he managed to stave off disaster until he came into his inheritance when he reached his majority.'

'Playing any sort of game for money is against the

rules in the army,' Ruth said thoughtfully. 'Although I'm quite sure a lot of it goes on anyway.'

'In the rarefied atmosphere that Arthur works in, it's expected that the men visit clubs, drink and gamble. I don't know why he's not been found out. He's already run through his substantial trust fund – if he gets into debt again, God knows what will happen because neither of us can pay it off.'

Ruth put her arm around Jill and held her while she cried quietly. How awful it must be for her friend to be in love with Arthur, knowing that he was seriously flawed. She didn't really know Sam, and decided before things progressed between them that they'd sit down and ask each other questions, make sure that they were in fact the ideal couple and perfectly suited. She'd allowed his charm and good looks to move things on far too quickly.

7

Sam wasn't sure if Ruth had left him alone because she knew he had to speak to Arthur in private or whether she was shocked by what he'd said. Whichever it was, he'd sort it out later. He returned to the room, walked in without knocking and quietly closed the door behind him. He leaned against it and looked at the other man. Arthur was taller than him, but Sam was broader and tougher.

'You have to resign, you understand that, don't you?'

Arthur shrugged and smiled in a superior sort of way, and Sam's fists clenched involuntarily.

'I don't have to do any such thing, Sergeant. Do

you really think anyone will believe you, an NCO, and not me? I'm part of the club, old boy, and you're not. That's all that matters in the world I occupy.'

Sam shrugged, abandoned the door, and kicked around the nearest chair so he could sit. He was damned if he was going to stand whilst he argued the toss.

'I might be a working-class bloke, not as well educated as you, but one thing I do know is that somebody with your gambling problem will have a history. It didn't just happen overnight – there must be dozens of people in your past who can verify what I say. It's better to resign with dignity than be humiliated in public, surely?'

Arthur appeared unimpressed by this irrefutable logic. 'You really don't understand how things work. Officers and gentlemen support each other. Whatever nonsense you think you can uncover, it will be ignored.'

The man's supercilious smile almost made Sam get up and punch him. He took several deep breaths, forced his hands to relax and breathed the tension out of his shoulders before he risked answering.

If he attacked this man, he would be the one in the clink – lower orders should know their place. This was what the overconfident, slimy bastard was hoping for, and he wasn't going to give him the satisfaction.

'You're on very thin ice, mate, and I intend to make sure you fall through. You might think you've got away with it...'

Arthur laughed. He was certain he had the upper hand and Sam decided to let him think so. The man might be a spook but where his addiction was concerned, he wasn't as sharp as he thought he was.

'I think it would be wise for you to find somewhere else to sleep, Sergeant, I've no intention of sharing this room with you. As it was booked in my name, you have no choice but to leave if I don't want you in here.'

'Not a problem, mate, I'll sleep with the girls.' He deliberately called his opponent mate as he could see him flinch every time he said it. 'I'll leave you to contemplate your future – I can assure you it's not a happy one.'

Sam stood, picked up his bag, and sauntered to the door. As he opened it, Arthur spoke again.

'I'm not a traitor, I'm not putting our country in any sort of danger, I have everything under control. My expertise is irreplaceable – my value to the war effort far outweighs any risk I might present.'

Sam didn't bother to answer. His mind was made up. As far as he was concerned, it didn't matter how bloody good the man was at his job, it was only a matter of time before he succumbed to his addiction again and he couldn't risk this man being blackmailed for state secrets.

Only as he was halfway down the stairs did it occur to him that there'd been no comment on his outrageous suggestion that he shared the room with Ruth and Jill. This was strange to say the least. Had Arthur not protested because he didn't care or because he knew when it came to it that Sam wouldn't dream of compromising the girls?

God, he really needed a beer. He bounded out into the evening sunshine and heard voices coming from the direction of the river. He'd go that way as that's where he and Ruth had intended to walk before his outburst.

He jogged though the pretty garden at the rear of the row of houses and emerged on the water. His eyes brightened when he saw the girls sitting on a bench just ahead.

Would he be welcome, or should he wait and hope Ruth saw him and let him know if he could join them? He lurked for a few minutes and began to get some funny looks from passers-by. He reached down, picked up a small stone and lobbed it at the bench. He'd intended for it to bounce in front of them but his aim was off and he hit Ruth on the back of the head.

She yelped and he raced over, apologising and explaining. She swivelled and his panic subsided. She was laughing.

'Golly, you made us jump. Couldn't you just call out like a sensible person?'

He grinned. 'Sorry, I didn't want to intrude. Can I join you?'

Jill was on her feet. 'I'd better go back. There's a pub a bit further up, you two go and get that drink.'

Sam dropped onto the bench beside Ruth – it would be easier to talk to her here than in a crowded pub.

'I've got to find somewhere else to stay. I told Arthur I would go in with you and Jill but obviously I can't do that. Do you mind if I go in search of a bed instead of a drink?'

'Makes perfect sense to me. We'll collect my things and then find somewhere for both of us. I feel so sorry for Jill. It must be incredibly difficult being in love with someone like him. How did your talk go?'

He quickly explained and she listened and then told him what she'd learned from Jill.

'Even if we could find anybody who has the

damning information I want, I doubt they'd be ready to talk about it. He's right saying that his lot stick together. I've heard about men like him gambling their entire estates away, leaving their families destitute, and then shooting themselves rather than face the consequences.'

'I think someone in Aunt Jemima's family did exactly that, which is why she was so against any form of gambling. Are you saying that you're not going to take this further?'

'I've got to even if it means I get my card marked. The lieutenant in charge of our section might listen as he's not from that sort of background – he went to grammar school, joined the officer cadets and then volunteered when this lot started. I think somebody told me his father's something in the church so he might be a good bloke to talk to.'

'Right, let's not discuss this any further. We'll go back and get our bags and then leave Jill and Arthur to pay the bill. After all, the rooms were booked in their names and if we're not staying then things are just as they would have been on any other visit.'

Sam remained on the pavement whilst Ruth collected her belongings. She was only gone a few minutes.

'Jill was with Arthur, I could hear them talking, so

I grabbed my bag. I don't quite know what I'd have said if I'd met Mrs Fredericks.'

'As we've both got to leave from King's Cross the day after tomorrow, it makes sense for us to find somewhere near the station.'

'Grace and I once stayed in a commercial travellers' B & B and it was fine. We were the only girls there but didn't have any trouble with the other guests. Basic accommodation but very clean and the breakfast was scrumptious.'

An hour later, they'd booked two rooms in a decent little place and, hand in hand, they went in search of a pub. After walking into three and being told only regulars were served, they abandoned the search.

'It's getting dark, there are no cafes open now and it's too late to go to the cinema. We could go to a nightclub, but I really don't like those sort of places – although I do like to dance.'

'Noted, love, I know the perfect place for tomorrow evening. They always have a first-class band and drinks aren't too prohibitive.'

They didn't have a key to enter the front door but had been told to knock, and as long as it was before eleven o'clock, they would be let in. They had an hour in hand. He wished he didn't have to say goodnight to

Ruth so early, but she seemed happy enough to turn in.

As he raised his hand to knock, there were heavy, running footsteps heading their way. Instinctively, Sam stepped in front of Ruth and turned to face whoever was approaching. A middle-aged bloke puffed up behind them.

'You going in or going to hang about outside? Marge serves cocoa and biscuits at ten – I ain't going to miss that and neither should you.'

'We didn't know that, just what we wanted,' Sam said.

He banged on the door and it was opened by a spotty youth with bad teeth. 'Just in time, me ma's just taking the jug into the dining room.'

They weren't allowed to take their mugs upstairs but there was ample room to sit, even with a dozen other guests eagerly slurping their hot drinks.

'This cocoa is super, made from milk and sweetened too. The biscuits might be broken but they taste just the same as the whole ones,' Ruth said as she munched half a chocolate bourbon with obvious enjoyment.

They were sharing a bench, which suited him just fine as it meant he could slide closer. They'd been welcomed by Marge but ignored by the men who knew each other and probably stayed there regularly.

'It's been a long and somewhat unusual day, Sam, but I've enjoyed it. Actually, I'm glad that we ended up on our own. We can get to know each other better. I've a lot of questions for you tomorrow and I expect you've got some for me.'

Sam rested his chin on the top of her head, knowing that there was one question he wanted to ask but couldn't. He thought he was already falling in love with her, but Ruth was different to any girl he'd ever met and he didn't want to mess things up by telling her too soon.

* * *

Ruth was in a tiny room on the top floor and Sam was on the floor below. She'd have preferred him to be next door – not so he could creep in, but in case somebody else tried to.

Her only concern was that her friendship with Jill might be ruined because of what had happened today, but she hoped that wouldn't be the case. As she fell asleep in the narrow, hard bed, she smiled.

She might not know a great deal about Sam, but she did know he was a good man, kind and intelligent.

Plus, added to these excellent attributes was the fact that he was startlingly good-looking. This made him an absolute catch, not that she was looking for a husband at the moment. She wanted to succeed as a gunner girl before she even considered anything more serious than being his girlfriend.

* * *

The next day they went to see the Tower, walked along the river, had fish and chips for lunch, then sat on a bench staring at the boats.

'What are these questions you mentioned yesterday, love? Fire away...'

Ruth smiled. 'Good word choice. You answer these first and then I'll do the same. I want you to tell me about your family, how you see your life in twenty years, what you'll do when the war's over and you leave the army.'

'Crikey, you don't want much, do you.' He held up a hand and waggled a finger in the air. 'One, I've a sister and a brother – both serving. Betty's in the WRNS, Billy's in the RAF. He's not aircrew but a fitter, looks after the bombers. He's twenty-one so a year younger than me, and Betty's three years younger.'

'What about your parents?'

'Mum's a leading light in the WVS and WI, Dad's a builder by day and firefighter by night. What about you?'

'Right. Well, I've almost certainly got siblings but they don't know about me and I don't know about them. I'm illegitimate; a shameful secret who was bundled off to be brought up by a spinster aunt. I don't care too much; I had a wonderful childhood and couldn't have been happier. But I've no one left now as Aunt Jemima died a few months ago.'

He nodded and waved a second finger. She loved his sense of humour but really didn't want to have fallen in love with him. She wanted to do her bit for the war effort.

'I see me married with a family and living in the countryside somewhere.' He pointed a third finger at her and continued. 'I'm a qualified electrician as well as a builder. I thought I'd told you that. I didn't put it on my application as I wanted to be a gunner and do something different for a few years.'

'I see myself as married with a family as well, I'd like to be an author and write books; it would be something I could do whilst running a home.'

He smiled. 'In case you're wondering, I'm vaguely C of E, but not a firm believer, and I'm a working man and not a supporter of the Conservative party. Not a commie, too extreme for me.'

She hadn't asked him about religion or politics but was pleased he'd volunteered these views. 'I'm C of E too, but probably more enthusiastic than you. I like Churchill but am not sure who I'll vote for when I'm actually allowed to do so next election.'

She was happy with his answers and thought he'd been very sensitive to her feelings by not asking who she saw herself married to. She noticed he was looking thoughtful.

'If you're underage, love, are you a ward of court? Who makes decisions for you?'

'I make my own. My aunt arranged things so I'm financially and legally independent. Emancipated, you might say. She was a suffragette, did I mention that?'

'You didn't, but that explains a lot. I wondered why you wanted to be in a mixed artillery section and now I understand. Your aunt brought you up to think that women are the same as men.'

This comment gave her pause for thought – had she said she thought women were equal? She didn't think so. 'Not really – she just believed we should have the vote. There are a lot of things we can do and are proving so at the moment, but we'll never be the same as men, who are generally physically stronger. I think it will be generations before women are treated equally but having the vote was a start.'

He chuckled. 'One day we might have a female Prime Minister – imagine that!'

'Not in our lifetimes unfortunately. I honestly believe that there'd be fewer wars if women were in charge as we're not as belligerent.'

'Fair point. What I'd really like is a cuppa and wad. Shall we go in search of them?'

'Yes, that's a good idea. I doubt there'll be any buns but we should be able to locate some tea.' Ruth was happier now she knew more about Sam but she was going to try not to let his physical attraction make her do anything rash.

* * *

They couldn't return to the B & B until the evening so headed for the pictures and saw *Band Wagon* with Arthur Askey, Richard Murdoch and Patricia Kirkwood. It was funny and Ruth was glad they'd seen the more depressing Pathé newsreel before the film so they came out smiling.

'We just need to get a bit of supper and then we can head for the dance hall in Farringdon Road – it's perfect as it's not far from where we're staying,' Sam said as he took her hand. 'Do you want to walk, catch a bus or take the underground?'

'Let's walk halfway then find something to eat – hopefully there'll still be a cafe open – and then it won't be so far. Some of the girls where I was training used to walk three miles there and back just to dance. It was through a dense wood and I wouldn't have done it even if I'd been able to, but they seemed to think it was worth the effort.'

After eating, they headed towards the dance hall and soon it became clear to Ruth that this place must be popular. There were dozens of couples walking in that direction as well as groups of girls and men eager to enjoy an evening of band music and energetic dancing.

'I can do all the ballroom dances, but I've not done any of the recent American imports. Do you know how to jitterbug?'

'I do indeed,' Sam said, 'and I'll be happy to teach you. It looks as though it's going to be busy. They limit the numbers for safety reasons – the shelter in the basement can only hold so many – and I don't want to be turned away.'

Ruth glanced over her shoulder. 'There are as many behind us as in front, I'm sure we'll be okay.'

They were and the band was still tuning up as they stepped into the surprisingly large dance hall. It wasn't the Palm Court – where the grand people danced at the Ritz hotel – but it was good enough for her.

Sam led her out onto the floor even though the music hadn't started. 'I want to dance every dance with you. Is your shoulder fully restored? I don't want to swing you about too vigorously and dislocate it again if it's not.'

'I'd forgotten about that so I think it might be best if we stick to the foxtrot and so on and leave the more energetic American dances to next time.'

'I've heard this band before, they're really good.' Sam's arm was around her waist and she was proud to be standing next to him and relieved that she didn't have to dance with a series of strangers.

'I only want to dance with you, Sam, so if anybody taps you on the shoulder, ignore them, please.'

He grinned. 'Don't worry, I'm not letting you go. I've only just found you and know how lucky I am.'

The next three hours literally whirled past and they emerged from the dance hall in time to run to the B & B so they didn't miss their cocoa and biscuits.

'I enjoyed that so much,' she said. 'My shoulder aches a little bit but not too badly and it was worth it.

You're a really good dancer and made me look much better than I actually am.'

They skidded to a halt outside the door, which was just about to close.

'Just made it, Ma's taking it through now,' her son told them as he closed the door firmly behind them.

Ruth recognised a couple of the men but one couldn't expect to see the same faces. It would have been nice to have had another girl there, but she knew she was safe with Sam.

He was gentle with her but if anybody offended her, they'd regret it. As she sipped her cocoa, she smiled. This was the best day of her life so far and she couldn't wait to write to Grace and tell her all about it.

The other guests were talking about something that had happened at Chelmsford. They were pointing at a photograph in what looked like the *Evening Standard*. One of them glanced over at her. 'Look, Redge, we've got one of them ATS girls here.'

Her curiosity piqued, Ruth stood up and with Sam close behind her went across to the table. 'Oh, my goodness – look at that, Sam. That's my friend Grace and her new husband, Squadron Leader Chris Holloway. George, her brother, is a fighter pilot, and has miraculously returned from the dead. How absolutely spiffing!'

She was now the centre of attention and instead of being ignored, they clamoured to hear the full story and she gave them a brief version.

'Crikey,' one of them said, shaking his head. 'That's a wedding present and a half, having a dead brother turn up on your honeymoon.'

'Imagine if he'd arrived during his own memorial service – that would have been even more extraordinary,' Ruth said as she finished reading the story.

She extricated herself from the crush around the newspaper and she and Sam returned to their bench in the corner.

'I'm not surprised it's made the national newspapers,' he said as he handed back her cocoa. 'Good news is in short supply. I expect there's a letter chasing you around the country. I wish now that we'd gone to Chelmsford as you suggested, as then you could have met this brother and congratulated your friend.'

'I'm glad we didn't as if we had then I'd have missed having such a wonderful day with you.'

'That's true, but you'd have avoided the unpleasantness with your friend Jill and her fiancé.'

'I've put that from my memory. These last two days have been for us – we haven't known each other long but one thing I do know is that I believe you might become someone rather special in my life.'

They'd been talking quietly, making sure their conversation couldn't be overheard by the others around the table and on the far side of the room. Instead of answering, Sam grabbed her hand and almost pulled her out of the room. What was he so excited about?

8

Sam guided Ruth to the small vestibule where guests signed in and out. 'I'm sorry to drag you away from your cocoa and biscuits but there's something I need to say to you.'

He hadn't intended to tell how he felt but she'd given him the perfect opportunity, admitting that she felt there was something special between them.

'I feel the same way as you, I knew the moment I saw you beside the train you were going to be important to me. I know you don't want to get engaged or anything like that and I respect your views. But I hope that one day you'll be ready to hear me ask you that very important question.'

Ruth was facing him but in the gloom of the dimly

lit space he couldn't decide if she was dismayed or de-lighted by his words.

'It's too soon to think about anything permanent, Sam, but ask me that question next year and I'm pretty sure you'll get the answer you want.'

He pulled her closer and kissed her, his mouth hard against hers. She responded so passionately that he almost lost control. His heart was hammer-ing; he'd never felt like this about any girl and had never wanted to go all the way, but now things were different. She was as innocent as he and he wanted their first time to be something special.

Gently he untangled her arms from around his neck. 'I'm sorry, I've just got to say it. I love you.'

'I know you do, and I'm pretty sure that I feel the same. But I'm not quite ready to say those words as it will mean we have to make a commitment that might be difficult to hold to. I'm posted close to you at the moment, but that could change. When the invasion of France takes place, who knows where either of us will be.'

'We'll take it slowly, put our duty first and when the time's right we'll make this official.'

She reached out and touched his face. Her finger was smooth, the feel of it sent him wild with desire.

He wanted to snatch her back and do more than just kiss her. He held his breath, not daring to move.

'I promise you that if we're still together in two years then I'll be more than happy to marry you.'

A surge of joy almost made him shout out but he restrained the urge and was glad he'd done so when she continued.

'A lot can happen in two years. We might have lost touch, met somebody else, one of us might be killed by a bomb – for the moment, let's just enjoy each other's company and the fact that we're young, healthy and doing our bit in the army.'

He swallowed his disappointment and hoped she hadn't seen his expression before he'd hidden it. 'God, if you put it like that, love, I don't know why we're bothering to go out together at all.'

'We're going out as we like each other, because you're the handsomest man I've ever met and also the kindest.' She tilted her head on one side and pursed her lips. 'I have had an occasional date but never a real boyfriend.'

'So I'm the first bloke you've liked?'

'Don't make assumptions, Sergeant Johnson, I might have wanted to be a girlfriend to one of them and been ignored.' She smiled and he chuckled.

'Don't fish for compliments, love. I hope to be your

first and last too.' He grinned and smoothed back his hair in what he hoped was a dashing manner. 'After all, if I look like a film star, I doubt you'll find anybody better looking than me.'

'Looks aren't everything. What if I meet a wealthy, aristocratic officer? I think a good bloodline and a large trust fund trumps looking like a film star.'

'Don't use the word trumps – I don't want to be reminded of playing bridge,' he scowled at her but his eyes were dancing.

'Is that all you can say? I've just told you I might run off with a rich lord and you're worried about my reference to yesterday's debacle.'

'I'm not worried about anything you said as it's all complete balderdash. I can hear the others coming so we'd better get going if we want to use the bathroom first.'

He kissed her once more before she vanished into her tiny bedroom and then prowled about outside to make sure none of the other guests rattled the door or caused her any embarrassment. Whatever she thought about things, as far as he was concerned, she was his girl now and he was going to keep her safe.

* * *

They didn't go down for breakfast until the guests who were going off to work had finished, which meant they had the dining room to themselves. The breakfast was just as good and the tea freshly made.

'I've just got to pay the bill and then we can head to the station. What time did you arrange to meet Jill?'

'I've already paid – don't look so disapproving, Sam, you paid for everything yesterday and it's only fair that I pay my share.'

'The bloke has to pay. It's how it's done. I'll reimburse you – how much was it?' He tried not to sound cross, but he was. Ruth kept saying that she was an independent woman, but she didn't seem to understand stepping on his toes was making him feel inadequate.

'No, my aunt brought me up to—'

'Be independent – I know that, you've told me often enough,' he said and her smile slipped.

'I'm sorry if you disapprove of my upbringing, Sam, but that's how things are. If you don't like it, then...'

He reached across the table so suddenly she recoiled and the precious piece of sausage she had just speared on her fork flew across the room.

'God, I'm sorry.' He was on his feet and collecting it before she could react.

She started to giggle. 'Are you apologising to me, my sausage or the Almighty?'

He had the missing item on the end of his own fork and looked down at it solemnly. 'The sausage, of course – he didn't deserve to be tossed across the dining room.'

'I'm not eating it after its unexpected adventure so I'm kindly donating it to you.'

He looked down at it – it hadn't done more than fly across the table so wasn't a health hazard. 'Thank you, your generosity is noted and appreciated.' He pulled it from the end of his fork and chewed noisily.

She was still laughing and he prayed she'd forgotten she'd been about to send him packing. He certainly wasn't going to mention it.

When he was seated, she took his hand. 'I wasn't going to suggest that we stop seeing each other.'

'That's a relief.'

She raised an imperious hand and he raised both eyebrows, which made her laugh again.

'Please don't do that, I'm trying to be serious. I was going to say that if you don't like the way I am then you'd better hurry up and get used to it because I'm not going to change.'

He closed the distance between them and kissed

her thoroughly. They were interrupted by the land-lady, who'd come in to collect the dirty crockery.

'Well, what a palaver! I can't remember the last time I've seen two people so much in love. Good for you – you deserve to be happy.'

Sam didn't look at Ruth in case she decided to explain how things really were between them. 'I'm sorry, ma'am, a bit much at the breakfast table. We've enjoyed our stay here, thank you for making us so welcome.'

'I second that. We don't get a lot of time together and staying here has been perfect.'

'Ta ever so, it was lovely having you here for a couple of nights. Do you want any more toast or fresh tea?'

'That's kind of you but we've got to get to the station.' Sam pushed his chair back and Ruth did the same.

They stood on the pavement holding hands, both sad that their leave was almost over.

'The brilliant thing about today is that we're going to travel together. I wish I'd made a firm arrangement with Jill but all we said was that we'd get the mid-morning train. I'm hoping she'll be at the left luggage office as it might be difficult to find her otherwise. The trains seem to be a mile long nowadays.'

He insisted he was going to carry her kitbag and after some hesitation she agreed. 'I don't want you to feel awkward in front of your section, so obviously in public you must do whatever you think's appropriate.'

'Fair enough. It's going to take a bit of getting used to, having a girlfriend with a mind of her own.'

She nudged him with her elbow and he stumbled sideways dramatically, which made her laugh again. He loved to see her happy.

* * *

Ruth handed in her ticket to the elderly man behind the counter and he produced her bag. 'I'm hoping you can tell me if any other ATS girls have been to collect theirs recently?'

They couldn't see Jill outside the office, and Ruth hoped she was already on the train that was due to leave in twenty minutes.

'Half a dozen of them a few minutes ago. I reckon you're all going on the same train.'

The station was full of uniforms, but most of them were the blue of the RAF and the WAAF, only a sprinkling of khaki.

'I should have realised the other members of our

section would probably catch this train. I'm not sure if I should go in search of them or travel with you.'

'You're not on duty until you reach the base so you can do what you want. I'll understand if you want to find Jill and the other girls, but I hope you don't.'

'I don't – I intend to spend every possible minute in your company. I've had such a lovely time, have you?'

His answer was to snatch her off her feet. The fact that he did this one-handed whilst holding her heavy bag in the other was almost as exciting as his kiss. Her hat was askew, her cheeks pink but her eyes were sparkling.

'Come on, we're going to be lucky to get a seat. We really should have got here a bit earlier.' Sam shouldered her bag, took her hand and they jogged through the crowds, waved their travel warrants at the guard, and then started searching for a space.

This train had no corridors, just individual compartments that stretched the width of the train with a door on each side. Ruth much preferred to travel in the ones where you weren't stuck with the seven other passengers for the entire journey.

Halfway down, Sam stopped. 'Plenty of room in this one.' There was only one adult passenger inside but there were also two screaming, very smelly toddlers.

Their arrival stopped the noise and the two of them – obviously twins – stared, round eyed. The mother, heavily pregnant, appeared to be asleep. No wonder the little ones were so unhappy.

'I'm good with children; strangely this is the second time I've travelled with distressed kiddies.' He was talking quietly, not wanting to wake the mother. 'I've not delivered a baby before, though, so let's hope that skill won't be needed on this journey.'

Sam put his hand back on the door. He was looking down the platform.

Ruth had expected him to shake his head, close the door and offer to help too, but he dropped her bag on the floor and was gone. The door slammed behind him. The sudden noise scared the twins and they screamed, waking up their mother.

'What? Please stop that noise, Lily, Iris, please give me a minute to rest?' the poor young woman, her face grey with fatigue, her light brown hair limp and un-kempt, said desperately.

'Hello, I'm Ruth, shall I change them for you? Are there nappies in that bag?'

The woman jerked upright and stared at Ruth. 'I'm sorry, I didn't realise you were in here. Yes, everything you need's in that. There's also biscuits and juice for them.' She managed to sit a bit straighter, but it was an effort. 'I'm Rose Drummond, this one's due any day and I'm desperate to get home before it comes so my family can help out.'

Now wasn't the time to ask why Rose had left it so late in the pregnancy. Neither could she dwell on Sam's behaviour. There must be a reason why he'd deserted her and this family and she wasn't going to make any hasty judgements until she'd spoken to him later.

Changing both children wasn't pleasant but once they were dry and clean, had been given a drink and handed a biscuit, they were happy to sit on the bench seat quietly next to their mother.

'Let me help you put your feet up, Rose, nobody else is going to get in with us and you'll be so much more comfortable like that.'

'You're being so kind. I know you must think me completely mad to be travelling on my own so near to my delivery date, but it took me far longer than I'd expected to sort things out at home.' She stopped and tried to hide her tears. There was more going on here than just a sudden move to join her mother.

Ruth picked up the twins and put them on the other seat. 'Lily, Iris, I'm going to make you comfortable over here and you can have a nice nap. When you wake up, I'll tell you a story – how's that?'

The little girls, now comfortable, fed and no longer scared, made no objection. She tucked blankets she'd found in the bag around each of them. She was puzzled that they hadn't got a rag doll or teddy – there was something odd going on here but it was none of her business.

'I really do appreciate your help, Ruth, you obviously know a bit about babies.'

'Not much, but enough to change a nappy. I'm getting out at Lincoln – what about you?'

'Me too, my father is Dr Munson and still has petrol for his car so he'll be meeting us. Let's hope my daughters sleep for most of the journey.'

Ruth helped Rose get comfortable, pushing her own haversack under her head as a pillow. With a sigh, the young woman closed her eyes and fell asleep. Ruth wondered how long it had been since Rose had managed to do more than close her eyes for a few seconds.

If Sam had stayed, it would have been so much easier taking care of the babies and their exhausted mother. Although she hadn't known him very long, she was still shocked and hurt that he'd not been prepared to help.

The train was picking up speed, the chuff-chuff of the engine soothing the girls and they fell asleep almost immediately.

Ruth wasn't sure how far it was between stations but knew her journey would be around four hours so there was no need to worry at the moment. Her knowledge of this route was non-existent, she'd have to open the window later and lean out in the hope that the guard would shout out the name of the station. Sam was familiar with this line and would have known exactly when to get off and it was rather selfish of him to have abandoned her.

She'd positioned the twins with their backs to the wall so was confident they wouldn't roll off unless the train stopped suddenly. Her kitbag was in the narrow gap between the seats so if they did fall before she could reach them, they would land on that and not the floor.

Although she had carefully wrapped the smelly nappies in the rubber sheet, she'd found the whiff was still quite noticeable. Should she have put this sheet underneath the twins? No – they had rubber pants over their nappies and that should stop any leakage.

Now everything was calm, her three companions sleeping peacefully, she had time to study them more closely. The babies were clean, their clothes looked expensive and they were definitely well-nourished. Rose was equally well dressed, and despite the pallor of her skin and her unwashed hair, Ruth could tell this wasn't a family without funds.

Why were they travelling alone? Surely someone like Rose should have had a nanny or maid to accompany her. Also, wouldn't they have been in first class where there was a dining car and waiters to take care of their every need? It didn't make sense this family was travelling in third class.

They'd been steaming along for half an hour and the compartment remained peaceful when Ruth heard the brakes being applied and the train began to slow. They must be approaching a station but as Lincoln was still many hours away, there was no need for her to get up. The main problem was that fresh passengers might want to get in with them and that would mean waking Rose and the girls.

The train rocked to a halt. She'd been observing carefully and hadn't noticed many passengers on the platform so didn't bother to stand up. She could hear the guard shouting at someone and then the carriage door opened and Sam jumped in.

The guard slammed it behind him and they were in motion again. To her astonishment and relief, none of the sleepers woke. She wasn't quite sure what to say to him so just sat silently, waiting for him to speak.

He wasn't looking at her but busy opening a large cardboard box he'd somehow acquired. 'God, that was close. I'd noticed there was WVS cart and wanted to get something for them to eat and drink. I just had time to get all this when the whistle went and had to jump in the nearest compartment. I wasn't popular, I can tell you.'

Ruth was so glad she hadn't said anything as she'd completely misjudged him and the situation. 'I didn't know where you'd gone and I can't tell you how happy I am that you're back and with supplies.'

He was perched on the end of the seat where Rose was stretched out. Like a conjurer getting a rabbit from a top hat, he held up two small knitted teddies. 'Look what I managed to get! The ladies were reluctant to part with them until I told them who they were for. I hope the tiddlers like them. How did you get them all to sleep so peacefully?'

'They're exhausted, especially Rose. Once I'd made them comfortable, nature did the rest. They don't have any personal possessions and only biscuits and juice.'

They'd been talking in whispers, her head close to

his. Instead of replying, he cupped her chin and kissed her softly.

'I didn't have time to tell you what I was going to do. I bet you thought I'd abandoned you. I wouldn't do that. This family needs our help – as I scrambled into the compartment, I noticed a man in a suit and two ruffians race to the platform. I think these three and those three could be connected.'

Ruth hadn't been going to admit that she had doubted him but decided honesty was important. 'I was very cross but then decided I'd wait until you explained what was going on before making a decision. How could you possibly know the man in the suit had anything to do with Rose and her daughters?'

'Instinct. One glance at these was enough to see they were running from something – a well-dressed young woman wouldn't travel without several suitcases and all she's got is that bag. I bet it's just things for the babies.'

She nodded. 'You're right. Gosh, I do hope those men didn't manage to get on the train.'

'Not a chance, they were arguing with the guard and wouldn't have had time. That said, I reckon if I'm right they'll be on the next one.'

Rose had woken up and had been listening to their conversation. 'I'm so sorry, I should have been honest.

Was the man in the suit tall with fair hair and the two men with him swarthy, like Italians?'

'They were. There must be a good reason for you to be on this train and you don't have to tell us. I promise we'll keep you safe.'

Ruth interrupted. 'Rose told me her father's collecting them at Lincoln station. Those men can't possibly get there before us, so I hope we've got nothing to worry about.'

9

Sam settled himself more comfortably on the seat and was finally able to relax. 'You're right, Ruth, I'm worrying unnecessarily. Do you want to see what I've got here?'

He was clutching the cardboard box on his lap and despite the fact it had been more than half an hour since he'd bought these items, he could still feel the residual warmth from the meat pasties and mug of tea.

'Yes, show me. Did you manage to get something suitable for the little ones?'

Rose stirred again and opened her eyes. 'I thought I heard you say you had something edible in your box? I feel a bit better now I know we're safe and my stomach is gurgling, which isn't good for the baby.'

'I've got just the thing. I've also got a mug of tea, which is still just about warm enough to be drunk.'

He carefully removed the tea, impressed that he'd managed to transport it without spilling more than a couple of drops. He grinned at Ruth, who was looking with interest, and handed the mug to her.

'It's easier for you to give it to Rose, I don't want to wake up the babies.'

Every drop of the tea was consumed eagerly and then Rose ate a meat pasty and a jam sandwich with equal enthusiasm.

'I can't tell you how grateful I am to you both. Aren't you going to have anything from that miraculous box?'

'We had a massive breakfast not long ago,' Sam said. 'Also, neither of us will eat until we're quite sure you and the children have had enough.'

'Do you know if I'll have time to use the loo at the next station? I'm surprised I haven't had an accident already.'

Sam nodded. 'Yes, the train will stop for ten minutes. Anyway, I'll make sure it doesn't leave before you're back. Don't worry.'

Ruth checked both girls were comfortable and then returned to her seat. 'You don't have to tell us,

Rose, but I would like to know why you're so desperate to get away from that man – is he your husband?'

'I owe you that much, I suppose. Brian seemed the ideal husband, he was wealthy, worked in the Foreign Office and my parents loved him, as did I.' Rose paused, her fingers clenched, but after a few seconds she continued. 'Everything started to change after the twins were born. He became more demanding, insisted his old nanny took care of them, even though he knew I wanted to do it myself.

'Initially I just thought it was because he loved me, but as he became more controlling, I realised he was jealous of our babies and didn't want to share me with anyone else. He didn't want me to see my parents or go out without one of those horrible men he employs trailing along behind me. Too late, I was seeing the true character of the man I'd married.'

'Did he physically abuse you?'

'It depends what you mean by that. He didn't beat me, but he did push me, slap me occasionally if I annoyed him, but never hard enough to leave marks.'

'How absolutely horrible for you,' Ruth said sympathetically.

Rose, once started, wanted to tell them the entire story. 'He ignored the twins and I only got to spend time with them when he was at work. Their nanny was too old to look after the babies once they were mobile and she was only too happy to let me take them as long as Brian didn't find out. I think she'd been living in poverty and was determined to stay warmly housed and well fed for as long as possible.'

Sam wanted to know what had finally driven the young woman to flee. 'Why did you leave today? What happened?'

Rose looked at him, her eyes wide, and he could see the fear in them. 'He said this baby wasn't his and that it would be taken away and adopted as soon as it was born.'

Ruth gasped. 'No wonder you ran away. I think your husband sounds unbalanced. You'll be much happier with your parents.'

One of the twins woke up and started to grizzle, interrupting the conversation. Ruth was there to comfort her and after being offered a portion of meat pasty, the little girl stopped crying and tucked in.

'This is Iris and her sister is Lily. Iris has a purple ribbon around her wrist and Lily has a white one, otherwise I wouldn't know the difference.'

Ruth, who had Iris on her lap, looked across at Rose. 'How can you tell them apart when undressed?'

'I struggle sometimes too! But Iris has a small birthmark on her back and Lily doesn't. I'm hoping as they grow, their personalities will make it easier.'

'We'll be stopping soon, Rose, so you need to get your shoes on so you can use the WC.'

'I think you'll have to go with her, Sam, I'll stay here with the babies.'

'I'd be really grateful for your help, I'm not very steady today.' The young woman shrugged. 'To be honest, I've not been able to walk safely for the last two weeks. I was able to get a taxi to the station and a porter kindly allowed me to put the girls on his trolley, otherwise I would never have got here.'

Sam accompanied Rose to use the facilities and he didn't have to ask the guard to hold the train for a few extra minutes as he took one look and nodded sympathetically.

'Bless you, when my Beryl was expecting she was in and out the bathroom like nobody's business. The train won't go without you, madam, don't you fret.'

The bloke obviously thought Sam was the husband and there was no need to disabuse him. Whilst he was waiting outside the ladies' room, something that had been niggling at the back of his mind occurred to him.

He beckoned the obliging guard over. 'Would it be possible for somebody to ring ahead and ask for a message to be given to a passenger?'

'Not here, but at one of them big stations, yes. People what have missed the train can ask the station-master to transfer the message.'

'Thank you, we were just discussing this and I said I'd find out the answer.' Sam smiled and turned to take Rose's arm as she emerged.

'Off you go then, I don't want to keep the train waiting if I can avoid it,' the guard said.

Rose was just seated when the whistle blew and the train steamed out of the station. Sam needed to discuss something with Ruth that he didn't want overheard.

'Lily's eaten her pasty and they've both had a drink of water and a few slices of apple. They still seem sleepy, Rose, do you think they'll go down for another nap?'

'Definitely. Come along, girls, we're all going to sleep for a while. Mummy is very tired.'

The girls didn't speak but they seemed to understand.

'Here you are, cuddle your nice new teddies,' Sam said and handed them over.

The toys were a huge success and the twins hugged and kissed them before happily snuggling down for a second time. He watched Ruth talking softly to them, tucking them in, even giving both of them a kiss and he was moved by the scene. She was going to make a wonderful mother some day and he prayed it would be to his children and not somebody else's.

Rose was already asleep and he joined Ruth on her side of the compartment. 'This Brian sounds a nasty bit of work. He might have rung the local police in Lincoln and told them that his wife was unstable and had kidnapped his children, or something like that.'

She stared at him. 'My God, you're right. They could be waiting at the station for them. What are we going to do?'

'I think we'll have to get off at Nottingham. If we book us all into a hotel, we can wait until her father can drive down and collect them.'

'We're both going to be late. As a sergeant you'll probably get away with it, but I doubt that I will,' she said.

'You're a bombardier now, love, gives you a bit of clout. With any luck, we'll be able to report back before curfew. I don't think it would help to tell them what we're up to. We'd be told in no uncertain times that duty comes first and this is none of our business.'

'I know that, but we can't leave Rose and her babies until we're sure she's safe.'

They'd been talking quietly and every few moments he'd been checking that Rose was asleep. Time enough to tell her what they planned when they were approaching the station.

* * *

Ruth was happy to spend the time playing with the babies whilst their mother remained asleep. She was delighted that Sam joined in. They used the two teddies to tell stories and there were plenty of funny voices, silly faces and songs to keep the twins entertained.

'We'll be pulling into Nottingham in about fifteen minutes, so do you want to wake Rose?'

'I'm still not sure we shouldn't have told her we're actually getting off at a different station,' Ruth said.

'The stations don't have names, she'll be none the wiser until we're safely away from the train. We'll explain then. Can you manage the two little ones if I take the bags and hold her arm?'

'I can take care of the children as long as I don't need to change their nappies as there aren't any more in the bag.' She had a tentative feel of the nearest bottom and nodded. 'They're a bit damp but nothing too disastrous. I don't know about you, but I'm concerned Rose has slept through everything. I do hope she's all right.'

'Her father's a doctor. What did she say his name was?'

'Munson, but we still don't know hers. We really ought to be able to tell the hotel her name,' Ruth said.

'We can ask her later. Dr Munson should be with her by this evening and can take care of her. All we've got to do is keep them safe for now.'

'It's occurred to me that we might be making a horrible mistake and just making things worse. What if her father is there, no sign of the police, won't he think the worst? Could we be arrested for interfering?' Ruth was worried.

'Don't be daft, Rose will tell them what's what. Better to be safe than sorry, love.'

'We don't want to put too many eggs in one basket and a stitch in time saves nine,' she said, just managing to keep her face straight.

He looked at her for a second and then nodded

solemnly. 'A bird in the hand is worth two in the bush and – blimey, I can't think of any more.'

'I'm sorry to tease, but you did say I was daft.'

The twins had soft button-up shoes and a set of leather reins each. Whilst he put these on, Ruth gently woke the sleeping woman.

'We'll be getting off soon, Rose, you need to sit up and put your shoes back on. I'll take the twins and Sam will help you and carry the bags.'

'I desperately need to pee. I assume that there'll be a ladies' room.'

'I'm sure there will,' Ruth said and glanced across at Sam, who nodded. 'I expect Lily and Iris will enjoy toddling up and down the platform whilst you go. Then I'll have to do the same before we leave the station.'

Sam put the bags down on the platform first then lifted the babies out and she jumped down and took hold of their reins. Next, he assisted Rose from the train and guided her to the building with the WC. The train had already steamed away by the time Ruth was back and they were making their way to the exit.

Nottingham station was busy, a fair number of passengers had alighted from the same train, which meant the ticket collector only gave their travel warrants and Rose's tickets a cursory glance. This was fortunate as if he'd told Rose they weren't at Lincoln, she might have panicked.

The interior of the station was smoky, noisy and crowded and at first Rose didn't notice this wasn't where she was supposed to be.

'I've not been here for years but it really doesn't look familiar. Have we got off at the wrong station?'

'I'm afraid we must have,' Sam said, taking his cue from her. 'I'm sorry, I was convinced it was Lincoln. It must be Nottingham.'

Instead of being upset, she shrugged. 'Don't worry, I know this town well. There's an excellent hotel we can wait at until my father arrives. Would you be kind enough to telephone the house? He'll ring home when I don't appear with the girls.' She handed over a piece of paper with the telephone number on it.

'Be happy to. Now, direct us to this hotel, we could all do with a decent cuppa and a bun.' Sam smiled at Ruth, and she nodded. Better to lie than worry Rose with the real reason they'd not remained on the train.

Rose suddenly grimaced. 'Actually, I'm so glad we got off early. I'm think I might be going into labour.'

Ruth exchanged a horrified look with Sam. This was the worst possible news.

To her relief, the twins were able to walk without stumbling and seemed solid on their feet. Maybe they were older than she thought. She didn't know a lot about babies. It was Rose who was having difficulty and Sam now had his free arm firmly about her waist. If this hotel wasn't close, Ruth feared they wouldn't make it without mishap.

Perhaps if she talked to Rose about her delightful daughters, this might help. 'How old are your girls?'

'They're eighteen months – Iris is five minutes older than Lily. I just pray I'm not having twins again this time. Brian wouldn't let me see a midwife or doctor as he said it didn't matter because the baby or babies would be put up for adoption as they weren't his.'

'Why ever would he think that?'

'He insisted that he'd used protection, but I know that at least twice he didn't.' Rose stumbled and Sam barely managed to keep her upright.

'Less talking, concentrate on moving your feet and not falling over, Rose,' he told her. 'Ruth, I can see the hotel just at the end of this road. Can you carry the babies and get there quickly and see if they've got a wheelchair. We're going to need it.'

She didn't argue that the children were too heavy but scooped them up, and with one on each hip she jogged, much to their delight, the remaining distance, arriving red-faced and breathless in the large hotel foyer. The concierge immediately hurried towards her.

'We need a wheelchair – their mother's heavily pregnant and about to collapse further down the street.'

'If you'd care to sit on the sofa with the children, miss, I'll make sure that their mother arrives safely.' The middle-aged, grey-haired man snapped his fingers and two uniformed young men appeared with a wheelchair as if they'd been waiting somewhere for just this summons.

Ruth produced the teddies which she'd tucked into her uniform jacket. 'Look, girls, your teddies have come too. They need a big cuddle after all the rushing about.'

She handed over the toys and the children cooed and kissed them and then began to babble in what sounded like complete nonsense, but they seemed to understand each other. Her aunt had once told her that twins could develop their own private language.

Another man in a tailcoat was approaching. He looked even more important than the concierge. 'Could you please make an urgent telephone call? The details, name and number are on this piece of paper. Please ask Dr Munson to get here as fast as he can.'

She handed him the paper Rose had given her and he read it, nodded and strode back to the imposing mahogany reception desk. She heard him making the call and prayed that Rose's father would get the message. Then something dreadful occurred to her. They'd got off the train half an hour before it was due to arrive in Lincoln. Dr Munson would still be waiting and not even know his daughter and granddaughters needed him so desperately.

'Stay where you are, Lily, Iris, I just have to speak to the kind man behind the desk. I won't be a moment.'

They looked up then resumed their babble and weren't upset when she dashed across the acre of Axminster carpet. 'Excuse me,' she said to the man behind the desk. 'Could I also ask you to call the nearest local doctor? Dr Munson might not be here soon enough.'

'Soon enough? Are you suggesting that his daughter is about to give birth? Would it be better to take her to the hospital? We don't have the facilities here for delivering a baby.'

Ruth glared at him. 'Don't be ridiculous. If you get the doctor, and a midwife if there is one, all that's needed is a room, towels and hot water. A hotel is the perfect place to have a baby if you can't be at home.'

He looked about to argue the point, but at the same moment the operator answered his call and with considerable reluctance he asked for another number. Ruth waited, glancing constantly over her shoulder at the twins, whilst this second call was connected. She heard him ask the doctor to come at once and to bring the midwife if possible. He replaced the receiver and turned to continue his protest, but Ruth didn't allow him to speak.

'I must have somewhere quiet for those two, so we'll need adjoining rooms. Their mother can have one and I'll go in the other.'

As he hesitated, she leaned forward. 'I'm sure you don't wish me to make a scene, but I can assure you that I will if you don't do what I want immediately.'

She turned her back on him and stood tall, praying this would convince him she was prepared to start yelling for somebody to help because he wouldn't.

The twins saw her and started to wriggle off the sofa. Ruth ran across and was just in time to prevent them from tumbling to the carpet, not that they would have come to harm as that would have been a soft landing.

'Right, you two, your mummy will be here in a

minute and we're going to find a lovely room where you can play.'

The manager arrived at her side, looking a little more conciliatory. 'Corporal, Dr Otter is on his way. Billy over there is going to take you up to your rooms and I'll bring the expectant mother. I can see that she's just arriving. Is the sergeant her husband?'

'No, Sergeant Johnson is my boyfriend. We only met this family on the train and are acting as good Samaritans until her family arrive.'

Leaving him to mull over what she'd told him, she took a little hand in each of hers and led the toddlers across to the lift. Billy grinned, closed the lift door behind them and pushed and pulled the appropriate levers.

The room they'd been given overlooked the main street but was spacious, well-appointed and more than adequate. There was a bathroom that was obviously shared with the adjoining room, which was even better.

She removed the toddlers' reins, shoes and socks in order to let them run around barefooted, when there was a knock on the door. 'I'm coming, just a minute.'

When she opened the door, a smart woman in a navy-blue dress marched in, followed by two chambermaids carrying baskets. 'I'm Mrs Rigby, the house-keeper here. I've brought clean nappies, towels and so on for the children. I'll have tea sent up in half an hour. I'm going to prepare the room for their mother.'

'Thank goodness. I don't really know much about looking after toddlers.'

10

Sam assisted Rose into the much-needed wheelchair and then shoved the bags into the willing hands of the two flunkies.

'Thank you, I doubt I could have reached the hotel without this,' Rose said as she collapsed into the waiting chair. 'I'm almost sure that I'm in labour. My father isn't going to be here in time to deliver his next grandchild.'

Sam was pushing her at the double and he tried not to think about how much trouble he and Ruth were going to be in. If Rose did have the baby, it was unlikely they'd be able to reach their respective sections today and would almost certainly be considered as AWOL. Being absent without leave was a serious offence but he was fairly confident they wouldn't be classed as deserters, which would be even worse. A deserter could be shot.

The doorman was there to help carry the patient and chair up the steps and into the foyer. Sam caught a glimpse of Ruth and the twins before they vanished.

'Mrs Drummond is in labour. Is the doctor on his way?' Sam spoke to the man in charge. Rose was gritting her teeth and clenching her hands, unable to speak.

'Yes, Sergeant, all arranged. The housekeeping staff are making a room ready. The lift is waiting.'

Rose looked up at him, her eyes wet, and nodded. He squeezed her shoulder. 'You'll be somewhere comfortable soon and the doctor will be here any minute.'

After a short journey, the lift rattled to a stop and Sam followed the manager towards an open door a little way down the wide carpeted corridor. This was an expensive establishment and he was glad he wouldn't have to foot the bill.

He heard the lift descend behind him and hoped it was going back to collect the doctor. Just then, a youngish man in a rumpled suit arrived at the head of the stairs, swinging a battered medical bag.

'Right in the nick of time, I'd say. I'll take it from here, Sergeant.' The doctor smiled down at Rose. 'How close are the contractions?'

Sam didn't hear the answer as the wheelchair and medic whisked though the open door and it was kicked shut behind them.

'Blimey, that was close,' he said to the manager.

'Mrs Drummond will be well taken care of. Dr Otter is an excellent physician. He attends to any of our guests that require medical aid.' The man smiled and looked less stiff. 'This will the first baby born here and hopefully the last.'

Sam slapped him on the back. 'Chin up, mate, it might be two babies. I believe Mrs Drummond has stayed here before; her father is Dr Munson from Lincoln.'

The man's expression changed. 'Good heavens, I'd no idea who she was. Thank God you weren't turned away.'

'You know the family?'

'The Munson family own this hotel; her grandfather opened it fifty years ago. I've worked here for twenty years but Benson, under manager, on the desk only started last year and wouldn't have recognised the name on the note.' He straightened, looking shell-shocked, and rushed off. No doubt to ensure everything possible was thrown in their direction.

Sam wanted to find Ruth and thought she'd probably be with the children in the adjacent room. He knocked and a uniformed maid opened the door.

'Come in, sir, Miss Ruth is just changing the babies in the bathroom. They'll be out in a minute.'

'Good, neither of us have eaten since breakfast...'

The girl beamed. 'Don't worry, nursery tea will be arriving at any moment and then Gladys is going straight down to fetch you and Miss Ruth a tray.'

'I prefer tea but Bombardier Cox is a coffee drinker. If you've got the real stuff, a jug of that would be perfect. By the way,' he said with a smile, 'I'm Sergeant Johnson – makes it easier to address us correctly, don't you think?'

'Beg your pardon, Sarge, I'll mind me Ps and Qs in future,' the girl giggled and dashed back into the bathroom to offer her assistance. From the racket in there, it was urgently needed.

* * *

The food for the babies arrived and also two highchairs – this hotel was certainly well equipped.

Small wonder Rose had said she knew of an excellent hotel – why hadn't she told them it was a family-owned business? Mind you, he couldn't complain about the service he'd got, even when they hadn't known exactly who they were dealing with.

Sally, the maid who'd let him in, was looking after the children, who were gabbling, laughing and eating, not at all bothered about their missing mother. Rose had said she hadn't spent a lot of time with them so perhaps they were used to her not being there.

Gladys had brought up a tray with tea, coffee, and a delicious array of sandwiches, cakes and savoury items. Ruth joined him at the table on the far side of the room that had been set out with a white cloth and silver cutlery.

'Golly, this is a spread – the concierge wasn't too pleased to see me initially but has obviously mellowed for some reason.'

He quickly explained and she laughed.

'I bet Benson's worried about his employment after the way he behaved when I first arrived. I hope Rose is going to be all right and the baby too. I can't believe that anyone could be so cruel to an expectant mother.'

'She'll be safe now and if I'd realised how important her family are, I'd not have insisted we got off the train early. I think it highly unlikely the Lincoln constabulary would have interfered, don't you?'

'Well, we didn't know and acted in what we thought were her best interests. Anyway, imagine if we'd had to try and deliver a baby on the train.'

'Then we did the right thing.'

Ruth poured herself another brimming cup of coffee. 'We can't leave until her father gets here and then it might take us hours to get to our bases. Are we going to be AWOL?'

'That's exactly what I wanted to talk to you about. I think we should telephone our respective officers and explain why we're going to be late. Even if they demand that we return instantly, they won't be any the wiser if we remain here until Rose's father turns up.'

'I agree, in fact I've been thinking that myself. What a shame we weren't travelling with Jill as I covered for her and I'm sure she would have done the same for me. I hope she's all right.'

'She's the least of our problems right now. As the senior NCO, I'm going to volunteer to make both calls. You stay here in case the babies need you.'

'I gave them a top-to-toe wash standing up in the bath and the housekeeper found those nighties from somewhere. After they've finished their tea, I'll let them play for a while and then put them to bed. Gladys and Sally have been assigned to take care of them. I think, on balance, all we've got to do is have a brief chat with Dr Munson and then we can leave. Lily and Iris will be perfectly safe without me here.'

'You're right, we've done everything we can and must now put our duty first. I'll go and make those calls.'

'I'll send for more coffee and another pot of tea. Good luck – I think you're going to need it.'

Sam ignored the lift and took the stairs. He headed for the reception desk and was somewhat taken aback to be immediately escorted into the office at the rear.

'How fortuitous, Sergeant Johnson, I was just coming in search of you. I've spoken to Sir John – Sir John Munson that is – Mrs Drummond's grandfather and explained the situation and told him how much worse things would have been if you and your friend hadn't stepped in to help.'

'We just did what any decent folk would do.'

'You've done far more than that. Sir John is contacting someone senior in the War Office on your behalf. He assures me that however late you and Corporal Cox are reporting for duty, there will be no charges laid against you.'

'Crikey, that's the best possible news. I was just coming down to ask if I could use your telephone and make the necessary calls. We didn't want to be AWOL, or worse, considered deserters.'

The telephone on the desk jangled and Mr Reynolds – he'd now identified himself as the manager – immediately picked up the receiver. He listened, nodded, smiled and then turned and held it out to Sam.

'Sir John would like to speak to you, Sergeant.'

* * *

Ruth had just got the twins settled – one in each single bed – pillows and cushions strategically arranged in case they rolled out, when Sam appeared at the door and beckoned her.

'Can you two sit with them, please? I won't be long.'

The helpful maids nodded and shooed her out.

Sam looked elated and took her hand, shaking his head when she asked what was going on. 'We're going to have a large drink on the house – in fact we can have anything we want on the house.'

'Gracious, has Dr Munson turned up?'

'Not as far as I know. I've just been speaking to –

wait for it – Sir John Munson, Rose's grandfather, who owns the hotel.'

'That's all very interesting but did you manage to speak to somebody at our bases?'

The manager was waiting to escort them to the bar, where a bottle of champagne was waiting. Ruth didn't really like this but was hardly going to say so.

'I know you've both had sandwiches,' the manager said, 'but the kitchen will be available to serve you dinner whenever you're hungry.' He bowed and backed away.

Sam was grinning. 'Sir John knows people in high places and has squared things for us. We don't have to report until tomorrow – as long as we're back before curfew, they don't mind what time it is. Therefore, we're spending the night here in the lap of luxury – how about that?'

'That's absolutely spiffing. Couldn't be better – all we need now is to hear that Rose has delivered a healthy baby and that both of them are doing well.'

'I'm sure someone will come and tell us when there's any news.' He nodded at the unopened bottle. 'Shall we ask them to bring something else? Pity to waste it if neither of us like it.'

'How did you know I wasn't keen on champagne?'

'You've a very expressive face, love, and didn't hide

your distaste quickly enough. I want a beer – preferably a pint of bitter – what's your tipple?'

'I don't like strong alcohol as it makes me feel peculiar, but I do like a lemonade shandy. Do you think such a grand place as this will have bitter and shandy available? The guests here are more sherry and champagne drinkers, I suppose.'

A smart waiter was approaching them, presumably with the intention of opening the bottle and pouring them both a glass. Sam explained they didn't want it and gave him their fresh order and he smiled.

'No problem at all, Sergeant Johnson, whilst you're here you can have anything you want.' The young man – more a youth really, and probably too young to be conscripted – grinned. 'Even if it means I've got to nip down to the local pub and get your order.'

Ruth laughed, as did Sam. 'How long is that likely to take?'

'You've got time to explore the hotel, as I think I'll be gone for fifteen minutes.'

'Right, Ruth, let's do that.' Sam glanced down at his somewhat rumpled uniform. 'At least because we're not in civvies we don't have to feel inferior to the other guests in their mink and dinner jackets.'

There was music from what sounded like a string quartet coming from an open door on the far side of the bar. 'Shall we investigate? It doesn't sound like something we can dance to, but you never know.'

The quartet were playing in the dining room and they listened for a while and then took another door and found themselves in a second salon – this one with booklined walls.

'This is more like it. I'd love to sit here and read but I suppose we'd better go back to the bar or our drinks will never reach us.'

Sam ignored her suggestion and flopped out in one of the deep-seated leather armchairs. 'He'll find us – we're the most important guests here apart from Rose and her children.'

Ruth squeaked. 'Golly, I'd forgotten all about them. I said I'd only be a few minutes. Look, you stay here and I'll run back and check everything's tickety-boo. I won't be long.'

He went to stand but she waved him back. 'No, you've done all the heavy lifting, literally, today. You deserve a rest.'

It took her a few minutes to find her way back to somewhere she recognised and she was crossing the foyer when a man carrying a medical bag bounded through the front door.

He saw her at once and rushed over. He threw his arms around her and she was lifted from her feet in a bear hug. 'My daughter probably owes her life to you, and possibly that of her babies. Whatever I can do for you and Sergeant Johnson now or in the future, you only have to ask.'

'Babies? Has Rose had twins again?'

'She has, this time one of each. Considering the lack of maternity care she had, it's a miracle they've all survived. Excuse me, Corporal Cox, I want to meet my new grandchildren. Where will I find you and your young man?'

'In the library.'

He pumped her hands and then raced off and vanished up the stairs, taking them two at a time. This was the best possible news. Ruth had expected Rose to be in labour for hours and yet now it seemed she was the proud mother of two more children.

Ruth almost forgot the reason she'd left Sam but dashed after Lily and Iris's grandfather, like him ignoring the lift as it was quicker to use the stairs.

The bedroom was quiet apart from the gentle breathing of the babies. The door to the communicating bathroom was closed and there were bangs and the sound of water running coming from there.

She crept across the room using the glimmer of light from under the bathroom door to guide her. 'Any problems?'

'No,' Sally whispered back. 'The two of them are sleeping like little angels. The housekeeper came in to check and two of us are in charge tonight.'

'Thank you, Mrs Drummond has had a little boy and girl and they're all doing well.'

'That's grand. You go off, Corporal, you don't have to worry about these babies any more.'

Ruth whispered her thanks and left them to it. She retraced her steps to burst into the library to see Sam happily slurping a brimming pint of beer. A pint of shandy waited for her on the table next to him.

'Twins again – and all of them are well. I just met Dr Munson.' She paused and frowned. 'I don't understand how he could have known about the babies when he must've been travelling in his car. They don't have telephones in cars, do they?'

'Some military vehicles have two-way radios, but I don't suppose he's got one of those. Does it matter? Shall we drink to the new arrivals?'

An hour later, a maid came in and drew the blackouts. 'Mrs Rigby has asked me to show you to the suite you'll be staying in. Your belongings have already been transferred.'

The suite was on the second floor. Ruth wasn't quite sure she and Sam should be sharing even something as large as a suite. However, when they were ushered in, she saw it was a similar layout to the one she'd shared with her friend Grace – but much more luxurious and larger. This meant it had two bedrooms separated by a large sitting room. There was bound to be a lock on the door, but she was certain she wouldn't need to use it.

The girl who'd taken them pointed to the left. 'That's your room, Corporal, got its own bathroom too.'

'Thank you, I'll go and explore,' Ruth said.

She used the facilities, washed her face and hands and re-pinned her hair. By the time she emerged, Sam was waiting for her.

'This is a bit of all right, I've never stayed anywhere as posh. Do you think you could eat again? I don't want to miss what could be a memorable dinner.'

'What I'd really like to do is see Rose and the new babies – do you think it would be acceptable to knock on the door so soon after delivery?'

'Don't ask me – I'm just a bloke. But there's no reason why you can't knock – they can always say no.' He smiled. 'Count me out, though, I'll wait in the bar for you. Shall I ask for a couple of menus so we can see what's on offer?'

'Yes, do that. Even if I'm allowed in, it will only be for a few minutes so I won't be long.'

He strode off and she turned left and knocked tentatively on the door, not wishing to wake Rose up if she was having a much-needed rest. The door opened and Dr Munson stepped out, beaming.

'Good, I hoped it might be you. My daughter's exhausted, as you might imagine, she's not up to visitors tonight but was most insistent that both you and your young man pop in before you leave tomorrow.'

'I'll be delighted to do that but Sam's a bit skittish about babies and new mothers.'

'Then he'll just have to grit his teeth because he's not leaving without speaking to Rose. Now, have you had dinner?'

'No, we were just about to do so. It would be lovely if you could join us and then we can tell you how we came to be involved and you can tell us about Rose's situation.'

'Splendid, I was going to suggest that myself. Lead the way, young lady, I've not eaten since I got a telephone call from my daughter that she was finally leaving that vile man at five o'clock this morning. I've been on tenterhooks since then.'

* * *

Ruth had no idea what she ate but it was all delicious. She was more interested in the conversation with Dr Munson than the food.

'I did wonder why Rose had left it so late to run away but understand that today was the first opportunity she'd had. Could you not step in earlier and help them?' This probably wasn't a tactful question to ask but she wanted to know.

'If I'd known what was going on, of course I'd have intervened. Rose didn't tell me until this morning what that miserable little bastard had planned.' He was lost in thought for a moment before continuing. 'My wife and I tried to dissuade her from marrying him but he was charming, handsome and plausible and as she was overage, we couldn't stop the wedding.'

'Did you even know she was having another baby?' Sam asked.

'No, that too was a shock.' He dropped his cutlery noisily on his empty dinner plate and sat back. 'Drummond's a ruined man. My father and I will make sure he's homeless and destitute by the time we've finished with him.'

'I'm curious as to how you knew about the babies before you arrived,' Ruth asked.

'I stopped and made a telephone call, Ruth, no mystery involved. That young Dr Otter did a splendid job. Sam is 5 lbs and Ruth is 5 lbs 4 oz. Excellent weights for twins.' He smiled at their stunned faces. 'Rose insists that they're called after you and wants you to be their godparents. I hope you won't say no.'

Ruth was overwhelmed at this piece of news. Having a child named after her was amazing.

11

Sam looked at Ruth and she nodded. If she was okay with being a godparent then he would go along with it.

'That's so kind of Rose,' Ruth said, 'we'd be honoured to be the new twins' godparents, wouldn't we, Sam?'

He nodded. 'Not sure what it entails but I'll do my best.'

Dr Munson laughed. 'Good heavens, young man, we won't expect you to do anything apart from turn up at the church for the christening. That's if you can both get permission to leave your post on the day.'

They said their goodnights and he and Ruth retired to their suite. Neither of them were ready to turn in, so they removed their jackets and shoes and flopped onto the sofa.

'I've been thinking,' Ruth said, 'Rose now has four children under two years old – it's a good thing she's not on her own. I can't think of anything worse – I'm beginning to wonder if I'm cut out for motherhood.'

'Do you have a history of twins in your family?'

'I've no idea.' She looked hurt at his tactless question.

'God, both feet in as usual. Of course you don't know. Anyway, I'd think the odds of anyone having two sets of twins within two years are negligible.' He grinned. 'Must make Rose the luckiest woman in Britain.'

'I really don't know why I'm worrying about it as I'm not intending to have a family until I'm married and that won't be for a while.'

They were sitting close, not touching and as if to soften her words, let him know that when she did get married it would probably be to him, she shifted sideways and leaned against his shoulder.

He swivelled slightly, leaning against the arm of the sofa, making room for her. She obliged by putting both feet on the cushions and settling back with a sigh of contentment.

'It's been an extraordinary couple of days, hasn't it,

Sam? I know you said you didn't want to think about Arthur, but I want to know if you've decided to report him or let it go?'

'I hoped you wouldn't ask me that question as it's going to make things difficult with your friend. I don't have a choice – he might well not be a risk to national security at the moment, but after Jill told us he'd run through his inheritance and had no more resources to pay any debts, I think he definitely could be at some point.'

'I suppose you're right. If you want me to give a statement then I'll do so, however awkward it might make things with Jill. I'm more concerned about the damage it might do to your career prospects than anything else.'

'Don't be, we signed up to protect our country and that's what I'm doing. So far I've not been in any physical danger and thousands of poor buggers have already lost their lives or limbs – especially the RAF aircrew – so putting my career prospects at risk is nothing compared to that.'

'I have a horrible feeling Arthur won't be touched but you'll be posted somewhere remote as a punishment for reporting him. His friends will close ranks, probably deny everything you said...'

'I know that, love, but I've still got to do it. You don't have to be involved.'

'I do. Whatever happens, even if we both end up in disgrace, we'll know we've done the right thing.'

Having her so close was making it difficult as his body was telling him something he was trying to ignore. Gently he extricated himself from behind her and stood up, keeping his back firmly towards her.

'I'd like a jug of cocoa and some of those little sweet things we had after dinner, what about you?'

'Petits fours? Yes, that would be scrumptious. Why don't you ask room service to bring it up – I doubt we'll ever be in this position again.'

'What position?'

'Being VIP guests in a top hotel,' she said.

'So let's make the most of it – is there anything else you fancy?'

She put her arms around his waist from behind him and his pulse rocketed and a pulse of heat made him catch his breath.

'Right, I'll ring down. Do you think they have any boardgames in that cupboard over there?' His voice sounded odd but she didn't seem to notice.

'I'll have a rummage whilst you order our supper. I don't usually drink strong alcohol but why don't we have a brandy to go with our cocoa? That's if they've got any.'

'The sort of people who stay here can have whatever they want. No such thing as rationing for the rich.' Sam picked up the receiver and was immediately answered by reception. He placed his order and was told it would be with them in a few minutes.

'Eureka!' Ruth yelled from the other side of the sitting room. He supposed he should refer to it as a drawing room as they were in such posh place. 'I've got backgammon, Monopoly, snakes and ladders and chess. There are also a few others that I don't recognise. Which one shall we play?'

Sam had everything back under control so walked across to see what she'd found. They agreed Monopoly would take too long, he'd no idea how to play backgammon, disliked chess so snakes and ladders it was. There were packs of cards, but they avoided these as they didn't want to think about the aborted bridge game they'd had a couple of days ago and how it had changed everything for both of them.

Eventually it was a mutual decision to turn in. She put the tray outside the door for the chambermaid to collect whilst he turned out the lights.

'What time are we going down for breakfast, love?'

'Whenever we wake up. It's after midnight now

and from tomorrow we'll be up with reveille. Let's make the most of it,' Ruth replied. 'Whoever's ready first can knock and then read or listen to the wireless. It's a shame we didn't notice until just now that we had one as I'd like to have listened to the evening concert.'

'Right, that's one thing settled. We've got to see Rose and the babies – our namesakes – before we leave. I'll find out what time the trains go tomorrow afternoon. We might as well have lunch here, don't you think?'

'That seems a bit greedy – we've already had so much from them. If you don't mind, I'd like to get a train in the morning just in case it's difficult to get to my posting. There won't be any transport laid on and I might have to walk and I want to leave myself enough time.'

'Bloody hell, you can't walk thirty miles carrying your kitbag.'

'Of course I can if I have to. Don't fuss, I'm part of a mixed artillery section and our officer treats ATS in exactly the same way as the men.'

He took her hands and held them for a moment, then moved closer and kissed her. 'Goodnight, love, it's been a spectacularly good leave for me. I hope you feel the same.' Her smile told him everything he needed to know.

'I don't want to, I'm trying hard not to, but I've a nasty suspicion that I'm falling in love with you. Horrible man – stop being so irresistible.'

Sam was still smiling as he cleaned his teeth. He cocked his head and looked at his reflection. Would Ruth feel the same way if he was ordinary looking? He hoped so – as loving someone because of their looks wasn't a good way to start a long-term relationship. He hoped she liked him for himself, for the man he was and not just for his appearance.

* * *

Ruth was up at seven and enjoyed a long, leisurely shower. She was pretty sure she must have used far more water than if she'd had a shallow bath but today wasn't a day for sticking to the rules.

She was fortunate that she had her full kit and was able to wear fresh clothes. After a quick brush down, her uniform was smart. Her shoes responded to the polish and shone as they should. She wasn't a vain girl, as her aunt had always told her it was what was inside that counted most of all. Even so, she nodded, satisfied she looked her best. Her eyes were shining, her skin glowed and it couldn't just be the fact that she'd had a wonderful night's sleep in the most comfortable bed. Her sparkle, she was pretty sure, was because of Sam.

She'd been out on dates with other young men but he was the first that had kissed her, had held her hand or walked with his arm around her waist. Aunt Jemima had told her that she'd not been lucky enough to meet anyone who made her want to give up her independence. That said, Ruth had been told firmly that although she shouldn't go searching for love, if it found her, she mustn't reject it.

It didn't take long to repack her kitbag and then she was ready to wake Sam up. She glanced at her wristwatch – plain but serviceable and a gift from her aunt – and saw it was almost eight o'clock. High time he was up and taking her down to breakfast.

She adjusted her tie and headed for the door, eager to see the man who, by some twist of fate, had burst into her life. As she opened the door, she walked right into him.

'You're up, I was just coming to wake you,' she said, and he was so close it seemed silly not to step into his embrace and enjoy a good morning kiss.

'I've been up for an hour but didn't like to disturb you. There's a train at eleven so we'll both be able to report for duty in good time.'

She was relieved he hadn't offered to accompany

her to Binbrook, as it was thirty miles further on than Skellingthorpe where he was stationed. Even carrying her kitbag, she was sure she could manage to walk that far without collapsing.

'I'm going to have egg and bacon and coffee, plus lashings of toast.'

'That'll do me,' Sam said. 'Look, Rose's dad is waving to us.'

They headed to the same table as last night and Dr Munson beamed. 'Good morning, I've just ordered a kipper. Too many bones but I love the taste. My wife won't have them in the house so I always have one when I can.'

A waiter was rushing in their direction so Ruth sat down hastily, not wanting to have her chair pulled out for her or her napkin flapped into her lap as if she wasn't capable of doing either thing for herself.

'How are Rose and the new arrivals? I could hear Lily and Iris laughing and playing so didn't go in. The chambermaids are obviously taking excellent care of them.'

'Perfectly splendid, both latched on and Rose is determined to feed them herself as she wasn't allowed to last time. She's asked me to send for Nanny Joseph, the old biddy who was helping with the girls. That's in hand, as well as a younger woman as it's going to be too much to manage four children under two. My wife will be getting everything organised at home.'

Sam had quietly ordered their breakfast whilst the doctor was speaking.

'When will you all be able to go home? Will your daughter and grandchildren have to stay here for a week?' Ruth asked.

'Good God, not at all. Arrangements are being made to transport them all back this afternoon. Rose will be much happier in familiar surroundings. Do you know, yesterday morning I'd never even met Iris or Lily and now I've got Sam and Ruth as well.'

'Is it unusual to have two sets of twins? There must be twins in your family, surely?' Ruth asked.

'My wife's a twin but sadly her sibling didn't survive. It's a nothing short of a medical miracle my darling Rose has produced two sets of healthy babies.' He beamed and looked ten years younger. 'I always wanted a big family and now I've got my wish. I shouldn't say so but in some respects I'm glad that Drummond turned out to be such a rotter, otherwise I might never have got my grandchildren and daughter back.'

Sam winked at her and then said solemnly, 'There's always a silver lining, sir.'

Ruth followed his lead. 'It's an ill wind that blows no good.'

The doctor looked at them both as if they were deranged and then pointed to the tray arriving with his breakfast. 'Good show. Here come my kippers.'

Breakfast over, Ruth and Sam followed Dr Munson to make the obligatory visit to Rose and the new arrivals.

'Before we go in, I'd like to say good morning to the girls,' she said, and the doctor nodded.

'They'll be delighted to see you. Happy little souls, let's hope they start talking properly soon and don't continue to babble in their own version of language.'

The children just glanced up and smiled and returned to their game. The hotel had produced a toy box and what was inside was obviously far more interesting than the three adults in the room, even if one of them was their grandfather.

'Lily and Iris are obviously tickety-boo,' Ruth said.

'I think they must be used to being looked after by a series of adults. Shall we go next door?'

Ruth wasn't quite sure what to expect and was relieved that Rose was sitting up in bed, looking radiant. Considering she'd just had her two babies, her tummy was still mountainous – there was so much Ruth didn't know about pregnancy, childbirth and babies and hoped she didn't have to find out for a while.

'Congratulations, Rose, I'm so glad everything worked out well for you,' Ruth said with a smile and walked over and embraced her.

Sam remained hovering at the door. 'Congratulations, Rose, and thank you for calling them after us.'

'I wanted to do something that would remind me how lucky I was that you two were travelling to Lincoln yesterday.'

Ruth looked around for the babies but couldn't immediately see them. Rose laughed.

'They are on the other side of my bed – we've had to use a drawer from a large chest. This might be a remarkably good hotel but finding two cribs at short notice was beyond even them.'

Tentatively Ruth moved round and stared into the makeshift cradle. Two very small bundles were sleeping peacefully, one at either end. Imagine having to look after something so tiny – helping to fire a giant artillery gun was so much easier and less stressful.

'Which one is Sam and which one Ruth?'

Rose leaned over the bed and pointed to the one nearest to her. 'That's Sam, obviously Ruth is the other baby. I promise you that when you come back for the christening they'll look much more interesting.'

Ruth flushed. 'I've never seen such small babies. Have your girls been introduced to their new brother and sister?'

'No, plenty of time to do that when we're settled. I'm not having the christening until nearer to Christmas. I hope you can arrange to get a day off.'

Sam spoke from the far side of the room. 'We should be due a forty-eight-hour pass by then. If we're both still in Lincolnshire, then we'll be there.'

Dr Munson cleared his throat. This was the welcome sign for them to leave. Ruth said goodbye and felt guilty to be relieved to be out of the overpowering smell of new babies.

They shook hands with the doctor, collected their bags from the luxurious suite they'd occupied for a night, and were ready to leave.

It was only just after nine and the train they'd intended to take didn't depart for another two hours. Neither of them mentioned that until they were standing on the pavement outside the hotel in the early-autumn sunshine.

'We could have had a coffee or something, Ruth, if you'd wanted to,' Sam said as he hefted her bag onto his shoulder.

'No, I'm more than ready to get away from domesticity and drama. I hope there's an earlier train as the sooner I get to Binbrook, the better.'

'I expect there's one every hour at least.'

They were almost at the station when a three-tonne army lorry hooted and rolled to a halt beside them. The ATS driver leaned out of her window.

'Where are you two going, Sarge? I've got a load of equipment I'm taking to the other side of Lincoln if that's any use.'

The girl was tall, blonde and reminded Ruth of her friend Grace. She rushed up to the driver. 'Sergeant Johnson is stationed at Skellingthorpe but I'm headed for Binbrook. Bombardier Ruth Cox, pleased to meet you.'

'Corporal Clara Felgate, glad to be of service. You'll have to travel with me as there's not a smidgen of room in the back.' She grinned. 'I'm delivering to Binbrook so you're in luck, Ruth.'

Sam tossed Ruth's kitbag in first, then she scrambled up and he followed, slamming the door behind him. The bag made an excellent footrest.

The driver engaged the gears smoothly and the lorry moved out into the traffic. Ruth didn't attempt to involve her in conversation whilst she negotiated the narrow streets, pedestrians and occasional horse and cart. Once they were safely on the more or less open road, Ruth turned slightly sideways so she could talk to her.

'Thanks for the lift, Corporal! You remind me of my best friend, Grace Sinclair – now Grace Holloway,' she said.

'Crikey, you must be Ruth, Grace has told me all about you but she didn't mention you'd got a handsome sergeant in tow.'

Sam smiled. What a coincidence that they'd got a lift from someone Ruth knew about.

12

Sam listened to the two girls catching up with news of their mutual friend but didn't feel excluded. They were soldiers like him and Clara was a bloody good driver and handled the lorry with ease. He wasn't really paying attention until he heard Binbrook mentioned.

'I can take you all the way, Ruth, shame I can't do the same for your chap. This is my last run as a normal driver as from tomorrow I'm transferring to a motorbike and becoming a dispatch rider.'

'That sounds like fun,' Ruth said. 'Almost as exciting as being part of an actual mixed artillery section. There aren't very many, you know.'

'Lucky you – that's one of the reasons I'm becoming a dispatch rider. It's done by men and women and I might be posted overseas at some point. That's what I'd really like to do.'

Sam checked that the door was firmly closed before leaning against it – he didn't want to end up on his backside in the road when they hit a pothole. By turning slightly sideways, it meant that Ruth could lean against him and he had his arms around her, ostensibly to hold her steady but they both knew the real reason. Too soon they'd have to say goodbye and only God knew when they'd be together again.

He dozed, letting the girls' chatter drift over his head and only started to take notice as the lorry slowed. He straightened and saw they were approaching a town; they must be in Lincoln.

'The turning to Skellingthorpe, Sarge, is just ahead. I can't take you any further but it's only a few miles down that road. It's a large barracks and I'm sure you'll be able to hitch a lift. Good to meet you.'

'Thanks for the ride, Corp, much appreciated.' He dropped to the ground with his haversack over one shoulder and Ruth leaned out so he could give her a quick kiss. 'Good luck, love. I'll let you know what happens with the other business.'

'Take care, Sam, I hope we'll be able to meet soon.'

He stepped back from the lorry, slammed the door

and saw it trundle off, wondering how long it might be before he saw her again. If things went badly with the young lieutenant he intended to speak to as soon as he'd signed in then he might be posted to the back of beyond – Scotland or Northumbria – somewhere too far away for them to meet.

He was used to marching in full kit, so doing so with only a haversack was no problem at all. He set off fast, covering the distance quickly with his long legs. A Tiger Moth flew over and the pilot waved. It was a girl, so he waved back. This airfield was new so he hoped the accommodation should be good.

As he approached the barracks, it was already late afternoon. He'd made good time walking the three miles. As he'd walked, he'd contemplated how much had happened and how it seemed longer than four weeks since he'd left to become a sergeant. He hoped to remain here for a few months at least and was looking forward to his new role. Skellingthorpe had 50 Squadron, which originally flew the obsolete Hampdens but they'd been given first the new Avro Manchester and the planes he could see on the apron were Lancasters. These had four engines and longer wings. He liked aircraft, he and his section were expected to know all the different types the bomber boys flew. It wouldn't do to shoot down an RAF plane by mistake.

* * *

This was a big barracks as far as Royal Artillery went, well equipped and housing not only the four sections needed to protect the base but also numerous orderlies, clerks, cooks and drivers. Section A was billeted a short distance from the gun park, B further in and C and D at the rear of the barracks, but they were only there alternate nights.

HQ was halfway around the perimeter of the base, C and D had their gunsite more or less opposite the barracks but on the far side of the base. They had to go at the double across the runways in order to man the guns and return in the same way twenty-four hours later when they swapped from manning to general duties.

Sam approached the guard, showed his papers and the barrier was raised so he could march in. His first task was to report at the admin office where his officer would be. A small squad of men in full kit jogged past and he smiled. These were defaulters made to run around the base for hours as a punishment for some misdeed.

There would be around two hundred soldiers living on this site, his section was one of the four based here. They had an evening off every eight days and a pass every twelve. Better than being on the front line and certainly better than during the heavy bombing last year.

Everything was either in a Nissen hut or a wooden building. Nothing brick built. As new RAF airfields were built, the RA sites were hastily constructed close by to protect them.

It didn't take him long to reach his billet, change clothes and check on his men. They seemed to have settled in and the moaning was no worse than usual. In fact, they were happy to be within walking distance of Lincoln, which had cinemas, pubs and a station. Their accommodation was basic but no different from other places.

There were two officers attached to A and B. Sam wasn't expected to interact with the one in charge of the other group but they shared the same office. He headed to the main building, a larger structure which housed offices, lecture rooms, the post room and a basic medical centre.

Sam wasn't on duty until six the following morning but wanted to get what was going to be a difficult interview about Arthur Humfrey done.

Unfortunately, the lieutenant he'd intended to speak to, the officer whose father was a vicar, had been posted and his replacement was a young man straight from Sandhurst. Sam thought his report probably wouldn't go any further. A new bloke wouldn't want to rock any boats and he couldn't really blame him. Probably better to wait until the man he wanted, Lieutenant Simpson, returned to his office and not accost him when he was busy.

There was a NAAFI on the site, small and with only room for a dozen tables, but adequate. He walked into the steamy interior and immediately saw the other sergeant now attached to his section, Ronnie Smith, a decent sort of bloke and only a couple of years older than himself. He was sitting in a corner where there were three small tables crammed together. There were a couple of gunners at one and the other was empty. He smiled at Ronnie.

'Afternoon, Ronnie, how are things going, then?' Sam said.

'Ain't complaining, Sam, and I'm billeted with you now. The new officer's going to need knocking into shape. He ain't got a clue. So wet behind the ears you could wring them out.'

'Not surprised. They send them somewhere they can't kill anyone to learn how to lead and then ship them off to a front line posting if they're any good. Can I join you? I'll get myself a cuppa and a wad. Anything else for you?'

Ronnie pointed to his enamel mug and Sam picked it up. When he returned to the table, he handed over the tea.

'Always tastes better served from a teapot,' he said. Anything liquid was presented in a metal bucket by the army caterers and you had to dip your mug into it.

Sam decided to share the information concerning Arthur Humfrey as he was conflicted about what he should do. Ronnie listened in silence and was shocked.

'If I report him, I'm ruining his life, the repercussions might ruin mine as well. No one likes a snitch.' But he trusted Ronnie, had known him for months, and a trouble shared and all that. He smiled thinking about Ruth and their enjoyment of old proverbs – if that's what they were called.

'Bleeding hell, mate, that's not good. You've got to tell someone but for gawd's sake not Simpson. Go further up the chain. A warrant officer would do.'

'I think you're right. I'll leave it for a few days, get settled back, before speaking to an officer. No urgency, after all, the bloke's not about to blow the country up. Not many German spies in Britain.'

His friend nodded and they drank their tea in companionable silence.

'Have you met any of the Brylcreem boys? I wasn't

here long enough to speak to any.' He grinned and shook his head. 'That's not true, I was commandeered into an ENSA entertainment and did speak to a few then.'

'The ones we come into contact with seem okay, but we "brown jobbies", as they call us, tend to keep away from them.' Ronnie looked serious. 'Wouldn't want their job, casualties are horrific for the bombers, even worse than for the fighters during the Battle of Britain.'

'Too true. They've got far better facilities than us, though, and half of this barracks actually works on their base, so it seems daft we don't mix a bit more than we do.'

Ronnie drained his mug. 'I'd better get a move on, back on duty in fifteen minutes. You taking over from me at two tomorrow as I've got a pass?'

'Certainly am. At least if I'm shelving the report for now, I won't be on my way to the wilds of Scotland.'

'Are you on duty today?'

'No, free until reveille,' Sam replied.

'Lucky bugger, swanning about like a blooming officer now.'

Sam didn't like being idle so decided to volunteer – not something anyone of any sense ever did – and marched back to the admin block. Lieutenant Simpson, the new officer, saw him approaching.

'There you are, Sergeant, I was expecting you to call in and introduce yourself.'

Sam stopped and saluted, annoyed the lieutenant didn't bother to return the gesture. Sloppy disregard for regulations in his opinion and just confirmed what Ronnie had said.

'Sorry, sir, you weren't in the office when I reported. I was on my way to try again. Sergeant Johnson reporting for duty.'

'Then you'd better get on with it. Don't stand about wasting time.'

'I'm not on duty until tomorrow, sir. Thank you, sir.' He snapped to attention a second time and marched off, biting his tongue. If he'd stayed, he'd have been insubordinate and put on a charge. He could have told Simpson he was about to find something to do but the man wasn't worth the effort.

* * *

Ruth really liked Clara and the fact that they shared the same best friend gave them an immediate connection.

'I wish I'd been able to go to her wedding but I was

in the middle of my training. It's absolutely miraculous that her brother George turned up alive and well. She was devastated when she thought he'd died.'

'I wish I'd been there for her but you looked after her. She doesn't really need either of us now as she's got her handsome squadron leader husband to do that. Also, she's gone for officer training and won't have time for anything but her position,' Clara said. 'I don't know exactly where I'm going to be but if you've got my service number and I've got yours, we can stay in contact.'

'I'd like that. Do you have a serious boyfriend? I only met Sam a few weeks ago but we seem to have already become more involved than is sensible. We might only be thirty miles apart but unless there's a good bus service to Lincoln, I can't see us being able to meet very often even if our free time coincides.'

'I'm sure you'll find a way if you want to. There's a bus of some sort – there must be a thousand or more people working on the RAF base and they'll all want to go to the nearest town. And yes, I do have someone special.'

Clara was right – she was worrying unnecessarily. 'Why didn't you do the same as us? Grace told me you had the same high standard of education as we did.'

'I was going to but changed my mind. Dashing

about on a motorbike taking important messages is just my cup of tea. We'll be invading France at some point and I intend to be with them.'

'Golly, I've got quite enough excitement being on a mixed artillery site. I don't want to venture overseas. I admire your spirit, though.'

Clara laughed as she began to slow down. 'We're getting near Binbrook – you might well see a bomber or two taking off.' Her expression changed and became sombre. 'Last month they had terrible losses here. Nine Wellingtons, five of them from 142 squadron based here, were lost in a raid on Kassel. I don't know how the aircrew can keep flying with so many deaths.'

'That's absolutely tragic. From what I've read, there haven't been many attacks on RAF bases since last year so I think we might well soon be redundant.'

'I know what you mean but Hitler could change his mind again and send his bombers and fighters here instead of to the cities. We have to be ready just in case.'

'The thing is,' Ruth said suddenly, realising she might have made another mistake by becoming a gunner girl, 'that I left my first post because it wasn't an active one and now I think I've moved from the frying pan to the fire, so to speak.'

Ruth had changed direction because she wanted an exciting life and had thought being a gunner girl would give her this.

'Then apply to become an officer – they need more ATS in command positions. They've asked me twice, but I've refused.'

'I might well do that, but after them spending so much time and money training me, I'd better remain where I am for a few months.'

The lorry slowed to turn into the gates of the RA site HQ, Clara showed the necessary papers and while she was doing so, Ruth jumped out and walked up to the guard as the lorry roared away.

'I'm Bombardier Cox, I need to join Section C. I know this is our HQ but I'm hoping you can point me in the right direction.'

He grinned. 'Your driver will be going to both sections. You should have stopped inside.'

Ruth shook her head at her stupidity. The friendly guard by the barrier pointed down the road. 'Your lot, Corp, are about a mile down this road on the left and A and B is on the other side of the base.'

Being late, being new, was making her confused and she prided herself on her clear thinking. 'Thank you, I'll wait over there on the left for my friend to reappear.'

Feeling decidedly foolish, she hefted her bag over her shoulder and attempted to march away but the weight made her somewhat unbalanced. She hadn't been waiting long when the lorry emerged from HQ and pulled up beside her.

'Golly, I wondered where you'd gone. Sorry, I should have stopped you getting out. I'm going to your section now.'

Ruth shoved her bag in and clambered up after it. 'Is there a town or village nearer than Lincoln?'

'Yes, Market Rasen is the nearest decent-sized town and isn't that far away. No cinemas but a few pubs, shops and definitely at least two cafes. I think it's about twelve miles – bit far to walk.'

'Then I expect we'll have to catch the bus. Thanks for the lift, Clara, good luck with your new challenge.'

Ruth showed her papers to the guard and the barrier was raised. She viewed the place that was to be her home for the next few months. It was bigger than she'd expected with several wooden buildings, as well as Nissen huts. The massive guns loomed over the site but were a hundred yards away. Close enough to reach if an alarm went. Everywhere was tidy; it wasn't going to be a luxurious stay, but it would certainly be interesting.

The ATS sergeant looked less than thrilled to see

her. 'Better late than never, Bombardier. What it is to have friends in high places. Everybody else was here on time but there you are – I can't put you on a charge for being AWOL.'

'I'm not due to report until tomorrow morning but wanted to get here as soon as I could.' Ruth hid her annoyance well.

'Fair enough – your billet's on the left. The ATS in your section are housed together, Section D in another hut. A and B are at the other emplacement. The canteen's shared; it's the large building on the right. Ablutions and latrines directly behind your billet.'

'Thank you, Sarge, I apologise for my tardy arrival.'

The woman had softened a little and almost smiled. 'It doesn't hurt to show the ATS in a good light to the general public so I suppose arriving late this time can be forgiven.'

Ruth had dropped her bag outside the door and collected it on the way past. She didn't see any of her friends doing general duties, so they must be at the gunsite. There was a NAAFI, but she didn't stop to investigate, a series of other buildings and as many ATS as there were men.

The hut she was to share had, thankfully, the usual metal framed beds and not rickety bunks. There were already a few personal items on the lockers beside each bed and one or two jolly pictures cut from magazines stuck on the wall. The only vacant bed was on the right as she walked in and had a wall around it to make it private. She had forgotten that as a bombardier she'd have a separate space.

There was an identical cubicle opposite, which must be for the other NCO. Sergeants, presumably, had their own billet and didn't have to share with the gunners.

It didn't take her long to stow away her belongings and she pushed her laundry into the bag and hung it on the end of the bed. Until she knew the routine, it would be safer there. Hopefully there was a drying room on this site where they could do personal laundry.

Every bed was correctly stacked, the bedding and biscuits arranged as they should be. No beds were to be made up until after five o'clock.

The sides of her tiny room were solid but there was only a curtain to draw across at the foot end. She left this open, as had the other bombardier. The hut was more than adequate for the dozen sleeping in it and there was a large table with chairs around it at the far end. There was also a sideboard and on investigation she saw it had a selection of board games, packs of cards and a dozen dog-eared books. This must be where they spent their free time because there obviously wasn't a designated recreation room for ATS. She bet the men had one.

Ruth wondered where Jill was sleeping and was about to investigate when her friend rushed in.

'I've been so worried about you, Ruth, there's been all sorts of speculation and gossip. What happened? Have you been put on a charge?'

'No. Are you free? Would you like to show me around whilst I tell you where I've been?'

'There's not a great deal to see, but I'll be happy to be your guide. I've got half an hour to grab something to eat as we all missed dinner through no fault of our own.'

Ruth was relieved that she'd been greeted so enthusiastically. Arthur and his gambling addiction certainly wouldn't be mentioned by her. Maybe Sam would change his mind and they could all forget about it and get on with doing their duty.

Jill was eager to fill her in and tell her what she'd missed. 'There's a loud bell in every hut so if there's a raid it rings and we're up and dressed in minutes. There's a triangle hanging outside the mess and that's banged as well until we're all deafened.'

'Battledress over pyjamas, boots unlaced, I suppose,' Ruth said with a smile.

'Yes, we had a drill last night and we were fastening our respirators as we ran. One girl, Daisy, almost knocked herself out with her steel helmet as she'd not attached the strap correctly.'

'Gosh, that sounds like fun. I hope they repeat it soon so I can participate.'

'We didn't actually go to the guns, just had to turn out fully equipped in three minutes. They will definitely be doing it again so we can practise doing our actual jobs in the dark and in silence.'

Ruth caught up with the other members of the section and even the men seemed happy to have her back. That evening, she settled down but couldn't sleep as she expected the bell to ring at any moment. It didn't, and she got up at reveille tired and not her best after very little sleep.

13

Sam was pleased that his section was performing perfectly. The bombers flew out as darkness fell to destroy Germany and each morning there were fewer returning, which meant dozens of brave young aircrew were lost. The Luftwaffe stayed away and after a week of inactivity he decided to run a night drill to keep his men on their toes.

Those not on general duties didn't man the guns until the alarms sounded – there was no need as they could be in position in minutes. When the bombs had been dropping constantly, it would have been different, but now only the cities were being attacked and even those not every night. In fact, folk were beginning to behave as if they'd nothing to fear.

He waited until he was sure everybody would be heavily asleep before sounding the alarms. This was for his section alone, the others had been told to remain in bed. As the camp came alive, it occurred to him that he'd neglected to tell Lieutenant Simpson and as the officer was ostensibly in charge, he really should have run it by him. Too late to worry about it now.

The men had to be in place, the guns loaded, those working the predictor at the ready, the man on the range finder standing by and the one with the binoculars staring into the night sky. All this had to be accomplished in absolute silence and without any lights.

'Well done, two minutes thirty seconds – that's a record,' he said. 'There's cocoa and a wad in the mess for anyone who wants it before they turn in again.'

Sam had organised this, knowing it would make the men less garrulous about having their beauty sleep disturbed. In good spirits, happy they'd broken their own record, his section carefully stowed their equipment and then headed for the mess.

Obviously, Ronnie had known about the drill and should have been looking happy when he came over, but he wasn't.

'Where's our bloody officer? Should have been out here first – I'm going to roust him out. You coming?'

'I forgot to tell him. But he should still have turned out with the men.' This was going to be an interesting encounter. 'Too bloody right I am. He was quick enough to reprimand me and I'd like to see what excuse he's got.'

The lieutenant had his own billet – a wooden structure little more than a shed but probably more comfortable and warmer than a metal hut.

'Not even a bleeding sound, lazy bugger,' Ronnie said as he banged loudly on the door.

They stood to attention, waiting for their officer to emerge, but the hut remained silent. Slightly worried that the young man had been taken ill and was unable to respond, Sam tried the door.

'It's locked. Now what the hell do we do? Do you think he's in there unconscious? Should we break in?'

'Shut your gob for a minute and let me listen.' Ronnie put his ear against the door and shook his head. 'I don't reckon there's anyone in there. But we don't have a choice – if he's kicked the bucket and we do nothing, we'll be for the high jump.'

One of the gunners had seen them and wandered over to see what was going on. 'You looking for our officer, Sarge?' This gunner was well spoken and could have been an officer himself but for some reason had refused any promotion offered.

'We are, Chalky, can you elucidate?' Sam asked him.

'He's AWOL, Sarge, he was picked up by a luscious young lady in a red sports car a couple of hours ago.'

'Sod me! Now what do we do?' Sam hadn't expected to be faced with such a dilemma so early in his new position. Ronnie was senior to him as he'd been a sergeant for several months so it was up to him to make the decision – whatever that might be.

'Buggered if I know. There ain't nobody to report him to.'

'Forgive me for interrupting, gentlemen, but might I make a suggestion?' Gunner Jeremy White – known as Chalky – said politely.

'Go ahead, we're stumped. If we report him, we'll be unpopular and if we don't, we'll still be unpopular,' Sam said with a shrug.

'We're the only ones who know about his night-time excursions. Yes, this isn't the first time. It might well come in useful at some point to have this knowledge.'

Sam immediately got his drift. 'Right, let's get an official report down, date and stamp it, but not file it, that way we've got him over a barrel if needs be.'

'I can type reasonably well, so would you like me to do it?'

'Yes, ta, that would be just the ticket,' Ronnie said and the three conspirators shook hands.

'I'll bring the report to your billet, Sarge, and slip it under the door. Then I'll join you and the boys for a scrumptious mug of army cocoa.'

The cocoa was made with water and even adding sugar didn't make it a pleasant drink.

* * *

The following morning, their officer was marching about just after reveille as if he'd been there all night. Sam wondered how long it would be before someone mentioned the drill. He didn't have long to wait. He was checking a piece of equipment when Simpson beckoned him over.

'Sergeant Johnson, you failed to inform me that you were holding a night drill.' The bloke drew breath to continue to complain but Sam forestalled him.

'And you, sir, failed to mention you were AWOL last night.' He nodded. 'Will there be anything else?'

'No, dismissed.' Simpson stalked away and Sam knew the officer was angry at being caught out.

Sam hid his smile and returned to the task he'd been doing before the interruption. None of the men mentioned the absence of the section CO and by the end of the day, Sam believed no one had noticed. After all, it had been dark, and they were concentrating on the drill. Officers didn't join the men for cocoa either. Better that way as he didn't want Simpson to be court martialled. Hopefully he'd learned his lesson and there'd be no further excursions unless the man was criminally stupid.

That night he wrote to Ruth, knowing she'd enjoy hearing his news, especially about the officer. He'd had only had a short note from her since they'd said goodbye but it was sufficient to tell him she was happy, settled and hadn't changed her mind about him. There was no mention of Jill or Arthur, and the time they'd spent in London, and he wasn't sure if that was a good thing or a deliberate evasion on Ruth's part.

It was his evening off and he decided to walk into Lincoln and treat himself to a decent coffee. If he was lucky, he might also be able to buy shampoo, tooth-paste, shoe polish and razor blades – all of which he could do with.

A bus ran past the entrance to the site and then stopped again at the RAF gate. He might be in luck and be able to catch one and save himself a three-mile walk.

He was approaching the entrance to the RAF base when a red sports car hurtled towards him on the wrong side of the road, hugging the hedge, leaving him no room. He threw himself into the prickles to avoid being mowed down. Despite being embedded in the greenery, the car still clipped his ankle, sending a wave of agony up his leg.

The driver didn't react. She must have seen him but just raced past. The car didn't stop.

He was turning the air blue. His foot was bloody painful and it took him several excruciating minutes to extricate himself from the hawthorn bushes. His hands and face were bleeding and he couldn't put weight on his injury. When he eventually emerged, dishevelled and furious, he was determined to bring the manic driver to justice.

He knew who the culprit was and where she was heading. His problem was that he would have to hop back to his base, and she would probably have already departed by the time he got there.

The welcome sound of boots pounding on the road alerted him to the arrival of assistance. Three RAF boys arrived.

'Are you all right? We saw what happened from the other side of the hedge. Have you broken anything? Bloody stupid woman,' a flying officer said as he offered his shoulder for Sam to lean on.

'How the hell did you see through this bloody

hedge?' Sam had meant to say thank you but had to know how these friendly blokes had come to his rescue.

'It's higher on the other side, we were playing cards outside our billet. It's too far for you to get back to your site so we're going to take you back to our medics.' The red-haired flying officer grinned. 'I'm Ginger, obviously, that's Beaker and that chap over there is a disgrace.'

Only then did Sam notice that the one called a disgrace had come with a wheelbarrow. God knows where he'd found that.

'Your chariot awaits, Sarge. Hop in, there's a good fellow, and we'll wheel you back in fine style.'

The three waited to see if he'd refuse but he laughed. 'Why not? I'm too heavy for you three puny specimens to carry and I can't walk.'

The wheelbarrow had been used for some sort of building work and was liberally coated with brick dust – at least it wasn't something worse. He needed the support of Ginger and Beaker to fold himself into the makeshift wheelchair.

'Right, you chaps, better to pull than to push, don't you think?' Beaker said.

'Good show, I'll hold the poor fellow in place, you two do the pulling,' Disgrace said cheerfully.

'Tally ho!' Ginger yelled as he grabbed one metal arm and Beaker took the other. This battle cry was used by fighter pilots before going into a dogfight. Sam braced himself and clung onto the sharp metal edges of the barrow, praying this wouldn't end as an even worse disaster.

They set off at the double and without the third bloke pressing on his shoulders, Sam would have been flung out. They were all drunk, he'd realised a little too late, and he was more likely to be killed in this ridiculous escapade than saved.

The racket the three of them were making attracted the attention of the two guards at the gate. Instead of stopping them, they laughed and waved them through. God knows what a senior officer would make of this spectacle. An army sergeant sitting in a wheelbarrow liberally covered with greenery being raced along by three very drunk airmen.

He was being bounced and rattled and his injured ankle was being flung around, which did it no good at all. He gritted his teeth, closed his eyes, and doubted that he was going to arrive at the medical centre with only an injured ankle to worry about.

* * *

Ruth was proud to be a gunner and being part of a mixed artillery section was even better. She was kept busy with her new responsibilities as a bombardier and scarcely had time to think about Sam that first week. She'd dashed off a quick note and posted it but wasn't counting the days until his reply arrived – at least she thought she wasn't.

Being on general duties was not enjoyable. They hadn't been told they would be peeling vegetables, digging holes and scrubbing the ablutions when they'd been doing their training. The men wore sensible overalls but the girls had to wear khaki denim dungarees which were too short in the leg and body and meant you had to almost undress to use the WC.

Every day there was PT, it wasn't the actual exercise Ruth objected to, but the brown divided skirt and orange, short-sleeved flimsy top and black plimsoles they had to wear. Soldiers had to be in peak mental and physical fitness at all times. Thank goodness ATS wore the same battledress as the men: steel helmets, boots, gaiters and respirators in a satchel when on the gun park. This made sense but Ruth thought all the marching, parading and unnecessary duties were just to keep them from complaining. Things were supposed to be equal, but they weren't really.

The food was adequate, but the men enjoyed it

more than most of the girls. Often a half-finished dinner was scraped onto the plates of the men on the same table. Breakfast was usually porridge, this filled you up nicely, or egg and fried bread or bacon and fried bread – never both at the same time.

Dinner, at midday, was stew with unrecognisable but edible meat in it somewhere and pudding was often a dismal sort of affair. Tea, however, was her favourite, corned beef fritters or cheese dreams alternated with bread, cheese, jam and a slab of cake.

Initially, she'd been a bit of a celebrity in her hut because of helping Rose but after a couple of days, no one mentioned it any more. Jill behaved as she had at training, no mention of what had happened in London, and this was fine by Ruth.

She was sitting at the table in their hut with some of the other girls a week after she'd arrived, chatting about this and that.

'Goodness,' one of them said, 'I'd no idea actual guns are so loud. I'm going to be deaf by the time I leave the army.'

'At least we're safe enough here. I counted the bombers out last night and was on my way back from the ablutions this morning as they returned,' Ruth said sadly. 'Five didn't make it. That's thirty young men possibly dead in one night on just this base.'

The happy smiles and chatter faded as the girls digested this awful information.

'If you think how many RAF bomber bases there are just in Lincolnshire,' Jill said, 'that's a staggeringly horrible death toll.'

'Soldiers die too,' Ellen, a tall, fair girl said as she wiped her eyes. 'My brother died at Dunkirk and my boyfriend is somewhere overseas and doesn't reply to my letters any more. I don't even know if he's dead or just changed his mind.'

'Well, I'll try and find out for you,' Ruth said. 'Give me his name, rank and number and I'll set things in motion.'

'Would you? Thanks, it's the not knowing that's so hard.'

Ruth was sympathetic and knew she was lucky to have Sam so close.

* * *

Every morning after breakfast parade at 7.30 a.m. there was the hut inspection. This was carried out by the orderly officer, accompanied by an NCO. Ruth stood to attention like the other girls at the end of her bed. The officer checked everything and if even a corner of a banket was out of place, the stack was dismantled and the unfortunate girl had to redo it. No one could leave until all beds were passed. Today everything was tickety-boo and the inspection was over quickly.

After the obligatory PT – luckily the men and women exercised separately – they had half an hour to change, wash and get off to whatever duty they had been allocated.

Ruth's first job was to collect the mail and take it to the various huts. It didn't take long to deliver them to the huts in her section. This was the first time she'd had to go into the men's quarters. She marched across and walked in, head high, not looking right or left. She nodded and put the pile of letters on the table by the door and marched out, not wanting to hear any of the possible derogatory comments that might be made about having a girl doing a man's job.

Her heart was pounding, her palms wet, but she'd acquitted herself well. Her girls would be thrilled to get so much correspondence. Ruth pointed to the pile of envelopes when she'd dropped them on the table. 'Lots of mail for us today.'

There were plenty of smiling faces as the girls were hastily scrambling into their uniform. There was just time to glance at letters before rushing off.

Ruth opened her letter and Jill did the same with hers. Ruth's was from Clara and she was pleased to now have another friend. However, a letter from Sam would have been better.

'Oh dear, this is not good, not good at all,' Jill said under her breath.

'What's wrong? Can I help?'

'These are both from Arthur. I've only read one and in it he asks if I can lend him money as he's over-spent his allowance. He also says he has urgent debts to pay that won't wait.' Jill collapsed on the nearest bed. 'After what happened in London, he promised me he'd stop gambling so if Sam did report him there'd be nothing for anyone to see.'

'By debts he means gambling debts, I assume?'

'Yes, I'm afraid so.' Jill looked up with tear-filled eyes. 'I didn't dare ask if Sam had reported him. I didn't want to ruin our friendship.'

'He hasn't so far. Jill, I think you'd better open the second letter.'

Jill quickly scanned the contents and then looked up with a smile of relief. 'It's all right, a friend has stepped in and helped him out; also he's been pro-moted and is being posted to Cairo.' Her eyes were moist and she held the letter to her chest. 'He doesn't go until next month and said he'll try to come and see me before he leaves.'

Ruth was horrified. Jill clearly didn't know that

Cairo was a hotbed of intrigue and spies. The very worst place in the world someone like Arthur should be sent. Should she tell Jill that this was bad news or pretend that him being sent to Egypt would make his problems vanish?

'Does he say who the friend was who paid off his gambling debts?' Ruth wasn't sure why she'd asked this question but had to say something.

Jill scanned the letter again. 'Yes, it was a friend of his father's – not somebody I know. Why do you ask?'

'I was just wondering how he was going to pay the loan back if he was abroad but if it's a family friend then there's no urgency, I suppose.'

'To be honest, Ruth, I try and stay out of his financial woes,' Jill said with a smile.

'I think that's an error on your part. It's none of my business but are you really sure that being married to a gambler, and not one that wins either, is something you want to do? However much he says he won't gamble, he obviously can't help himself. You could spend your entire married life being in constant fear of losing everything. Is that a sensible way to live?'

Jill stood up abruptly, snatched her letters from the table, rushed to her locker and put them in. Then she left without another word. Ruth didn't regret telling Jill the truth but was sorry she might well have lost her friendship. Nobody likes to be told their decisions are questionable.

She needed to write to Sam and tell him that he couldn't postpone reporting Arthur any longer. But there wasn't time now, she had to report for guard duty. And that was more important.

14

Sam was trundled, much to the amusement of those that they passed, to the medical centre on the base.

'Here you are, Sarge, no one can say that we boys in blue don't help out the brown jobbies,' the bloke, who didn't appear to have a name apart from being called a disgrace, said as they unceremoniously tipped him out onto the concrete.

Sam's appalling language expressed his feelings about this manoeuvre. Unrepentant, the three drunken aircrew fell about laughing. Then, as Sam heaved himself up, trying to keep his injured foot from the ground, he watched Ginger drop into the wheelbarrow and his two friends grab the handles and race off with him. If one of them didn't break something, he would be very surprised.

A doctor had been watching this performance with bemusement. 'Right, I take it you're the injured party. It will be a first to treat a soldier. Put your arm around my shoulders, young man, and I'll get you inside and have a look at that ankle.'

Several extremely painful minutes later, his ankle was declared badly sprained but not broken. It had been securely strapped and he'd been given a pair of crutches – well – loaned them, to be more exact.

'I'll find a driver to run you back. You need to stay off that ankle as much as possible. Keep it elevated. I don't suppose you've got a medic on your artillery base?'

'No, sir, but we have medical orderlies who deal with minor things. We have a doctor at HQ but as he takes care of all four sections, he's not often there. We have to go to Lincoln for serious medical emergencies. Thank you, I appreciate you taking care of me. I just hope those three silly buggers don't have to fly tonight.'

The doctor shook his head. 'Afraid they do, young man. They shouldn't drink but who can blame them for doing so? They'll be sober enough to fly if there is an op tonight.'

True to his word, there was a car waiting to drive him back. The medic had offered to get one of his orderlies to ring Sam's headquarters so his officer knew what had happened and wouldn't mark Sam as AWOL, but this wasn't needed as Sam was off duty until the morning.

Hardly seemed worth the bother for the WAAF driver as they were there in minutes, she then had to turn round and drive back. He'd been gone so long he didn't expect to see the bloody woman who'd knocked him into the hedge but headed for the HQ speak to the lieutenant.

Using the crutches wasn't difficult and as he swung across the cleared area, Ronnie appeared in the door of the building which was used as the main office.

'Blimey O'Reilly, good job you didn't break it.'

'I didn't do anything to it – it was that bit of fluff belonging to our officer in her red MG. She must have seen me but made no effort to avoid a collision. I could have been killed – in fact, I would have been seriously injured if I hadn't been able to throw myself into the hedge.'

'Our revered officer has a twenty-four-hour pass and we're in charge. He buggered off at two after the guards were changed. You need to report the accident – any injury has to be recorded and the reason for it.

You can also make it very clear who did it and that it was entirely the driver's fault.'

'I'll do that now. Isn't it time for another practice run? God knows when we'll actually be called into action but we have to be ready,' Sam replied.

'As you're no use, so to speak, mate, you can do the admin and I'll do everything else.' Ronnie smirked, knowing he'd got the best of the bargain. Nobody liked to be buried in paperwork – the army wanted every form filled in in triplicate at least.

Sam found an old crate and put it under the desk so he could keep his foot elevated as the doc had suggested. It ached, but as long as he didn't move it or try and put any weight on it, it wasn't too bad. He was lucky.

He was a bit uncomfortable sitting in his absent officer's chair, especially as this room was shared with the one attached to section B. There were two ATS clerks typing away in the office next door and one kindly fetched his lunch on a tray so he didn't have to hobble over to the canteen. He was just eating the last spoonful of apple crumble and custard when a dispatch rider on a motorbike roared in with the afternoon mailbag. He recognised her as Clara, the driver of the lorry who'd given him a lift here – what a coincidence.

The door was open and he waved and the ATS girl waved back, kicked the bike onto its stand, removed the neatly tied bundle of letters and ran in.

'Golly, what happened to you, Sam?'

'I was run over but it's not as bad as it looks. I didn't expect to see you again so soon.' He grinned. 'Mind you, I've only been here ten days.'

'I'm delivering the mail all over Lincolnshire at the moment so do you want me to give a personal message to Ruth? I'm bound to see her eventually.'

'Yes, you can tell her about my accident and that I'm perfectly fine apart from a sprained ankle.'

'I'll do that. Cheerio, I'd better not linger or I'll be for the high jump.'

She rushed off, leaving him smiling whilst he rummaged through the letters. There was the continued clatter of typewriters in another room and the occasional ring of the telephone.

Eagerly he flipped through and found what he was looking for. A letter from Ruth – just what he needed to cheer him up. He put it to one side whilst he finished separating the letters into piles – one for each hut. There were a couple for the officer but he just dumped them in the empty correspondence tray.

A clerk had seen the motorbike and came through to collect and deliver the mail for him. He shouldn't read personal correspondence when on duty but as he was ostensibly in command of his section, he took the risk.

He opened the envelope carefully, not wishing to tear the contents in his enthusiasm. He was looking forward to hearing Ruth's news, but his eyes widened as he began to read.

Dear Sam,

The most dreadful thing has happened and I hope you get this letter really quickly.

Jill has just had two letters from Arthur. The first saying he was heavily in debt and asking to borrow some money – gambling debts.

The second saying that he'd paid his debts as a family friend had lent him the money then he said that he'd been promoted and was going out to Cairo at the end of the month.

We both know what it's like in Egypt and I'm afraid that you can't put off reporting him any longer. Jill thinks that him going to Cairo is a good thing and I didn't want to disabuse her.

I hope you're well. I've settled in and will write again about mundane matters.

Please let me know what happens and if you want me to make a written statement. I suppose

they could also ask Jill as I'm sure she won't lie
about it if asked directly by an officer.
   Best wishes

Sam scanned it again and it didn't make more comfortable reading. This was the worst possible time for this information to arrive. Simpson wouldn't be back until tomorrow.

He couldn't go in search of the officer in charge of another section with an injured ankle. He smiled wryly. The sections were connected by telephone so there'd be no difficulty speaking to whatever officer was in charge over there.

He heaved himself to his feet, grabbed his crutches and went in search of his friend. Ronnie saw him hobbling his way and came to meet him.

'What's up? You should have sent someone to fetch me.'

'You'd better read this letter from my girlfriend. You'll see why I didn't want to wait.'

Ronnie quickly read the letter and his happy smile vanished. 'Sod me. This isn't good – we've got Simpson over a barrel and he'd have to pass the information to the War Office. Bloody typical that he's not here just when we want him.'

'This Arthur Humfrey isn't leaving for two weeks,

so I don't think another day will make any difference. Our officer will be back tomorrow morning so it can wait until then.' He smiled grimly. 'Simpson isn't going to like the conversation I intend to have with him. I'm tempted to report that woman to the police as well as to the army – set things in motion.'

'Do it. You've got a telephone and I'm sure the operator will connect you to the local constabulary even if you don't know the telephone number.'

'Right, I'll get onto it. Everything tickety-boo up here?'

'No problems.'

Sam's injured ankle was throbbing by the time he returned to his desk. This made him even more determined to report the dangerous driver. After a few clicks and whirrs, he was connected to the police station in Lincoln.

He reported the incident and the constable who'd answered the telephone said somebody would be out to see him later today.

He was sharing a pot of tea and a plate of broken biscuits with Ronnie when a black sedan turned into the site.

'I reckon this is the bobbies. They've obviously sent detectives rather than a constable on a bicycle,' Ronnie said as he went to investigate.

Sam had written down exactly what took place, added the names and numbers of the RAF pilots and a full description of the car and the driver. He didn't want to get any details wrong in the official complaint.

He saw an oldish man with thinning brown hair, in a rumpled suit, emerge from the front passenger seat, closely followed by the driver, also in plain-clothes, presumably his sergeant.

The two of them headed straight for him, ignoring Ronnie, who mimed that he was going to fetch a fresh pot of tea. Sam had pushed himself upright, balancing on one foot by holding onto the edge of the desk.

'Thank you for coming so promptly, officers. I'm Sergeant Sam Johnson – the injured party, as you can see.' He gestured towards the two chairs already positioned in front of the desk. The older man took one and the younger one did the same and immediately got out his little black book and licked the end of his pencil.

'I'm Detective Inspector Brown – that's Detective Constable Reynolds. Now, Sergeant Johnson, please give me the details of what happened.'

Sam handed the detective constable what he'd written and the young man nodded his thanks. He also gave a verbal report and when he'd finished, the inspector frowned.

'Unfortunately, Sergeant Johnson, I know exactly the person and vehicle you describe as this isn't the first time I've had a complaint about her reckless driving. However, this is the first time she appears to have deliberately run somebody over. Are you quite sure she saw you?'

'Absolutely. In fact, I'm equally sure that she deliberately swerved so she hit me. She couldn't have known my injuries would be minimal.'

'Have you had any contact with this woman before?' The policeman was carefully not mentioning the driver's name, although he obviously knew it.

Ronnie arrived with Chalky – the private who'd told them about the MG – in tow, along with a fresh tray of tea and biscuits, which were received with pleasure by the visitors.

'This is Gunner White,' Sam said. 'He can tell you more about the driver.'

Chalky's story was also written down and the unauthorised absence of Simpson was also noted. Sam realised this had probably screwed his chances of getting any cooperation from the lieutenant as he'd inadvertently already dropped him in it.

Ronnie was trying to attract his attention. His friend pointed to the letter Sam had just received from Ruth and then nodded vigorously.

'There's another thing I need to ask you about. I'm not sure that it's your jurisdiction but I do know this information needs to be passed up the chain of command somehow.'

'Go ahead, Sergeant, I'll listen whilst I drink my tea and eat my biscuits.' The way he said this made it clear the DI would only remain until he'd finished both.

Sam was used to giving brief reports to his superiors and gave this information in the same efficient way. He then handed over the letter from Ruth for the officer to read for himself.

'Hmm. I can see why you're concerned about this. As it happens, I'm exactly the person to deal with this matter. Better it comes from outside the services as it will go directly to the person who needs to know.'

He drained his mug and stood up. 'Forget about the Cairo business – better you don't know what happens. I'm sorry you were run over by that woman. Yes, I do know who she is but she's the daughter of somebody very important and I think it best that I don't reveal her identity. There are going to be serious repercussions for your officer and this young woman. I give you my word that I don't intend to let this incident be pushed under the carpet.'

Sam gripped the edge of the table ready to stand up, but Brown shook his head.

'No, remain where you are. I'm sorry you were injured. I'll be in touch. I'm going in search of the RAF airmen to get their statements. Good afternoon, gentlemen.'

Sam relaxed after the inspector had gone. He'd done his duty and the problem was someone else's now.

* * *

Ruth was delighted to see Clara arrive on a motorbike with the next morning's letters. She was on admin duty today and envied her new friend the freedom to be racing around the county with correspondence or messages.

'Good morning, Clara, I didn't expect to meet up with you so soon. Are you now firmly established in Lincolnshire?' Ruth asked with a smile.

'I put my name down for overseas postings but was told that girls usually, unless they're nurses or doctors, remain in Blighty,' Clara said. 'We're bound to invade before long and then they'll need every soldier they've got, regardless of their sex.'

Clara handed over a neatly tied bundle of letters.

'Actually, I delivered to your Sam the other day. I expect there might be one for you in amongst this lot. He said to tell you that he's sprained his ankle but is tickety-boo. I expect he'll have given you the details.'

'Are you allowed to use your motorbike when you're off duty? I really need to see him as soon as I can. I'm entitled to a twenty-four-hour pass every twelve days and that's the day after tomorrow.'

'As you're an ATS bombardier, I don't see why not. I'll come and get you – I can't promise to be able to do more than take you there and you'll have to find your own way back.'

Ruth wanted to hug her but decided it wouldn't be approved of as they were being closely watched by Lieutenant Smithers, who wasn't enthralled to be in charge of a mixed artillery battery.

'You'd better get on as we're being scrutinised by my officer. He's convinced that we ATS spend most of our time chatting.'

Clara laughed and roared away. Ruth hadn't thought to ask her if she also collected letters, but it didn't really matter. Sam must have received hers by now and her stomach churned at the thought of the possible repercussions of reporting Arthur – definitely for Sam, but possibly also for her.

* * *

There was a dance in the village that night and those with an evening pass were off duty and going officially and some of those who should remain in camp were going to sneak through a hole in the hedge and catch the bus too. Jill, who was in high spirits, thinking her fiancé's problems were over, was also attending.

Ruth hadn't needed to make excuses not to spend time with her as Jill had pointedly ignored her since the incident with the letters. Ruth knew that when Jill discovered what had been set in motion, she was even less likely to want to continue the friendship.

She was on duty at the gun park tonight so couldn't go to the dance even if she'd wanted to. She would have to turn a blind eye to the illegal exit of some of the more daring girls.

Tonight she was the spotter, which meant she had the binoculars and if an alarm came through it was her job to scan the sky and locate the bomber or fighter that was approaching the base. She had to yell to the range finder and then whoever that was would twiddle her dials and the information would pass to the predictor and then on to the guns.

It was cloudy, hiding the late-evening sun, too light

for searchlights if there was an alarm so it would be down to her to call the direction for the range finder.

There was no alarm raised – and she spent the evening listening to the wireless. The girls who'd had the evening officially free, plus those who hadn't, returned in high spirits from the village dance just before curfew.

Was it wrong to wish that there would be an air raid so their highly trained section could put their skills into use? The bombers on the base had continued to have heavy losses and it was heartbreaking knowing how many of the brave boys who crewed these massive planes failed to return after each raid.

* * *

The following afternoon, just after the two o'clock parade, when the guard changed and those who'd been manning the guns swapped to general duties, there was the most extraordinary news. Ruth wasn't given it directly – a bombardier wasn't important enough to be included in the initial briefing – but was told that she had to collect a notice and pin it to the board outside her accommodation hut.

She read it with growing incredulity. It appeared that the Air Ministry had decided to lay concrete run-

ways at Binbrook and the squadrons were being transferred elsewhere. This meant that there was no
further need for the RA sites until the spring when
squadrons would return.

The girls crowded around and naturally they were
astonished that they were going to be posted somewhere else so soon after their arrival.

'When do you think we're going to go, Corp?' May,
a jolly girl, asked.

'I know no more than any of you. I'm sure we'll be
informed when those in charge of this sort of thing
have the information. Until then, we carry on as usual,' Ruth said firmly.

Jill grabbed her arm and drew her to one side.
This was the first time her erstwhile friend had
spoken to her directly. 'Do you think it will be in a few
days or a few weeks?'

'Days, I imagine. We'll know we're leaving when
the squadrons have left. To be honest, I'm glad the
poor boys are being sent somewhere else. Maybe
flying from a different base will improve their luck.'

'As we've been trained together, do you think that
we'll transfer as we are or be broken up?' Jill asked.

'We're part of a four-section Royal Artillery unit
and I'm pretty sure we'll be posted as we are.' Ruth

didn't know anything more than Jill did but hoped what she said was true.

'It would be spiffing if we were sent to London. There're a lot of RA sites protecting the city,' Jill said. 'I'd definitely be able to say goodbye to Arthur if that was the case.'

'London would be good but not for me as I wouldn't be able to see Sam when we get a day off.' Ruth smiled as she heard the distinctive roar of a motorbike approaching. 'I'm sorry, I've got to change and grab my things as a friend of mine is going to give me a lift to Lincoln.'

Clara didn't come into the site but waited outside the barrier. She waved as Ruth ran out to join her.

'I hope you've pinned your hat on really tight, otherwise you're likely to lose it,' Clara said.

'I thought of tying a scarf around my head but I'd probably be considered improperly dressed if I did. I've never travelled on the back of one of these and I'm really looking forward to it.'

She'd changed from her battledress into the uniform she had to wear when she left the base and wished she'd been allowed to keep the trousers on as it would be so much warmer and easier on a motorbike. Clara was wearing jodhpurs as asking her to ride a motorbike all day in a skirt would be silly.

'It's not far to Skellingthorpe and you're lucky that the weather's dry. It's beastly on a bike when it's wet.'

Ruth wriggled onto the pillion and put her arms around Clara's waist. Her new friend revved the engine and they took off smoothly. It was impossible to talk so she just enjoyed the scenery, even if it did speed past at a terrifying rate.

Almost too soon, they arrived at the barracks where Sam was based. They both presented their papers and the vigilant guard raised the barrier and they rode in. Ruth wriggled off, straightened her skirt and hugged Clara.

'Thank you so much for bringing me. I didn't have time to tell you that Binbrook's closing until the spring for proper runways to be put down. I don't know where I'm going to be but I'm sure we'll find each other.'

Clara had kicked the bike onto its stand, turned off the engine and had already removed the correspondence from the pannier and had it in her hand. She marched off to deliver it, leaving Ruth to go in search of Sam and hope that he had at least an hour off sometime in the day so they could talk.

15

After a couple of days, Sam was able to hobble about on his sprained ankle using just one of the crutches as a stick. He had to remain on general duties as turning out in a hurry if there was an alarm was still beyond him.

Lieutenant Simpson had failed to return from his leave. This meant that Sam had had to do the hut inspection after breakfast as Simpson was the orderly officer this week.

He'd had nothing to complain about and was returning to the office when he almost tripped over his crutch. Ruth was walking towards him looking even more beautiful than the last time he'd seen her.

Maybe not everyone would think her beautiful, but he did. She marched towards him, head up, arms swinging, and the blokes who saw her watched with admiration. He couldn't believe this lovely girl had come all this way to see him.

'Sergeant Johnson, when can we talk? I'll wait in the NAAFI until you're free.'

'My officer's missing, which means I'm doing his job today. I wish I'd known you were coming as I might have been able to arrange a couple of hours off.'

'I could help you with any administrative duties – I could be your runner. I don't suppose anybody would even notice that I'm not actually based here.'

He thought for a few moments and then nodded. 'Actually, that would be really useful. There're usually two clerks on duty but one's home on compassionate leave and the other's got chickenpox, so I'm on my own.'

Her smile lit her face. 'That's the best news. I'm sorry for your girls, of course, but I can't see even the stuffiest of officers objecting to me helping out on my day off.'

She followed him back to the office, one step behind him, not engaging him in chatter and he reckoned nobody would know they were going out together.

'I'll deal with anything in the clerk's office unless there's something else you want me to do?'

There was something, but suggesting that she kissed him would get them both in serious trouble.

The telephone on his desk jangled noisily and he picked it up, guessing what it might be about. He recognised the caller as Major Phillips – the senior officer in charge of all four sections, who was stationed at HQ.

'Good afternoon, sir, Sergeant Johnson here. I'm hoping you can tell me what's happened to Lieutenant Simpson.'

'I think you can probably guess, Sergeant, as you set the ball rolling. Simpson is a disgrace to the RA – he's been posted somewhere he can't do any further harm.'

This seemed rather harsh as the poor sod wasn't directly responsible for the accident. 'I don't quite understand, sir.'

'Your report that he was AWOL came to my attention. I know you were protecting your own officer by not informing me personally and I appreciate your loyalty. However, it just won't do. I've also received a report that you were involved in a traffic accident. What happened?'

'Lieutenant Simpson's girlfriend – apparently, she's

the daughter of somebody influential but I don't know her name – tried to run me over me with her car three days ago.' As soon as he spoke, Sam regretted having given the details.

There was an ominous silence, then his commanding officer made a noise that sounded like a growl. 'No, that information hasn't reached me.'

Sam's throat constricted. This wasn't good – in fact it was a bloody disaster. He hadn't mentioned in his official report that he knew the identity of the driver.

'I informed the local constabulary and they are dealing with the matter. I didn't think that it directly concerned Lieutenant Simpson but was intending to speak to him when he returned.'

To his surprise and relief, the major chuckled. 'I can imagine exactly what you were going to say, Sergeant Johnson; however, if the matter is being dealt with by the police then I'll leave it to them. It just confirms my decision that the further away from this particular young woman Simpson is, the better for him.'

'I have my friend, Bombardier Ruth Cox, assisting me in the office as my two clerks are absent. Is that acceptable?'

'I take it this ATS girl isn't stationed with you?'

'No, sir, she managed to get a lift from Binbrook and called in to say hello.'

'If Bombardier Cox is prepared to give up her leave to help you out of a difficult situation, I can see nothing untoward about that. Another lieutenant will be with you in a day or two. Until then, if you need an officer, speak to one of the chaps attached to the other sections.'

There was a click as the receiver was replaced. Sam smiled – the major was old school, a relic from the last war, but none the worse for that. He looked up to see Ruth standing in the doorway.

'You've got permission to be here. Why don't you fetch us both a cuppa and then you can tell me why you came and I can tell you what's been going on at my end.'

* * *

By some miracle, Ruth managed to buy two small bars of chocolate – they rarely appeared for sale in their small NAAFI and would be a real treat for both of them.

Sam had been shocked by her news that she was about to be posted and she was equally horrified by the way he'd received his injury.

'I can't believe anybody would do something so stupid. Do you think that she'd heard somehow about your report?' She shook her head. 'That doesn't make sense. How could she have known you were the one who made the report?'

'Good point. She might have had my name and description, I suppose, but not sure she could have identified me at the speed she was travelling.'

'Maybe she was so angry that anyone in khaki was fair game.'

'That could be it – it makes a bit more sense now. You're going to have to tell Jill that I've reported her fiancé and the reason for it. She needs to know why we did it.'

'I'm dreading having that conversation as Jill has only just started speaking to me again. I'll talk to her as soon as I'm back.'

'You don't have to report until two tomorrow – as you're temporarily assigned to me, I'm sure I can find you a billet for the night. I have to remain here, otherwise I'm free.'

'That's the best news. I have to leave first thing as it might take me hours to get to Binbrook.'

'Fair enough. I'm hoping you didn't just come all this way in order to speak to me about the Arthur business.'

She pulled a face and he laughed. 'Obviously, Sergeant Johnson, you were very low on my list of priorities.' She batted her eyelashes at him and he laughed again. 'I'm only too happy to postpone my return if it means I can spend extra time with you.'

'Good to know. Now we'd better get on with some work. Can you type?'

Ruth nodded. 'Yes, and I use all my fingers too.'

She turned ready to go to her own desk in the adjacent office, but her eyes were sad.

'Sam, it might be impossible for us to meet if I'm posted to the other end of the country.'

'When will you know?'

'One of the bomber squadrons was in the process of leaving this afternoon. I don't suppose it will be long before the others have gone too. Therefore, I should know tomorrow or the next day at the latest.'

'It's not likely to be anywhere in Lincolnshire,' he said. 'I was surprised and delighted when they sent your mixed battery to Binbrook. There's no point speculating, we'll just have to wait.'

The telephone rang and immediately he focused on that. When he replaced the receiver, he could hear her busy in the next room. It had been more than two days since he'd made his report to the DI, so it was possible he might hear what was going on whilst Ruth was here.

* * *

With no further opportunity for personal conversation, Sam had to wait until early evening to spend time with the girl he'd fallen in love with.

She was out delivering letters to the post room. She'd already handed the ones for HQ to the dispatch rider – this time it was a bloke, not her friend, Clara – and when she returned, the office would be closed until the morning. He remained on duty but hopefully nothing untoward would take place.

'I still don't know where I'm sleeping – I suppose that we should have organised that hours ago,' Ruth said.

'It's done. You're using the officer's billet as he's no longer with us. Don't frown, love, I've cleared it with HQ.'

'That's the ticket – better than finding a modest B & B somewhere. I'm absolutely ravenous. Do you think it might be corned beef fritters for tea?'

'I've no idea but let's head to the canteen and see for ourselves. The scoff's not bad here so it'll be something better than bread and jam.'

She didn't go ahead of him as he expected but stood behind the half-open door. He closed the gap and pulled her close. Passionate kisses were all very well, but he wanted to make love to her and knew that wasn't on the cards. She wasn't that sort of girl and would expect a ring on her finger first.

* * *

Ruth was breathless and glowing all over when Sam stepped back. His eyes were dark, his face as flushed as hers. He'd not kissed her like this before.

'I'm going to hate being on the other side of the country, Sam...'

'We don't know where you'll be going so let's not spoil our evening worrying about it,' he replied.

As they walked across the camp, Ruth wanted to hold his hand but knew she couldn't. 'I was toying with the idea of going for officer training, but if I did, we wouldn't be allowed to go out together.'

'It's only if we're in the same chain of command, love, as long as you're based somewhere different then we can do what we like. You go for it if that's what you want. You've got the right education, unlike me.'

'I thought you'd have gone to grammar school. You're very intelligent.'

'I worked from fourteen with my dad, he's a

builder. Never wanted anything else. I'll go back to it when this lot's over.'

'They'll want hundreds of builders after the war. Isn't it a reserved profession?'

'No, but I'd not have wanted to remain when others were fighting. Dad's too old to be called up.'

A shiver of fear made the hair on the back her neck stand up as she asked the all-important question, praying his answer would be no. 'Will you have to go with the invasion force?'

'I hope so. We're RA – anything to do with guns is our responsibility. I doubt you'll have to, at least I hope not.'

Ruth touched her white lanyard, the one that indicated she was a gunner. Even the girls were called bombardiers, not privates, in the Royal Artillery. She was proud to wear it but wasn't keen to be on the front line.

She changed the subject. Thinking about what might be coming for him was too depressing. 'I'm going to take your advice and put my name down for OCTU, although I doubt that I could jump straight from bombardier to being a subaltern.'

'Bloody silly keeping different names for your officers – you should be called lieutenants, same as we are. You go for it, love, now's the time to apply when your battery's being moved.'

* * *

It wasn't corned beef fritters but the beans on toast were almost as good. Ruth didn't want to sit with the male NCOs, who looked a bit intimidating, so joined the handful of ATS on the other side of the canteen.

She introduced herself and the girls seemed happy to have her there. Then a rather coarse girl with peroxide-blonde hair smirked and nodded towards Sam.

'He's your fella, ain't he? Wondered why he didn't look at none of us.'

'Yes, Sergeant Johnson is my boyfriend.' She left it there and began to eat her tea. Nobody thought this rude as food was consumed first and conversation came second. You never knew if you were going to be called away in the middle of a meal.

Ruth didn't join in the chatter but nodded and smiled when appropriate. They were all gunners, which meant they couldn't do anything to offend her. Sam had wanted to keep their relationship secret but it was too late to worry about that.

She stood, picked up her plate and irons and

walked across to the two buckets, one for the slops the other to rinse the plate, personal cutlery and mug.

Then she deliberately turned and smiled directly at Sam. He understood immediately. His smile was blinding. He left his own things as he couldn't manage them and his crutch and one of his friends collected not only his plate but his personal cutlery. They'd made it abundantly clear that they were more than just friends.

Although he didn't take her hand, he placed his free arm across her back briefly and she looked up at him and nodded. 'I'm sorry, one of the girls asked me directly and I wasn't going to lie.'

'Doesn't bother me, love, I'm the envy of every bloke here. Them knowing that you're my girlfriend makes me pleased as punch.' He winked at her and she tried to think of a suitable phrase to follow up with.

'I'm cock-a-hoop to be seen with you.' She giggled and he grinned. 'I know what both those phrases actually mean but have no idea where they came from. Why would anyone be pleased because they'd been punched and what does a cockerel and a hoop have to do with being happy?'

'Haven't the faintest idea – remember I left school at fourteen – I don't have your superior education.'

For horrible second, Ruth thought he was being serious, then he laughed. 'I reckon being able to build a house from the foundations up is more important than having a huge vocabulary,' he added.

'So do I. Did I tell you that I speak very good French as well as decent German?'

'I'd keep that information to yourself, love, they'll have you in the SOE and parachute you into France to help the resistance if they know about it.'

'That's why I've kept it quiet. I'm really not suited to that sort of life – Clara is different. I wish I was more like her.'

'I like you just as you are, love. Better a live coward than a dead hero.'

She laughed and so did he. 'Did you make that up? I'll remember that and use it one day myself.'

'Probably got it from somewhere. Better to be cautious than dead sounds more like it. No one likes a coward.'

He stopped and she realised he was having difficulty walking. 'Shall we grab a couple of chairs from somewhere and sit down and talk?'

'There are two in my hut. Hang on, I'll send someone to fetch them. Being a senior NCO does have its perks.'

A willing private brought them the seats and she

and Sam were just settled at the back of the main building, where it was quieter, when the same private returned at the double.

'Sarge, the rozzers are here to see you. Shall I send them round?'

'Yes, please do,' Sam said. He waited until they were alone and shrugged. 'I'm glad you're here. It will be news about my accident and possibly about Arthur too.'

He stood up, as did Ruth, as the two men in plain clothes came around the corner of the building.

'DI Brown, good to see you. Allow me to introduce you to Bombardier Cox.'

The older man in a rumpled suit nodded in her direction but didn't offer his hand. Sam didn't introduce her to the younger man.

'It's not good news, Sergeant, I've come to warn you to expect repercussions for making the report about Arthur Humfrey.'

Sam gripped the back of the chair; his knuckles were white. Ruth sat down.

'What happened?'

'I passed the information to the appropriate authorities but this Arthur Humfrey has very powerful friends in very high places. I was told in no uncertain terms to forget about it and not to pursue it further.'

'Bloody hell! Ruth, did you know Humfrey was so well connected?'

She shook her head. 'No, Jill didn't mention anything about his background. She's not from a grand family, I'm sure of it.' Her stomach was roiling, there was a lump in her throat.

'Sergeant Johnson, I've further bad news, I'm afraid. The young woman who ran you over is going to get off with just a warning. Her father made sure of that.'

Ruth was reeling from this barrage of bad news and looked at Sam with dismay.

'Her boyfriend has been sent away so maybe that will be punishment enough,' Sam said. The inspector looked confused. 'My lieutenant has been sent to the wilds of Scotland but for an unconnected misdemeanour.'

'I'm sorry things have turned out so badly for you. We'll just have to pray that even though nothing's being done in the Humfrey matter, at least the authorities have been alerted,' the policeman said.

Ruth finally found her voice. 'They already know he's a hardened gambler and yet are still sending him to Cairo. It makes no sense at all.'

'A lot of things don't, Bombardier Cox, a lot of

things don't.' The inspector nodded and was about to leave when Sam called him back.

'What exactly do you think "the repercussions" are likely to be for me?'

'I fear you might be joining your erstwhile officer in the wilds of Scotland.'

Sam shrugged. 'Can't be helped. I did the right thing even if it's upset some bigwigs.'

16

Sam watched the policeman go and tried to think of something encouraging to say to Ruth. She touched his arm and he looked down at her.

'Let's not worry about it now, we've got an entire evening to be together. I'm going to be posted tomorrow or the next day, so we knew we'd be unable to meet up easily.'

He smiled. 'You always make me feel more optimistic. Some poor sods are in Africa and haven't seen their families for years. We're the lucky ones, safe as houses in Blighty.'

'I agree, we have to count our blessings, don't we?' Her eyes twinkled and he chuckled. He'd used the proverb unintentionally, but his lovely, intelligent girl had picked up on it immediately. She was too bright for him, came from a different class and maybe it would be better for her if they were at opposite ends of the country.

He couldn't bear to think of her moving on, finding an officer instead of him but in that moment he decided that ending the relationship now might be the best for both of them. She could do better for herself. She could do so much better than him, find herself an officer, someone more like her.

She patted the chair next to hers and he resumed his seat, not intending to point out that RA batteries would follow the infantry troops when the allies invaded and then he'd be in the line of fire too. ATS were unlikely to go so she'd be safe and that's all that mattered to him.

'We can write every week, maybe telephone occasionally, and if we're lucky we'll get leave together one day,' she said as she snuggled up to him.

He was about to blurt out that he loved her but that would be cruel and selfish and make things so much worse. 'I was thinking that as it will be hard for us not being able to go out and enjoy ourselves without feeling guilty...'

'What do you mean? Of course we can both have fun with our friends, I intend to go to dances but that won't change how I feel about you, won't stop me being your girlfriend.' She shrugged off his arm and stared at him. 'Don't you trust me? Do you mean to flirt with other girls?'

'No, I don't, but I want you to be able to enjoy yourself, mix with a better class of blokes. I'm not good enough for you...'

She punched him hard, and he winced. 'How can you sit there and say something so stupid? I'm a bastard with a good education, so I'm the lucky one having a wonderful man like you prepared to ignore my birth and go out with me.'

Her language made him flinch. It was deliberate, but she'd wanted to shock him into seeing things from her side. He blinked back unwanted tears. 'I love you, Ruth, and had decided to let you go, let you find someone more suitable.'

Instead of being upset, she was furious. She tensed, and was preparing to launch a full-scale physical attack so he reached out, grabbed her arms and kept her in the chair.

'I'm sorry, love, I've got this horribly wrong, haven't I?'

She relaxed and tears trickled down her cheeks. 'You're a fool, Sam, but I love you anyway.'

For a second, her words didn't register then he

smiled, picked her up and put her on his lap. 'Are you sure? I know you could find someone better.'

Her eyes were fierce, she reached up and yanked his hair. 'If you dare say such a stupid thing again, Sergeant Johnson, I'll do you some real harm.'

He did the only sensible thing and kissed her. She responded passionately and if they hadn't been interrupted by the sound of boots approaching at the double for a second time, things might have got out of hand.

Hastily he put her back on her own chair and adjusted his uniform to cover his embarrassment and stood up, using the back of the chair to keep his weight off his injured ankle.

Thomas arrived. 'You're needed, Sarge, there's been an accident, I reckon Tiny Bates could be a goner.'

Sam snatched up his crutch and followed. He forgot about Ruth and concentrated on the emergency.

'What's happened? Details,' Sam said as they hurried towards the gunsite.

'Silly bugger was chatting to one of them telephonists in the dugout and lost his balance. Fell headfirst down the steps and ain't moved a muscle since.'

'Has someone sent for the medical orderly? Rung for an ambulance? Rung HQ?'

'Not sure, Sarge, chaos up there.'

Sam was about to yell for a gunner when Ruth called out from behind him. 'I'll do that, Sarge, I know where to go. I'll let HQ know what's going on.'

Ruth was efficient and definitely officer material. It was a pity there wasn't someone like her working here.

The gun park was behind a hedge but he could hear the panicked shouting. He was on general duties tonight so Ronnie should have been here. Where the hell was he? Those manning the guns should have been doing routine checks, not talking to the girls on the telephones.

Chaos was indeed what he found. The telephonists, who worked in the safety of a dugout so communication with the other sections and HQ was kept open at all times, were weeping in each other's arms and weren't where they should be.

He took charge and sent the milling crowd of agitated soldiers back to their posts and jumped down to see for himself and winced as his injured ankle hit the ground. The man was ominously still, his head at a strange angle. Sam dropped to his knees and checked for a pulse he knew wouldn't be there. Tiny had broken his neck in the fall. A bloody tragic accident that shouldn't have happened.

Tiny was so called because he was huge, over six foot and weighed twenty stone at least. It was going to be a bugger of a job getting him out of there.

As Tiny was face down, there was no need to cover him and Sam didn't want to move the body anyway. The MPs would have to be told, statements taken, but his biggest concern right now was the whereabouts of both Ronnie, the sergeant on duty, and his bombardier. They should both have been here overseeing the drills and the fact that they were absent was something he needed to investigate before an officer arrived from HQ to take charge.

If his friend was skiving, he'd be court martialled for gross dereliction of duty. This death could have been avoided if the men had been doing what they were supposed to be doing and hadn't been wandering about chatting.

The men in his section were a team, they stuck up for each other and wouldn't nark on the men who were missing. With any luck, they could cover for Ronnie and Dinger Bell, the bombardier who was missing too. Sam hoped they were just off having a fag and a cuppa somewhere and not actually AWOL.

He hopped up the short flight of steps that led

from the underground shelter, wishing he was fully fit and not hobbling about. Lance Bombardier Jimmy Sainty was waiting, ashen faced, to speak to hm.

'Sarge, them two what are not here went to sort something out with Section B. Been a lot of aggro between A and B earlier and it needed to be dealt with pronto before it got out of hand like.'

'Bloody hell, how long ago did they go?'

"Bout half an hour since, Sarge. Cycled across the fields so didn't go past no guards.'

'Right, ta for telling me.' Sam waved his arm and the men reacted immediately and were standing to attention in front of him moments later.

'Tiny broke his neck in the fall. Nobody's fault but his own. Jimmy, nip down in the dugout and ring B section. Tell them what's happened and make sure whoever you speak to gets the message to our two.'

The medical orderly arrived and after a quick look agreed there was nothing to be done for the poor sod. 'He'll need to go to the morgue in Lincoln, Sarge. Bombardier Cox is organising all that. I've covered Tiny with a blanket for now.'

'Good. Stay with the body. No rubberneckers. Got that?'

'Yes, Sarge.' The orderly pointed at Sam's foot.

'You're supposed to be resting that, not galivanting about the place.'

* * *

Ruth had informed HQ of the disaster and asked if an officer would be coming to deal with the incident. She'd been told that the MO – a Major Crossley – would be there in fifteen minutes. She was puzzled as it wasn't usual to have two senior officers at headquarters. Maybe this doctor was on a temporary assignment of some sort.

She'd been impressed by Sam's authority, his command of the situation and remembered what somebody had told her about senior NCOs: that they were the men – and presumably women – who were the true backbone of the army and that officers were just there for decoration.

Word had spread rapidly around the small barracks and soldiers from the other sections were drifting towards the gun park. The last thing Sam needed was a crowd of men gawping at what was going on.

'You men, there's been an accident in A section. Nothing to do with you. A section gun park is not part of your remit.'

Ruth spoke directly to the leader, keeping her eyes on his. None of them had stripes so she outranked them, but would it be enough?

One of the men smirked. 'We ain't taking no orders from no ATS girl, are we, Arnie?'

'Shut your trap, Fred, the bombardier's right. It ain't none of our business.' He nodded politely at her. 'Begging your pardon, we was just curious.'

She remained rigid, unsmiling, apparently in total command of the situation until they were walking away. She unclenched her fists and tried to swallow but her mouth was too dry. If they'd refused her direct order, she wasn't sure what she'd have done.

Relieved that things had worked out for her, she doubled to the gun park to see what she could do to help. There were two ATS girls – presumably the ones from the dugout – hovering on the periphery of the disaster area, obviously not sure what they should be doing. Now this she could deal with.

'You two, what are you doing up here? Get back to your positions immediately. I'm ashamed of you both for abandoning your posts.'

'There's a body down there, Bombardier...'

'I'm well aware of that. Have you forgotten there's a war on? People die but those that remain must carry on doing their duty regardless. You're bringing the

ATS into disrepute; if you don't resume your post then I'll have you both on a charge.'

The two girls exchanged a glance and decided Ruth meant what she said and that having to work with the mortal remains of a friend of theirs was better than the alternative.

She followed them to the steps that led down into the area where the telephones were manned. She nodded to the medical orderly, who was standing watch over the body.

'Blimey, I'm glad them two are back. That blooming phone has been ringing non-stop but it's not my place to answer.'

To prove his words were not an exaggeration, both telephones rang and Ruth was pleased to see the girls put on the headphones and answer them professionally.

Sam arrived and beckoned her up. 'Well done, I was just getting onto that.' He was limping badly and had lost his crutch.

'Lean on my shoulder, Sarge, and we'll get out of the way. The doctor from headquarters will be here any minute to take charge.'

'I just hope that our missing sergeant and bombardier are back before he arrives. Sod's law that they're absent when this took place.' He quickly explained why those two weren't there.

'I've a horrible feeling that an officer at the other gun park might well have noticed them. If there's bad blood between the sections then the men there won't feel any obligation to lie if asked.'

Sam's expression was grim but then he smiled. 'Thank God, here they come.'

Ruth turned and saw two red-faced soldiers leap off a battered bicycle and race towards them.

'I'll get out of your way, Sam, having me here won't help when the major arrives.'

He barely glanced at her and nodded. Before she left, she decided to go in search of his missing crutch and she found it immediately. It had been dropped just in front of the dugout and no one had noticed. She retrieved it, brushed it down and handed it to Sam as she walked past.

This time he smiled and was obviously happy to have his support back. Ruth was just returning to the office when a car roared in. The officer from HQ had arrived. Before he had time to emerge from the vehicle, an ambulance, bell clanging, screeched to a halt behind the car.

She hesitated for a second and then headed for the ambulance driver. She smiled and spoke to him through his open window. 'There's no emergency. The soldier's dead and needs taking to the morgue.'

The driver grinned. 'Ta, Bombardier, we knew that. Me and Tom like having the bell on so we can drive fast.'

The officer, a surprisingly young man to be a major and a doctor, didn't look too fierce. She wondered why he wasn't on the front line but promptly put those thoughts aside as he strode towards her.

'Bombardier Cox, I presume?'

She jumped to attention and saluted. 'Yes, sir.'

'Come with me and explain exactly what happened.'

Ruth could only suppose he wanted her to accompany him because she'd been the one to inform HQ. She gave him a succinct account and he listened silently.

'Right. Thank you.' He stopped so abruptly she almost walked past him. 'Tell me, Cox, why Sergeant Johnson was needed when there's already a sergeant on duty at the gun park?'

'I don't know, sir, I just followed orders.' Even to her, this sounded like an evasion. He stared at her for a moment. 'As I thought. You're dismissed.'

She saluted again but this time received no response as he'd turned his back, marched away, and was approaching the gun park. There was going to be trouble and she prayed it wouldn't include Sam. He was already in enough deep water to drown. Despite the dire circumstances, her mouth curved. Had she always used so many truisms and only being with Sam had made her aware of this?

* * *

Sam quickly told Ronnie what had happened and his friend was shocked.

'Sod me, how could the silly blighter break his neck falling down a few steps? What a bloody stupid way to die.'

A gunner hurtled up to them. 'Officer coming, he don't look too happy, Sarge.'

'Ta, get lost, you don't want to be asked to lie. Tell the others to play dumb when questioned,' Sam said.

'No, mate, this is my mess, I'll not let you take the blame.'

A voice spoke from directly behind them. How the hell had the bloody major appeared so silently?

'Wise move, Sergeant Smith, I'd already decided that you were absent from duty when this accident took place.'

Both Sam and Ronnie snapped to attention and

from the corner of his eye, Sam saw the men of his section suddenly find something urgent to attend to elsewhere. Major Crossley was new to him, the medic must have joined the battery very recently and as he was based at HQ, they'd not crossed paths until now.

He and Ronnie were left to stand like stuffed dummies whilst the major dropped into the dugout to examine the body. Sam exchanged a quick glance with his friend, who looked even more grey and worried than he had before. They didn't dare speak, even to whisper, as they were already in so much trouble.

The officer reappeared and issued orders before speaking to them. 'Right, you two, with me.' The ambulance men were lurking, waiting to be given permission to collect Tiny.

'You'll not remove the cadaver without help.' He smiled but it wasn't friendly. 'Get four men to assist you.'

'Yes, sir,' they chorused.

Then the major marched back to the office, knowing Sam and Ronnie would follow.

'Here, lean on me, Sam, you're a bit unsteady, is your ankle playing up?'

'Too right. Thanks, your assistance's appreciated.'

Even with the crutch to lean on as well, Sam was in trouble. He'd been warned to stay off his injured ankle and was paying the price for ignoring this. Men still fought the Germans on the front line with a bullet in them so a sprained ankle wasn't going to stop him doing his duty.

The major swore and stopped. 'For God's sake, Johnson, what's wrong with you?'

'I was run over a couple of days ago and sprained my ankle, sir. Shouldn't be walking on it.'

The look the officer gave Ronnie could have blistered paint. 'If you'd been where you should have been, Smith, Johnson wouldn't be in this state and that gunner wouldn't be dead.'

Ronnie shifted miserably but said nothing. There was little he could say in mitigation as leaving your post for any reason without permission was a heinous crime.

'Johnson, none of this is your fault. Hobble to the medical room and I'll take a look at your ankle. I'll not be long.'

Major Crossley nodded and strode off. Ronnie, shoulders slumped, trailed along behind. Sam knew what was going to happen. Ronnie would be demoted, possibly back to a gunner. Tiny's death wouldn't have happened if Ronnie had left his bombardier in charge, even if he'd gone AWOL himself.

Ruth appeared at his side. 'Let me help you, Sam. Aren't you going to the office?'

'No, to the medical room. Ronnie's for it now. I'm not sure how this battery will manage with an officer and sergeant short and me not fully fit.'

She squeezed his arm. 'This has been a dreadful week, especially for you and your section.'

He leaned heavily on her shoulder as well as the crutch. His ankle threatened to give way beneath him and hurt more than it had done when he'd first done it. He'd felt something go when he'd gone down the steps to check the body and had a nasty feeling he might have torn something else.

The medical orderly was expecting him. 'In here, Sarge, you need to elevate your leg. I reckon you might have fractured it.'

'When I went down into the dugout, something went then. The major's coming to have a dekko.'

'I'll get us some tea from the NAAFI,' Ruth said and immediately dashed off.

Sam crossed the room and flopped onto the examination table. Lifting his injured ankle up was excruciating but he wasn't going to ask for help. Using his hands, he shuffled back and leaned against the raised end of the table, wondering what was going on in the office.

He'd expected to wait fifteen minutes at least but was only just settled when the major arrived. It was as if a different man walked in – he was smiling and relaxed, quite different from previously.

'I expect you want to know what happened to your friend. He's lucky not to lose all his stripes but he has a good record so he's now a bombardier. Bloody nuisance that you're out of action.'

'Yes, sir, thank you, sir,' Sam said trying not to show his relief that his friend had got off so lightly.

The major pointed at Sam's booted foot. 'Good thing you've got your boot on. That will have helped to stabilise any fracture.'

'I saw the medic at the RAF base and he said it was just sprained and to keep it elevated and not to walk on it for a week.'

The doctor shook his head and tutted as if he wasn't surprised the RAF medic had got it wrong. 'Orderly, remove your sergeant's boot and do it very carefully.'

Sam gritted his teeth whilst this was done and was relieved when it was over.

17

Ruth persuaded the two jolly ladies serving behind the counter at the NAAFI to let her borrow a tray in order to carry the four mugs of tea.

'Here you go then, miss, can't say no to your handsome young man. Dreadful business up at the gunsite. Such a shame,' the one with scarlet lipstick said as she put the mugs on the tray.

'Yes, a tragic waste of a young life. Did you know that more people were killed by the blackout than by the Germans in the first year of the war?' Ruth didn't know why she'd told them this.

'Blooming heck, I'm not surprised. Blooming dangerous creeping around in the dark, especially in the winter. I reckon them Germans are suffering just as much as us so it's fair, ain't it?'

Ruth wasn't sure about that but nodded and smiled. 'If you've got any buns, biscuits or cakes, that would be wonderful.'

'Hang on a tick, I'll find you something,' the other lady said and vanished into the kitchen to return triumphantly with three iced fingers and a saucer full of broken biscuits.

'Thank you, that's so kind,' Ruth said and put a handful of coppers, plus two threepenny bits, on the counter to cover the cost.

She almost tripped over the step as she walked in the medical centre and found the terrifying officer already there examining Sam's ankle.

'Excellent timing, Bombardier, I'm in need of a strong cup of tea,' he said, with a charming smile. 'I'll understand if there isn't one for me.'

'I brought four, sir, just in case.' Ruth couldn't salute as she was holding the tray but nodded instead and he nodded back.

Sam looked pale but smiled at her. 'Major Crossley thinks my ankle was fractured, not sprained, which is why it's been so painful. I've made it worse by walking on it. I've got to go to Lincoln and have it X-rayed and plastered.'

'The ambulance hasn't left yet. If you don't mind travelling with the remains then you could go with them. I'll come too.' Ruth looked at the officer and he nodded.

'Good thinking. Nip out and make sure they don't leave. The orderly can wheel your sergeant out to them when he's drunk his tea.'

Ruth bribed the ambulance drivers with a shilling to get themselves a tea and then they were happy to hang about for a bit.

'Knackering work getting that bloke out of the dugout. We could do with a cup of char, couldn't we, Jimmy?'

'Not half, ta, Corp. We'll wait until your sarge's ready. No rush. Our passenger ain't going nowhere,' Jimmy replied.

When she returned, the orderly had vanished with his tea, leaving, to her surprise, Sam and the major chatting as if they were old friends.

'They're having a drink and are happy to wait until you're ready. Do you need to take anything with you? Will they keep you in?' Ruth wasn't going to spend the night on this battery site unless Sam was there too.

The officer answered from his chair where he was sitting perfectly relaxed. 'It's not a compound fracture, Bombardier, they won't need to do anything but X-ray and plaster. A fair amount of hanging about, no doubt.'

'I think I'll go back to my base tonight, Sam, seems silly not to as I'll be in Lincoln anyway.'

It was a bit awkward talking about personal things in front of a senior officer, but he seemed glued to his chair and didn't seem to appreciate that they wanted to be alone.

Sam grinned. 'I was going to suggest that you did that, love. I'm going to be on medical leave until the plaster comes off so will take my kitbag with me. I've sent someone to pack.'

The major was watching them both as if he knew something they didn't. He was making her feel uncomfortable. With a small smile, he drained his tea and put it down.

'I was waiting for you both to be here before speaking about this.'

He had their full attention now.

'This Humfrey business is a tricky one. You breaking your ankle is perfect timing, Sergeant Johnson. I'm sending you home to convalesce and by the time you return, it should have blown over. We don't want to lose a promising NCO like yourself.'

'What about Arthur Humfrey?' Ruth blurted out.

'His card has been well and truly marked. He's still

going to Cairo, but I'll be keeping a very close eye on him.' He grinned at their surprise. 'Yes, I'm being posted to the same place as him. That's why I've been made aware of the issue. When the DI reported your information to the War Office, they were furious with you and with him.'

'I was told by the DI that I was being posted to the Outer Hebrides,' Sam said. 'Humfrey said they all stick together and would ignore anything a lower-class bloke like me told them.'

'Unfortunately, there are many of that ilk in that particular department. However, not all of them that work there are old Etonians and so on. Word filtered down and things were set in motion.'

Ruth guessed the major was also a spook and the perfect man to make sure Arthur didn't become entangled in anything unsavoury because of his addiction.

'Were you posted here to speak to Sam?'

'Good God, not at all. Pure coincidence. I was marking time until I was needed elsewhere.'

'I'm sorry if I'm being obtuse, sir, but how is Sam going to get from Lincoln hospital to St Albans, where his parents live, carrying his kitbag and using crutches?'

'He's a resourceful chap, I'm sure he'll manage somehow.'

'My RA battery is being posted as Binbrook is being emptied of planes until next spring. Would it be possible for me to have compassionate leave or something to escort my fiancé home? I'm not needed on my site and have no idea where we'll be sent next. I'm intending to apply to attend an OCTU.'

The poor man was stunned by this barrage of words. He recovered and smiled. 'I don't see why not. I'd heard Binbrook was out of action. I'll see what I can do. I'll make a few telephone calls on your behalf.'

As soon as they were alone, she hugged Sam, who promptly pulled her onto his lap for a very enjoyable few minutes. Knowing they could be rejoined by their superior officer at any moment, she jumped off and beamed at him.

'I can't believe that this might actually work out for the best – it's an ill wind that blows nobody any good.' Ruth tried not to giggle and waited for his response.

'Every cloud has a silver lining,' he responded and waggled his eyebrows, which made her giggle even more.

'I'm very much afraid, Sergeant Johnson, that we are now engaged. Do you wish to break it off?'

His eyes flashed. 'I'd marry you tomorrow if I could. I love you, I knew it the moment I set eyes on you. Didn't think there was any such thing as love at first sight – but I know it's true.'

'I love you too, this has happened so quickly my head's spinning.' She pulled a chair over so she could sit next to him. 'It's the middle of October now; do you expect to have your leg out of plaster by the end of November?'

'I bloody well hope so. It's going to be chaos here with no sergeants or an officer. I might be posted somewhere else when I'm fit, and I think that might be for the best after what's happened.'

'If I get sent for officer training, that takes longer than being made up to sergeant so maybe we can meet in London like last time.'

He nodded. 'As you're accompanying me to St Albans,' he delved into his pocket and produced a notebook and the nub of a pencil, 'I'll write down my address just in case we get separated or something.'

'I can't see why that would happen, but you're right, better to be safe than sorry.'

He chuckled and scribbled the information on a page and tore it out. 'Here you are, love. A stitch in time saves nine.'

'This is becoming silly. We must stop using these sayings or people will think we're daft.'

'I think it's a laugh.' He smiled in way that sent a

wave of unexpected heat to a very strange place. 'I'll be able to introduce you to my parents. Now we're engaged...'

'You haven't actually asked me and I haven't given you my answer.'

'Will you marry me, Ruth?'

Her laughter echoed around the chilly medical room and the orderly poked his head around the door to see what was going on. He took one look at the pair of them and hastily retreated.

'Sam, that was the most unromantic proposal I've ever heard,' she said.

It was his turn to laugh. 'Good God, how many times has someone proposed to you? Are you a serial fiancée?'

Ruth was about to answer but Major Crossley strolled in and joined in the merriment.

'Good news all round. Congratulations on your engagement.' He remained standing, so Ruth got to her feet.

'You will report to the barracks in Regent's Park for OT three days from now, Bombardier Cox. Sergeant Johnson, you have six weeks' medical leave, and your new posting will be sent to your home address.'

'Thank you, sir, for arranging this for us. I think I'd better get a move on. It will be full dark soon.'

Ruth wasn't looking forward to travelling with a corpse but had no choice. She wheeled Sam to the waiting ambulance and the men lifted him inside.

'On the bench, Sarge, with your foot elevated. We'll strap you in,' one of the drivers said cheerfully.

This was accomplished without him yelping but it was a close thing as the pain was worse than before. He was worried the ankle might be more damaged than either medic thought. He'd find out soon enough so no need to mention it to Ruth.

The door slammed behind them.

'It's only a few miles to the hospital, love, hold my hand and don't think about who we're in here with.'

Sam ignored the throbbing of his broken ankle, the silent shrouded shape on the other side of the ambulance and just concentrated on the woman he was going to marry one day. She snuggled up to him and he put his arm around her.

'Have you worked out how we're going to get from the hospital to the station in the blackout?' Ruth whispered to him.

'You don't have to whisper, Tiny doesn't care,' he whispered back and she giggled, which was his intention. He raised his voice. 'To be honest, I don't think we've got the slightest chance of catching a train to London today. We can either find an empty waiting room at the hospital or go to the station and hope there's one there.'

'I was just thinking about the mechanics of you travelling on a bus with crutches and your leg in plaster and me with my haversack, respirator, tin hat and your kitbag.' She wasn't whispering but was still speaking so quietly he almost missed what she said.

'Okay – we've got to make a decision first about where we're going to spend the night then we can discuss how we're getting from A to B.'

'At the hospital, it's likely to be warmer and cleaner than the station.'

'In which case we don't have to worry about anything else until tomorrow morning. When do you want to get married?' His abrupt change of subject was deliberate. She wasn't fazed and replied immediately.

'Next summer if we can coincide our leave. Neither of us know where we'll be or what we'll be doing then but it's good to have something to look forward to.'

'I think as an officer you might have more say in where you're posted. If you ask for London then at least I'll be able to get to you from wherever I might be.'

'I'll do that. Shall we try and get time off together close to Christmas or the New Year?' She hesitated and then squeezed his hand as if she was about to give him bad news and his stomach dropped.

'There's something I've not told you and you might be upset when I do. I've got £3,000 in a trust fund, the interest comes to me each quarter. I can access the full amount on marriage or when I'm twenty-one.'

'That's amazing. Why did you think I'd be upset to discover I'm marrying a wealthy woman?'

'Hardly that, but it does mean we can buy ourselves a house...'

'Not bloody likely, we'll buy a bit of land and my dad and I will build a house for us.'

Her teeth flashed white in the darkness and she sighed loudly. 'How spiffing, as my friend Grace would say, having a house that nobody else has ever lived in. I grew up in ancient buildings and have never lived in a new house. I can't wait.'

They were chatting away in the gloom with as much enthusiasm as if they were sitting in a cafe rather than next to a dead body.

The ambulance rocked to a halt and it was a relief to have the doors open even though they could see bugger all in the dark as no lights were allowed in the blackout.

'Hang on, Sarge, we'll just deliver the body and

then get a wheelchair and take you in,' someone said, but Sam couldn't tell which one of the drivers it was.

'I'll get out, give you more room to manoeuvre,' Ruth said and slid off the narrow bench he was strapped into.

* * *

Sam's eyes had adjusted to the darkness and he could just make out the two men and then the shape of Tiny as he was gently removed from the ambulance. He expected Ruth to jump back in but she didn't. He wasn't sure how long it took to take a body to the morgue but he reckoned it would be half an hour at least.

'I found a wheelchair, Sam, if I bring it right to the doors do you think you could somehow get into it with my help?' Ruth said from outside the open ambulance door.

'I'll give it a go, if I can lean on your shoulder whilst I hang onto the door frame, I think I'll be able to do it without putting my foot down.'

He completed the transfer successfully but the pain left him speechless for a few moments.

'I'll wheel you around to the accident department, Sam, it's a bit creepy standing around outside the morgue.'

'You'll have to take it slowly, love, as I've got to hold my foot in the air.'

'No, you haven't. This is a wheelchair specially for broken legs and it's got a thingy I can pull out for you to rest your leg on. I couldn't do it until you were safely in the chair.'

She fiddled around under his thigh and despite his discomfort it made his pulse race having her so close.

'There, if we lift your leg this support will slip underneath, at least I hope it will.'

It did and immediately the pain lessened. 'I'm impressed, love, you're going to make a bloody marvellous officer,' he said and grabbed her hand and kissed the knuckles.

'I wish you'd not swear so much, Sam, I'm not used to it.'

He chuckled. 'Then you must be deaf as all soldiers swear and most of them a lot worse than me.'

There were no steps or slopes to negotiate and with him holding a torch in each hand and pointing it ahead of them, they found the entrance to the hospital that the ambulance men used to bring in patients.

'There you are, Sergeant Johnson, we were beginning to think you'd changed your mind,' a white-coated doctor with horn-rimmed spectacles and grey hair said with a smile.

'Sorry to have kept you waiting, Doctor, but I'm here now.'

* * *

The surgeon decided after examining the X-ray that his ankle would recover with just a plaster cast.

'I'm the bearer of good news, Sergeant, a few weeks and you'll be fighting fit. I'm not needed so will leave this to a junior doctor to do.'

'That's excellent news. It's going to be too late to find accommodation for tonight. Is there a room somewhere my fiancée and I can wait until morning?'

'I'm sure there is and I'll mention it to Matron. Goodnight, young man.'

Ruth was allowed to wait with him whilst a junior medic was located to plaster the ankle. 'The matron is going to sort out a place we can stay for the night.'

'That's good news. A nice student nurse is making us a cup of tea and will bring it to us. Isn't that kind?'

'Certainly is. I've been thinking, love, that it can't have been a coincidence that Crossley just happened to be the medic on duty at my battery.'

'I asked him, but he said it was a coincidence – but you're right. I'm sure he was posted there, temporarily, in order to speak to you specifically about Humfrey, even though he denied it. Just luck that you actually needed his medical expertise.'

'I know it's convenient for me to be out of action and so on but it's a bloody nuisance. I'd rather be posted to Scotland than this.'

'I'm glad you won't be sent away. Actually, I think you should think about suing the girl who injured you. She should be made to pay financially even if she's got away with the legal side.'

'I'm not sure I want to upset that girl's posh family any further,' Sam said.

'Remember you won't be in the vicinity if you start legal proceedings. I know a solicitor costs a lot of money, but I'll willingly pay the fees and you can refund me when you win your damages.'

Sam wasn't keen on borrowing money from Ruth but she seemed so set on getting him compensation for his accident that reluctantly he agreed.

'If I write a letter saying that you're acting on my behalf, do you think that will be enough? I really don't want to get involved, it's not my sort of thing but if you feel so strongly about it then I'd be happy for you to give it a go.'

18

Ruth was surprised that Sam wanted her to deal with this as usually a man handled this sort of thing. She was pleased that already he trusted her to act for him. Something belatedly occurred to her. 'I don't think I can act for you, now I think about it, a solicitor would need your signature and so on.'

'Fair enough, I'll consider doing it but not right now.'

'I've got to go back to Binbrook to collect my kit and say my goodbyes. I do hope they haven't already left. I've enjoyed being a part of a mixed artillery site but wonder if I'll even be allowed to continue as part of the RA.'

'Blimey, Ruth, they won't want to let you go somewhere else. Your training as a kine operator as well as range finder, spotter and predictor makes you invaluable. As our invasion of France gets closer, more men will need to be released for service overseas so someone like you will be essential.'

'The only thing I've not done is learn how to use the spotlights. Mind you, those girls are stationed in remote places and have to live in pretty dire conditions. I'm glad now that I didn't opt for that.'

Their chat was interrupted by the arrival of the young doctor to plaster Sam's broken ankle. Ruth left them to it and went in search of the promised tea. There was no sign of the student, so she guessed the girl had been called away.

A qualified nurse was walking briskly towards her. 'Excuse me, nurse, is there a public call box near this hospital?'

'Yes, Corp, just outside, but I wouldn't recommend you going in the dark. If it's urgent then you could always ask Sister if you could use her telephone.'

'Thanks, my section is about to be transferred and if they leave before I can get back then heaven knows what will happen to my kit.' Ruth didn't correct the girl's inaccurate use of the word corporal – being referred to as a bombardier when you were in a Royal

Artillery battery was something civilians wouldn't know about.

'That sounds urgent to me. Always worth a try, Sister Daniels is okay, not like some I could mention.' The nurse smiled and hurried off without indicating where Sister Daniels' office was located.

Ruth was faced with a long, empty corridor with several closed doors. She thought for a moment and then decided if she found the ward then this sister might well have her office close by.

Light was filtering onto the shiny linoleum further down and it was the same direction that the helpful nurse had gone – this would be a good place to start and she hurried towards what was hopefully the ward she was looking for.

As she approached, a nurse in navy-blue uniform and immaculately starched sparkling white cap and apron emerged. She didn't look particularly friendly, but Ruth had no option – if she wanted to use a telephone then she had to speak to someone.

'Excuse me, I'm looking for Sister Daniels, I'm wondering if you might be her?'

'No, I'm Sister Watson. It's not visiting hours so what are you doing wandering about the hospital?'

This wasn't an auspicious start, but Ruth decided to ask about the telephone anyway. She explained her predicament and expected to be told in no uncertain terms that only staff members could use the phone, but the reverse was true.

'Come with me, Bombardier Cox, you can use mine. My son's a sergeant in the RA and he told me that girls are serving alongside him. I'd never hear the last of it if I didn't help. He's stationed in London – maybe you'll be posted there after your officer training.'

They'd now reached one of the closed doors and Sister Watson pushed it open and pointed proudly to the telephone sitting on her desk. 'Just ask the operator to connect you. When you lift the receiver, the switchboard will answer immediately.'

'Thank you, Sister, this is so kind of you.'

She was connected to HQ at Binbrook RA battery immediately. She asked to speak to an officer and told him the problem.

'I've got a message here from someone further up the command chain that you won't be rejoining your section but are going immediately for OT at Regent's Park. I'll arrange for your kit to be packed and sent on there. There's no need for you to return here.'

'Thank you, sir, that would be really helpful. Could you possibly tell me where our battery's being posted? I've made some good friends in my section and would like to be able to keep in touch.'

'They're going to Liverpool. If you have the service numbers of your friends then, as you know, you can contact them by mail easily enough.'

This was more or less a reprimand for asking an unnecessary question. 'I shall do that, sir, thank you again.' She put down the receiver thoughtfully, not sure if she was relieved or sad not to have been able to speak to Jill in person and tell her that the authorities knew about Arthur.

She almost collided with the friendly nurse she'd spoken to earlier. 'Golly, you were brave. Did Sister Watson allow you to use her telephone? She's a bit of a tartar and guards it like a lioness with her cub.'

'Yes, and she was very accommodating. I think it's because her son is in a mixed artillery battery, as am I. Everything's been arranged perfectly, thank you.'

'Actually, I was coming to find you as I've taken a tray of tea and biscuits to your handsome fiancé. The plastering's finished and he just has to wait for it to harden and then you'll be taken to a side room where you can stay for the night.'

* * *

Ruth wasn't allowed to wheel Sam through the hospital – it was against regulations for some reason – so an unfortunate porter had been fetched and had to do it for them.

'What a palaver, anyone would think you were someone important. You must have friends in high places. I never heard of no one being allowed to spend the night in one of them posh rooms before,' the disgruntled man told them sourly.

Sam half-swivelled in the chair and fixed him with an icy look. 'Who we are and who we know is none of your concern. We don't require any comments from you.'

Ruth expected the porter to apologise but instead he released his hold on the wheelchair and stepped away.

'Then you'll find the bloody place on your own. I ain't one of your squaddies to be bossed about.'

The bad-tempered man stomped away, leaving them marooned in a dimly lit corridor and with no idea where they were supposed to be.

'Golly, that wasn't a good idea, Sam. You should just have let it go, you don't always have to step in like that,' Ruth said, more sharply than she'd intended.

'He's a porter, he's there to do a job and not pass judgement. This is obviously the more expensive part of the hospital where the wealthy are treated. We just have to look for an empty room and then we can use that,' he said without apology for his part in this debacle.

'That's all very well for you to say. Are you suggesting that I knock on these doors, disturb anyone who's inside, until we find a room we can use? I'm sorry, I'm not going to do that. There's a general waiting room for the outpatients I noticed on the way in and we'll just have to spend the night in there.'

They travelled the length of the hospital in uncomfortable silence. She was waiting for him to apologise, which he obviously wasn't going to do. If he was waiting for her to do the same, then he was in for a long wait.

* * *

Sam wasn't enjoying this perambulation down the freezing hospital corridors in a less than comfortable wheelchair. The strong pain medication he'd been given hadn't kicked in and it was making him bad-tempered.

He just wanted to be lying flat on a bed somewhere and he really didn't care where that was. What had Ruth just said? His mind was beginning to blur, his concentration slipping but she must have made some sort of reply but wasn't sure what they'd been talking about.

He closed his eyes and let the morphine do its job. From a distance, he heard voices – one of them he thought was Ruth's, but he didn't know who the other person was – and then more trundling.

To his immense relief, some kind souls lifted him from his wheelchair and put him onto a bed. As soon as his leg was supported, covers were put over him, and he was deeply asleep.

* * *

His eyes were sticky, his throat dry and his head was pounding when he woke up the next day. For a moment he was disorientated and then he dredged up the information he needed and immediately looked around for Ruth.

The room was pleasantly warm, containing only his bed, an armchair and a chest of drawers. Where the hell had Ruth slept whilst he'd been comfortable on the bed? He pushed himself upright and swung his legs to the floor.

His broken ankle no longer hurt and there were crutches leaning against the bed ready for him to use.

His first venture must be to the bog. He considered himself an expert and had no difficulty reaching the door, although opening it was a little more difficult.

He saw a student nurse hurrying towards him. 'I need the WC.'

'It's the door opposite, Sergeant, and it's unoccupied. Do you need any help?'

'No, ta, I'll manage.'

He heard her laughing as she vanished around the corner. He was in luck because there was a sink with a mirror and he sluiced his face with cold water and washed his hands; that cleared his head a little. He ran his hand over his bristly chin and knew he needed to shave but the thought of trying to find his wash bag in his kitbag didn't appeal to him.

He'd returned to the room and settled on the bed when Ruth came in carrying a tray with a pot of tea, two mugs and what looked like a pile of freshly made toast.

'I was worried about you, love, I woke up and you weren't here.'

'I was fetching us some breakfast. You look like a pirate and your uniform's horribly crumpled.' She said this without her usual sunny smile and for a moment he was puzzled. Then he remembered that he'd had a blissful night's sleep whilst she'd had to spend it in an armchair. This would make her a bit tetchy.

'I appreciate you looking after me. I'm gasping for a cuppa, my throat's like the bottom of a parrot cage.'

'Well, Sergeant Johnson, that will never do. If your throat's that dry, can you manage the toast?'

'Just try me, I can smell the melting butter from here.'

'No butter, I'm afraid, Sam, just margarine and jam. The nurses have been so kind and made this for us.'

He happily munched his way through four slices of toast and drank two mugs of tea and was a new man.

'I'm sorry you had to sleep on the chair, love, you could have shared the bed with me. Nobody would have been any the wiser.'

'I was perfectly comfortable in the chair. Look, I've been arranging things for you as I really don't think even with me helping that we could get you safely to St Albans. I managed to get hold of Clara and we've pulled some strings and arranged a car.'

'Crikey, that's impressive. When will it be collecting us?'

She looked away and then back and he finally understood that something had changed between them but he had no idea what it was or why it had happened.

'I won't be going with you, Sam, I'm catching the train to London as my OCTU is taking place near Regent's Park. I really can't go to St Albans without my kit – I hope you understand.'

He didn't – but he supposed what she said made sense. After all, she only had an overnight bag with her.

'Fair enough. I would have liked you to meet my parents but that can wait. I haven't given you a ring and I'd hoped we could choose one together. Until then, I won't feel that we're properly engaged.'

He waited for her to smile, hug him and say that a ring didn't matter, that she loved him, but she didn't. He didn't know a lot about women – she was his first real girlfriend – but he'd spent enough time with blokes to know when you shouldn't let things drift.

'What's wrong? Have I done something to upset you? Have you changed your mind about wanting to marry me?'

She didn't answer and his heart sank.

'Come on, Ruth, you can't have been in love with me yesterday and not today. Something's happened and you owe it to me to tell me. You've been giving me the cold shoulder since I woke up. I deserve an explanation, don't you think?'

'I am having second thoughts. We don't really know each other very well and I think we're moving too fast.'

'For God's sake, what are you talking about?'

'You bullied the porter and made him abandon us. You were rude to me and then you didn't apologise.'

Sam was stunned by her outburst. 'I was in a lot of pain, which made me bad-tempered. I'd no idea I was rude to you, and I couldn't apologise because the drugs knocked me out. I barely remember any of it and certainly not how I arrived here.'

He stared at her, not letting her look away. 'Do you honestly think I'd have let you sleep on a chair when I was lying in comfort if I'd known? You really don't know me and I obviously don't know you as well as I thought. Unlike you, that just makes me more determined to get to know you, not want to cut and run.'

'I see, I think I've overreacted. I was upset last night and it didn't occur to me there was a perfectly acceptable explanation. I'm sorry.'

'I'm sorry too, love. I'm proud that you want to become an officer and that doesn't make me feel in any way inferior.' He paused and something occurred to him that she hadn't asked and he'd never volunteered.

'I might not have my higher school certificate like you, but the army still thought I was intelligent enough to train to do exactly the job that you do. I could become an officer if I wanted to, but I prefer to be with ordinary people. Far too often, in my opinion, officers are appointed because of their social status, not their ability.'

This was the longest speech he'd ever made to her and she was looking at him differently, as if realising that he wasn't the man she thought him to be. The fact that he was – could be – on a par with her didn't seem to help for some reason. Had she wanted to marry him because she thought that being illegitimate made her unsuitable for someone better?

No sooner had he thought this than he swallowed a bitter taste. They'd both been swept along by some nonsense, love if you like, and ignored the reality. She would always consider herself a cut above him and he would always be apologising for something.

Finally, she smiled at him in the way she had before this misunderstanding. He had a nasty feeling too much had been said that couldn't be retracted and the damage to their relationship couldn't be mended.

'I'm sorry, love, but neither of us would have said the things we have if we didn't have doubts about this engagement. I do love you, doubt I'll ever feel the same way about anyone else, but you're right to want to end things...'

Her eyes widened and she flung herself into his arms. They closed of their own volition. He held her close as she sobbed against his shoulder. After a while, she began to recover, gulping and sniffing, then sat back and rummaged in her pocket for a clean hand-kerchief. After blowing her nose and wiping her face, she stepped away, her eyes were sad and he knew what she was going to say next.

'I think that I love you too, Sam, but I hadn't even considered ending things between us until you men-tioned it. It breaks my heart, but I think maybe you're right. Let's not be engaged, we've not told anybody so that won't be a problem or an embarrassment for ei-ther of us. I still want to go out with you, will write to you every week as before. If, when you're fit for duty, you still want to meet up in London then we'll do that.'

He'd been about to blurt out that nothing would really change his mind, that despite what he'd said she was the one for him, but pride made him keep this information to himself.

'That sounds tickety-boo. If after your officer training you want to meet up then I'd be happy to and see how things go.'

What he wanted to do was kiss her, show her that they were meant to be together, but he'd missed his chance. Now he had to let her go and pray she didn't meet a toffee-nosed officer and decide that she'd rather be with him than an ordinary bloke like Sam.

He was able to continue a conversation about nothing much whilst hiding his misery. He'd known all along that Ruth was too good for him, but he loved her so much that he wasn't going to tie her down to an engagement she wasn't convinced was best for her. It was a relief when she gathered up the dirty crockery and dashed off with the tray.

Thank God he hadn't told his parents about her – he'd not even mentioned her in his occasional letters. A porter arrived with a wheelchair to take him out to the car.

'I'm waiting to say goodbye to my girlfriend, I'm sure she won't be long.'

'The driver said if you don't come immediately, she won't wait, Sarge,' the porter said.

'In which case, I'm ready to go. If you'd be kind enough to dump my bag in my lap, I reckon I can hold it okay until we reach the car.'

He glanced back several times, hoping Ruth would appear, but she didn't. The ATS driver helped him into the front seat and then jammed his kitbag between his legs.

'I can't have you in the back, sorry, Sarge. I know it'll be a bit uncomfortable but better than being put on a charge. I'm taking you to Cambridge and then hopefully there'll be another lift waiting to take you to St Albans.'

She slammed his door, ran around the bonnet and jumped into her own seat. His throat was thick, his eyes damp, but he was determined not to show how devastated he was by this unexpected turn of events.

19

Ruth took longer than necessary washing up the cups, saucers and plates they'd used whilst trying to make sense of what had just happened. How could things between her and the man she loved have deteriorated so suddenly?

It was all her fault – she'd overreacted and made the arrangements for him to travel by car while she was tired and hungry. She really should have asked him before she'd done this. Not a good combination for making sensible decisions. She smiled and ran through what she was going to say to him, imagined his delighted smile and the joyous moment when they were in each other's arms.

She dried the final spoon and hurried back from

the small kitchen area that the nurses used, feeling it wasn't too late to put things right. She burst into the room, but found it empty. His belongings had gone – he had gone – he couldn't have made it clearer that he wasn't ready to forgive her. She collapsed into the armchair in which she'd spent a cold and uncomfortable night and despite her best efforts couldn't keep back the tears.

After a few minutes, she'd stopped crying but had been too miserable to move from the chair. She remained where she was until two student nurses arrived to put the room back to its original pristine state.

'Goodness me, I thought you'd already gone. The sergeant left ages ago,' one of them said.

'I'm sorry, I didn't get any sleep last night and must have dozed off. I'm going now. Thank you very much for letting us stay in here.' Ruth scrambled to her feet, keeping her tear-stained face averted, grabbed her haversack and respirator from the floor and was out of the room before either of the girls could comment.

* * *

Ruth made her way disconsolately to the station at Lincoln and discovered there was a train to London arriving in twenty minutes. She didn't have a travel warrant so would have to buy her own ticket and a perverse impulse made her ask for a seat in first class.

'There you are, Corporal. I expect you'll be wanting to have lunch on the train – they do a lovely hotpot and sticky toffee pudding.'

'Thank you, I'll certainly look forward to that.' Didn't the man see her white lanyard that indicated she was a bombardier?

The last thing she wanted was to sit in the dining room with everybody staring at her and then have to try to eat. Travel warrants for service people were always third class but today she deserved a little luxury. She really couldn't face being squashed in with other travellers at the moment.

She had a reserved seat by the window and was so comfortable and warm she immediately fell asleep and didn't wake until the train steamed into London. Ruth carefully straightened her hat, checked her hair was securely pinned, her stocking seams were straight, her shoes shining and was then ready to emerge into King's Cross station.

She wasn't expected at the barracks in Regent's Park for another two days but she was desperately hoping her belongings had already been transferred as she couldn't keep herself immaculate for much longer without access to her kit.

After sleeping for several hours, she felt better, but as she hadn't been able to eat any of the toast that morning she was now starving. She remembered there was a decent restaurant at this station where she and Sam had eaten before they'd caught the train together.

She bit her lip and blinked furiously. She was in the army now and personal disappointments must be put aside, and her duty performed at all times. She would cling onto the fact that they hadn't entirely broken up as Sam had agreed she could write to him and that he would meet her in London when she'd completed her officer training. He could always say he was unable to get a pass if he didn't actually want to come.

That would have to suffice for the moment – she would consider him her boyfriend and forget all about their brief engagement and just pray that somehow, one day, they could turn the clock back and things would be the way they were yesterday.

After a decent lunch and a large pot of tea, she was ready to brave the world. London was dreary, the sky grey, a steady drizzle falling. An umbrella wasn't part of an ATS uniform so she'd just have to get wet and jolly well lump it.

She took the underground to Euston station and

then went in search of the barracks. A helpful policeman told her the only barracks in Regent's Park were used by the horse guards and these were the Albany Street barracks.

She was sure that training ATS girls to be officers wouldn't happen in this place but she'd no option but to march across the park and walk boldly into the main administrative building.

The first person she saw was a Senior Commander Edmonds and this was a great relief. She saluted smartly and introduced herself.

'I was told to report the day after tomorrow, ma'am, but I need to reclaim my kitbag before then.'

'Bombardier Cox, you're in luck as your belongings arrived this morning. As you've turned up early, I might as well send you to Leicester today as that's where your OCTU is situated.' The officer smiled. 'They problay won't want you early but can hardly send you away.'

'Thank you, ma'am, I do want to get on with it.' Training to be an officer might distract her from missing Sam so much. The fact that Ruth could have gone straight from Binbrook to Leicester wouldn't have occurred to this officer.

* * *

Less than an hour later, with her travel warrant clutched in her hand, she walked briskly into St Pancras station. On enquiry, Ruth discovered there was a train leaving for Leicester but not for two hours. The large station clock showed the time to be just after three thirty.

'Sorry, Corp, this means you won't be there until some god-awful time. I hope somebody will be collecting you as you don't want to hang around in the dark, not a nice young lady like yourself,' the guard said to her.

'Never mind, as I'm so early with any luck I'll find a seat. Don't worry, I can take care of myself.'

She went in search of the platform where the train would be arriving eventually and to her surprise it steamed in after a relatively short wait, exhaling smoke and cinders. She stood to one side to allow the passengers arriving to disembark and was then given permission by the ticket collector to find third class and claim a seat.

After putting her kitbag firmly in the end seat by the sliding door so she was facing the way the train would be going, she left it and then went in search of the ladies' room. She was tempted to collect her tin mug and buy a cup of tea from the NAAFI trolley but decided that would defeat the object of having visited the WC.

Sam had bought them tea and cakes from a similar trolley and the reminder made her sad.

The compartment she'd chosen was closest to the exit doors and hopefully this would mean it wouldn't be too difficult to get off when she arrived at Leicester. Although she'd blithely told the guard she'd be perfectly fine in the dark, on her own, on an empty station this wasn't exactly true.

There wouldn't be any transport laid on for her for two reasons – one was that she was arriving two days earlier than expected and the other being that as an officer cadet she would be expected to use her initiative in order to get herself to her destination.

The train filled up rapidly and by the time it pulled out of St Pancras it was standing room only. The blinds were pulled down, a single very low-wattage bulb illuminated the compartment and there was no heating at all. She was pleased that she'd had the foresight to remove her greatcoat from her kitbag and had put it on before they left.

The small space was jammed with a miscellany of service personnel. The narrow passageway that ran down the side was equally crammed. There were two RAF groundcrew, one aircrew, two privates, one lance corp and a lonely civilian who looked like a tradesperson of some sort. The businessmen would travel in second and first class.

As a bombardier, she was the highest rank amongst them, which was an advantage, but being the only female wasn't. She wasn't uncomfortable surrounded by men after training and working successfully in a mixed artillery battery, but she didn't enjoy the blue fog of cigarette smoke that immediately enveloped her.

The train stopped a couple of times for no apparent reason before it reached the first station – at least she hoped the other stops hadn't been stations, otherwise Leicester wouldn't be where she expected it to be.

'Excuse me, Lance Corp, I need to get off at Leicester. I don't suppose you happen to know exactly when we're likely to arrive and how many more stops there are before we get there?'

The young man leered at her and she regretted her impulse to speak to him. The fact that he was sitting opposite had made him the obvious choice.

'I'm getting off at Leicester, you just follow me, lovie.'

'You will address me correctly. I am Bombardier Cox. Might I inform you that I've already made a note of your service number?'

His unpleasant smirk vanished and he attempted to look apologetic. 'I beg your pardon, Bombardier, just having a bit of a lark. I meant nothing by it. My mistake.'

His words were considered but his eyes were mean and it brought back the unpleasant memories of the man who'd attacked her on the train from Clacton when Sam had stepped in. She wished he was here beside her now.

Then the private next to him elbowed the speaker. 'Pack it up, Eddie, mind your manners. Not every pretty girl wants to flirt with you.'

Eddie's expression changed again and this time his smile was genuine. 'Can't help meself, Bombardier, and to be honest I never noticed your stripes when I spoke. No offence intended.'

Ruth's fingers unclenched. 'Apology accepted, Lance Corporal, but might I suggest that you check to whom you're speaking another time?'

She relaxed against the padded seat, closing her eyes, making it clear she didn't wish to continue the conversation – not with him or with anybody else.

* * *

Sam eventually arrived on the outskirts of St Albans mid-afternoon after a draining and uncomfortable journey. He'd had to clamber into the back of a lorry at Cambridge, much to the amusement of the platoon of soldiers already in there, none of whom got out and offered to help, even though he was a sergeant. He'd asked to be dropped adjacent to a telephone kiosk as that meant he could ring the pub, three doors down from his parents, and ask them to get a message to his dad to come and collect him.

His dad arrived twenty minutes later and unlike the soldiers, was out of the cab as soon as he stopped.

'Well, son, this a pretty kettle of fish. Broken ankle and not a German in sight.' Sam was warmly hugged, his bag tossed into the back of the lorry and then his dad assisted him into the front.

'Ta for coming, Dad, it will be good to be home for a few weeks. How's business? How's Mum? Have you heard from Betty or Billy recently?'

'I've got more work than I can cope with and not enough materials or labour to do it.'

'I'll not be any good to you with my leg in plaster.'

'Don't expect you to be. Mum's tickety-boo and, as always, busy with the WVS and WI meetings. Your sister has just got engaged to a sailor and your brother's been promoted to Leading Aircraftman.'

'That's good news.' The lorry bounced into a pot-hole and jarred his leg painfully. This gave him time to swallow the lump in his throat at the mention of his sister being engaged when he no longer was.

'Sorry, son, blooming big holes everywhere nowadays. That leg's bothering you. You'll be better once you're safe in bed with it off the ground.'

'I don't want to be waited on, I'm not an invalid, Dad, but you're right, today I'll be glad to be in bed.'

'They should have kept you in hospital. You're grey, don't look too clever at all. Your mum will be beside herself when she sees you.'

They rolled to a halt on the drive outside the family home. It was a solid, red-brick, four-bedroom detached house that had been built by Sam's grandfather forty years go. He'd not been home since he joined up and now regretted it.

His reason for remaining absent was simple, his parents shared the house with his grandparents, had never had their own home, and he didn't get on with either of them. They treated his mum like a skivvy and as children he and his siblings had to be seen and not heard. They'd spent their childhood playing in the large child-friendly garden and the treehouse Dad had built for them to keep them out of the way.

'Look, Sam, it's a bit tricky inside. Your nan's not

too clever, senile dementia the doctor says, and your grandad's spending all his time at the pub. He can't cope with seeing her like she is.'

Instead of feeling sorry for his grandfather, Sam was angry. 'Of course he is. Bloody typical. Mum's having to look after Nan as well as doing everything else as well. I'm not staying here for more than a couple of nights, Dad, I'll find a B & B, I'll not make extra work for her.'

Dad didn't swear, as his own parents were strict methodist and wouldn't have blasphemy or bad language in the house. Sam was shocked when his dad broke the rule of decades.

'You'll bloody well stay with us if I have to tie you to the bed, son. We've not seen you for more than two years and we're not letting you bugger off.'

Sam laughed and felt better than he had all day. He reached out and squeezed his dad's arm. 'All right, I'll stay, but you need to find someone to help Mum. I know they've refused to have any outsiders in up to now, but if you want me to remain then that's what's got to happen. I'll not add to Mum's workload unless she's got someone coming in to do the heavy work at least.'

'Fair enough, son, it's time I stood up for myself. My dad stopped working years ago, my mum's on her way out, so from now on it's my house and my rules.' He smiled sadly. 'I know why you three scarpered as soon as you could and should have done something then. I'm sorry, son, I'll put it right now.'

'Then this broken ankle was worth it. I'll back you up, I'm a sergeant, in charge of forty stroppy soldiers, so one old man won't bother me.'

His dad helped him out of the cab and collected his kitbag, Sam got himself stable on his crutches and was ready to move.

For the first time in his life, Sam was actually eager to enter his family home. His aversion to religion stemmed directly from his grandparents' narrow-minded view on life and their insistence that on Sundays only the Bible must be read and that there could be no fun of any sort.

His mother must have heard the lorry pull up as the front door slammed open and she was flying down the drive to hug him. 'Dearest Sam, I've missed you so much. Come in, come in, you look really unwell. I'll soon have you feeling better.'

He held her close for a moment, inhaling the aroma of freshly baked bread, lavender and hard work that he remembered so well. She felt insubstantial in his arms and he leaned back and looked down at her. Her hair was still a vibrant chestnut brown, her twinset and green skirt were immaculate as always, and when she smiled at him, his anxiety evaporated.

'I'm so happy to be home, Mum. Things are going to be different here from now on. Dad's going to sort things out.' He left unsaid that this should have been done years ago but she nodded and smiled. They'd always been in tune.

'I've got a lovely meal waiting for you, will you eat or go straight upstairs and have it on a tray?'

'I'll eat with you and Dad. Will my grandfather be there, and Nan?'

'He doesn't come back until your nan's safely in bed and then expects a hot meal on the table whatever time it is.'

Dad overheard this remark and snorted. 'Not any more, love. From now on, if he wants to eat, he'll be here at the same time as us or he'll make himself some bread and dripping.'

'Are you sure, Fred? I don't mind making him something if it keeps the peace,' Sam's mother said.

'I know you don't, but I do. As Sam said just now, things are going to be different. You get Ada from the council houses to come in every day to help with Nan and do the laundry and that. No argument, love, I've made up my mind.'

'Fred, I can't tell you how long I've waited for you

to say that. Thank you, it will make my life so much easier.'

Sam smiled as his parents embraced and exchanged a chaste kiss. It must have been hard for both of them to not be allowed to show any affection in their own home.

'Dad, why don't you convert the workshop for Nan and Grandpa? It's already got water and electricity, it wouldn't take much to make it snug and going upstairs must be hard for her now.'

'He wouldn't move, son, he'll not be alone with Nan since she got ill.'

'But would it be easier for Nan?'

'It certainly would. It takes two of us to get her to bed,' Mum replied.

'Then convert it for Nan and a live-in helper. If he spends all his time in the pub, it won't matter if he still sleeps here, will it?' Sam said.

He swung his way into the entrance hall, a decent space from which the kitchen, dining room, sitting room, front room and office opened. There was also a second bog downstairs, very grand and almost unheard of all those years ago.

One thing he would say for his grandfather was that he'd been good at his trade and the house he'd built was just the ticket even forty years later. His grandpa had been too old to be conscripted for the first war and his dad had flat feet so was exempt.

The last lot was supposed to have been the war to end all wars, and here they were again fighting the bleeding Germans.

20

Ruth had plenty of time to mull over what had happened between her and Sam as she travelled slowly to Leicester on a train that seemed to stop and start continually. He was quite right to say that nobody fell out of love with someone overnight and she wasn't surprised he'd been hurt by her actions.

They'd both had said things they didn't mean, neither of them had had the sense to put things right and here they were – with possibly the shortest engagement ever. She didn't think of him as a second-best option, but she could just about understand why he might believe that. Every time she spoke, the difference between their education and upbringing was evident. It didn't matter to her but men might be more touchy; it might make him feel inferior, which was absolute nonsense.

It could have been a problem if she'd had a family to go back to, but she didn't, and anyway, they were marrying each other, not their families. She smiled ruefully. Actually, Aunt Jemima would have loved Sam – she hadn't been a snob and there had been as many working-class suffragettes as there had been upper and middle class. The women had banded together to get the vote and that was more important than their so-called place in society.

The lance corp who was sitting opposite had taken the hint, as had his companions; not only had they talked quietly, refrained from swearing most of the time, but one of them had also got up and opened the window to let some of the blue smoke out.

Several tedious hours later, the train slowed and Eddie got to his feet. 'We're here, Bombardier, and only half an hour late, which is a record.' He nodded at her kitbag but she shook her head.

'Thank you, soldier, but I can manage my own kit. However, as you and your companions obviously know Leicester station, perhaps you could direct me to somewhere I can catch a bus to Dunwoody Hall.'

'We can do better than that, there'll be transport

waiting for us and I'll tell the driver to drop you off as we go past the OCTU.'

For the first time, she smiled at him. 'That would be a great help, I'm quite prepared to wait for the first bus but a lift even with you lot will be much better.'

They appreciated her feeble attempt at a joke and she let them out first and then followed as it was easier to negotiate the narrow doorway with an empty carriage. The lone civilian had got off ages ago.

She was rather dreading clambering down from the carriage with her kitbag on her shoulder but accomplished it without mishap. This was fortunate as the group of men she'd just travelled from London with had waited for her.

The rain was heavier, it was more like the end of November than the end of October, but it was always colder in the North than in London where she'd just been. With the help of the seven pinpricks of light from their torches, they made their way through the station and out into the forecourt where a three-tonne lorry, engine running, was awaiting.

The driver, an ATS, leaned out of the window when she saw her. 'Come up front, you don't want to travel with that lot. Nobody would.'

There were catcalls and the sound of laughter from the canvas-covered rear and Ruth realised the vehicle was already full. 'Thank you, the lance corp said you'd give me a lift.'

'Dunwoody Hall? I've dropped off lots of girls but not for a couple of days.'

Ruth pushed her kitbag into the cab first and then clambered up after it. It was blissfully warm inside, but this was just the contrast to the cold night air as there weren't heaters in a lorry cab.

'Thank you for this, I really wasn't looking forward to hanging about in the dark waiting for the first bus.'

'That's okay, Bombardier, I often pick up and drop off girls going for officer training.' The driver turned sharply out of the station forecourt and then drove rather fast through the blackout. The headlights on the lorry were reduced to a tiny beam and if anything appeared in their path, Ruth was sure they'd not be able to avoid a collision.

'I know nothing about Dunwoody Hall or OCT. I don't suppose you've picked up any snippets that would help me,' Ruth said as they hit a big pothole and her bottom left the seat and returned with a thump.

'I do know quite a lot, some of it not very good. For instance, some girls were chucked out of the course after two days because they didn't know which knife or fork to use at dinner. What's that got to do with being an officer?'

'Not a lot but those in charge still think that girls from a less privileged background shouldn't be officers. Giving them a dozen knives and forks and watching to see if they know which one to use is one way.'

The driver snorted. 'That's plain daft.'

'I agree,' Ruth said. 'It's unfair to dismiss candidates for such trivial reasons.'

'Last week I picked up someone who'd chucked it in. She told me being an officer wasn't what she'd expected and would rather remain a sergeant.'

Neither of the pieces of information Ruth had been given were particularly encouraging. She was tempted to remain in the lorry and then be dropped at the nearest station, but she couldn't do that because then she'd be AWOL and be put on a charge and possibly lose the stripes she'd already got.

No, if – when – she found out more about her responsibilities as an officer, they didn't appeal then she'd do something silly and fail the course. That way she could still progress as an NCO and hopefully without any black marks against her name.

'Here we are, I can't take you up the drive but it's no more than half a mile. You're lucky it's not raining.'

'Thank you so much, I really appreciate the lift. I've got my greatcoat on and my waterproof is in my bag so it doesn't matter if it rains.'

As the lorry rumbled off, she could hear the moans from the men in the back and smiled. Soldiers loved to moan and if they weren't doing so their NCOs would be worried. Probably they didn't moan when they were on the front line as they'd be too busy staying alive, but it was boring for those waiting in barracks for the invasion of Europe to begin.

Ruth marched with her bag on her shoulder down the drive. It was well maintained so there was no danger of her going headfirst into a pothole, which was a relief. She was walking for twenty minutes before the pinprick of light from her torch showed her she was approaching the house.

It was now very late and she thought it quite possible she wouldn't be able to gain entry but have to find a shed or outbuilding in which to spend the remainder of the night. She was in two minds whether to risk being horribly unpopular by banging on the door or risk being thought indecisive for not doing so.

The house was huge, late Victorian she thought, from the towers, gargoyles and crenelated roof. As she reached the imposing portico and front door, the heavens opened, which decided her next move. There was a brass knocker shaped like a dolphin and she grasped it and banged it twice.

Almost immediately she heard footsteps. She held her bag by the handles at her side so it would be easier for her to negotiate whatever blackout arrangements they had.

A male voice spoke from behind the door without opening it. 'Identify yourself.'

'Bombardier Cox, reporting for Officer Cadet Training.' This man was quite definitely an officer.

Ruth heard the door open but the entrance hall was as dark as outside so she couldn't see the speaker or if there were any curtains between her and him. The small beam from her trusty torch showed her it was safe to step in.

The door closed behind her and the man who'd let her in switched on the central light. Ruth blinked, screwed up her eyes, unable to see after the darkness.

'Are you going to stand there with your eyes closed for much longer, Bombardier?'

She turned, jumped to attention and saluted. Facing her was a captain, one arm missing, but everything else intact – including a perfect set of blindingly white teeth and flashing blue eyes. He obviously found her amusing.

'I apologise for arriving in the middle of the night,

sir.' She'd been going to ask if he could direct her to her room but something about his expression made her wary. Was this another trap to weed out unsuitable candidates?

'Exactly why is this? If the rest of your cohort managed to arrive at a seemly hour on the correct day, I cannot see why you failed to do so.'

'With all due respect, sir, I've arrived two days early, not late. The senior commander at Regent's Park was most insistent that I travelled immediately regardless of the time of my arrival.'

His false smile vanished and he glared at her. 'I see. In which case, Bombardier, you'll understand that your accommodation isn't available. I'm sure you will be comfortable in an armchair in the recreation room.'

She met his icy gaze without flinching. 'Thank you, Captain, an armchair indoors is far preferable to spending the night in an outbuilding, which I was quite prepared to do.' She saluted again, forcing him to reciprocate the gesture, which annoyed him even more.

Ignoring him was difficult, she could feel his eyes burning a hole in the back of her coat, but with commendable aplomb she marched past him and headed to the rear of the building where she was pretty sure she'd find the kitchen and be able to make herself a hot drink and something to eat.

Officers were supposed to be resilient, decisive and quick thinking and she rather thought she'd proved to be all three. The unidentified captain probably thought her insubordinate and a troublemaker but for some reason she didn't care. She was here to prove she was the sort of girl who could take command, could lead a platoon or section of girls effectively, and no supercilious young officer was going to put her off her stride.

* * *

Sam devoured his meal with enthusiasm. His mum had always been an excellent cook and this rabbit stew with dumplings followed by baked apples and custard was no exception. He'd been concerned that neither of his grandparents had joined them at the table.

'I know you said that Grandpa doesn't come in for his supper, but what about Nan? I should really have gone to speak to her before sitting down to eat,' Sam said.

'Your nan's in the front room, she's no trouble really apart from wandering off if we don't keep the door locked,' Mum said. His look of horror made her laugh.

'Goodness me, I don't mean she's locked in the front room all day, that would be unkind. No, I just have to make sure the front and back doors are locked and the keys put out of the way.'

'I'll come with you, Mum. I'd offer to carry the tray but I can't do that at the moment.'

The front room was warm and cheerful, a good fire burning in the grate, and the little old lady huddled in the armchair listening to the radio was scarcely recognisable as the stern, upright, sturdy grandparent he'd last seen three years ago.

'Hello, Nan, it's Sam, I broke my leg so I'm staying here for a bit.'

She looked up and her eyes focused. 'I know who you are and I can see you've got a broken leg. I might be old but I'm not stupid.'

The crockery rattled and Mum almost dropped the tray. 'Mother, isn't it good that Sam's home? I've brought your supper.'

'I'm not hungry. I don't want it. It smells nasty. I want jelly and cream.'

His grandmother's mental clarity had been short lived. 'If you put it on the table, Mum, I'll stay with her and see if I can persuade her to eat. From the look of her she doesn't eat nearly enough.'

He wished the words unsaid as his mother's eyes

filled. 'I know. I know it's my fault, but if I try and make her eat, she throws it on the floor or at me so I tend to leave it and hope for the best.'

'Right – she'll not be throwing anything whilst I'm here. Go, Mum, make yourself a lovely cuppa and leave this to me. Close the door, please, let's keep the heat in.'

He waited until this had been done and then propped his crutches against the wall and sat on the bentwood chair his mum had put next to the armchair for him.

'Okay, Nan, do you prefer to feed yourself or would you like me to help you?'

She ignored him and he smiled because he could see she was listening. Maybe having somebody else looking after her, someone she couldn't boss about, was what was needed to improve things.

There were no knives or forks on the tray and this saddened him. There were, however, three pudding spoons. He filled one of them with the tasty stew – bones and lumps carefully removed – and by rotating on the chair was able to hold the spoon against her mouth.

The old woman sniffed, then her mouth opened and he slipped the food in. She still didn't look at him, said nothing, but allowed him to feed her and to his delight she ate every mouthful.

'There's baked apple and custard, Nan, do you still have room for it?' He wasn't sure she understood what he was saying but it would be disrespectful not to give her a chance to express her wishes.

Finally, she looked round, nodded and opened her mouth like a baby bird. The pudding went down as easily as the stew and he could almost swear there was more colour in her cheeks already after having eaten a proper meal. He wondered how long it was since she'd eaten more than a few bites of anything.

There was a china cup with a spout on the tray which he assumed was for the invalid to drink from. He checked and it contained tea – not hot but warm enough to make it palatable. He offered it to her but she ignored the cup and just opened her mouth.

She drank the lot. He carefully picked up the table with the tray and placed it on the other side of him.

'I'm so pleased to see you eating and enjoying it, Nan. You'll feel so much better with good food inside you.' He leaned over and hugged her, put his bristly cheek against her papery thin face and she didn't pull away.

He sat back but kept hold of her hand and gently stroked it. Throughout all this she didn't look at him, but after a few minutes her fingers slowly closed over his and they were holding hands.

Sam had never liked his grandmother but seeing her so vulnerable, a shadow of herself, triggered a re-action in him. Maybe it was because he too was in a difficult place – had possibly lost the love of his life and had no idea where he would be posted when he was declared fit in a few weeks.

'Nan, I'm going to keep you company, help you to eat, whilst I'm here even if I can't do much else. I could read to you if you'd like me to. Not the Bible – what about an Agatha Christie?'

Her eyes were closed, and she looked more re-laxed, but he didn't think she was asleep. He con-tinued to chat to her, telling her about Ruth, about how he broke his leg and anything else he could think of.

Then her hand went slack and for a horrible sec-ond, he thought she'd passed away but she was just asleep. He pulled the comforter over her, reached out for his crutches and stood up. Something had oc-curred to him whilst he was nattering and he wanted to share it with his parents.

The handsome walnut clock on the mantelpiece struck nine. Sam was shocked he'd been in there so long, but surprised his mother hadn't poked her head around the door to see what was going on.

He pulled it open and heard angry voices coming from the kitchen. His grandfather was back and demanding his supper. He thought his father was going to sort this out but obviously this hadn't happened.

He shouldered his way into the kitchen, expecting to see the man he loathed as reduced as his nan was by age and illness. He hesitated, seeing that his grandfather was still as big and belligerent as he'd always been. His mother was almost cowering by the range and there was no sign of his father. What the hell was going on?

The old man was thumping on the table, emphasising every shouted word. 'You get my food on the table, woman, and do it now. This is my house and I'll turn you and my useless son out if you don't mind your Ps and Qs.'

Sam kicked the door shut behind him. The sudden noise made his mother look up and her tear-streaked face was enough to make him forget that for years this obnoxious man had bullied him and he stepped forward to put things right.

'Shut your trap, old man, or I'll bloody well shut it for you,' Sam snarled, his swearing and poor grammar deliberate. He wanted to turn the old man's anger against himself so his mother could escape.

'How dare you use such language in my house...'

'It's not your house, old man, it now belongs to my father and mother, as they take all the responsibility for it. It's you who can be turned out if you don't button your lip.'

His grandfather seemed to swell. Sam almost expected actual steam to come out of his ears. This ridiculous thought made him smile, which was the worst thing he could have done.

'I'll teach you a lesson you won't forget, I'll not be spoken to like that in my house.'

Suddenly Sam was confronted with a furious old bloke waving a carving knife and from the look on his face he'd every intention of using it.

He didn't back away. He advanced and swept the old man's legs from under him using his heavy plastered leg.

'Good God,' Dad said from the scullery. 'What the hell's going on in here?' He put down the two full coal scuttles, patted Mum on the arm and then leaned down and heaved Grandpa back to his feet.

'I upset him and he was going to stab me. I think he's even more unhinged than Nan.'

Dad took his father by his arms and unceremoniously bundled him out of the back door whilst the old codger continued to yell abuse at them. God knows what the neighbours would think.

Dad slammed the door and locked it behind him. 'You can cool off out there, you miserable old sod. I'm not having you in here until you calm down.'

'I'm sorry, Dad, it got a bit out of hand. I heard him screaming at Mum and it escalated from there.'

'I didn't know he was back. I was in the coal shed and didn't hear anything over the shovelling. Are you all right, love? He didn't hurt you?'

Mum had already recovered – she was tough. She'd had to be to survive living with her in-laws all these years. 'I refused to make him any supper and he completely lost his temper. I shudder to think what might have happened if you hadn't come in, Sam.'

'Will he go back to the pub, Dad? He might be a miserable old codger but I don't like to think of him freezing to death.'

'I'll let him in again soon. In a way, I'm glad this has happened because from now on he's not having things his way. If there's any of that stew left, can you heat it up for him, Alice, just this once?'

21

Ruth passed what was obviously a formal dining room, a mess hall and then as expected, she found the kitchen. This was immaculate – as was always the case anywhere in the army and particularly where officers were being trained.

It didn't take her long to fill a kettle and put it on, then after further searching she found the where-withal to make herself several slices of toast to go with her tea. There was both jam and butter in the well-stocked pantry but she settled for beef dripping and salt – this was a particular favourite of hers, as Aunt Jemima had loved it.

As she was slathering the delicious dark brown jelly that you found under the white dripping on the last slice of toast, the kettle whistled. After carefully cutting the toast into triangles, she poured herself a mug of tea and sat down at the table, glad that she was indoors and not outside in the torrential rain.

Her tea slopped onto the table as the door swung open. The captain strode in and her stomach somer-saulted. She was probably going to be put on a charge or possibly sent packing before she'd even started.

'I could smell the toast from the office. Please say you're going to give a starving officer a slice.'

She could hardly stand to attention or salute as she was sitting at the table, so she smiled. 'There's plenty here, sir, and you're welcome to share it with me. I'll get you a cup of tea as well.'

He shook his head. 'No, Bombardier Cox, stay put, I've gate-crashed your midnight feast and will get my own tea. Don't look so surprised – I might only have one arm but I'm quite capable of filling a mug with tea.' He grinned and walked around the long table and she heard him doing just that behind her.

'Are you intentionally anonymous, sir, as I'd like to know with whom I'm sharing my meal.'

'Fair point. I'm Adam McAllister. I apologise for being so bloody rude to you when you arrived earlier. I'd fallen asleep on duty, which is a hanging offence in the army, as you know.'

'Apology accepted, sir, and nobody will hear about your heinous crime from me. I'm assuming that I won't be put on a charge for stealing my supper.'

'I'm still considering my options. Doesn't do to show favouritism to an NCO.'

Ruth was enjoying this conversation rather too much and wondered why that was. He wasn't particularly handsome and probably ten years older than her. Then she realised she was talking to him in the same way she talked to Sam.

'Is there really no accommodation for me until the day after tomorrow?'

'I expect there's a bed somewhere, but we can't wander about upstairs peering in bedrooms tonight. Why were you sent here two days early?'

'I think the senior commander took pity on me. I would have had to find a bed and breakfast somewhere as I'm now detached from my RA unit. How many cohorts are there being trained at any one time?'

'There are four groups of ten doing the twelve-week course, but we now have a two-day preliminary course which weeds out the unsuitable candidates and means that the majority of those here gain their pips.'

His matter-of-fact explanation rang warning bells.

'Am I to assume, Captain McAllister, that I'm going straight onto the full course?'

'Of course you are. I checked your record, Bombardier, and I doubt there's any other officer cadet as highly skilled as you. I'm wondering why you wanted to be an officer – you do realise you'll no longer be doing any of the things you trained for, don't you?'

Ruth frowned. 'I'm not sure that I understand, sir.'

'ATS officers are responsible for the discipline and welfare of those under their command. Once you're promoted, you won't be involved in range finding and so on – it will just be discipline, welfare and administrative work.'

Her heart sank. She'd sort of known this but had pushed the worries aside and now she was faced with a dilemma. She pushed her chair back and refilled the teapot from the gently hissing kettle to give her time to think about what he'd said.

Could she trust him if she asked him what he thought she should do? She poured them both a second mug of tea.

'Do I have permission to speak freely, sir?'

He nodded. 'Go ahead, Bombardier Cox, nothing you say will go on your record if that's what you're worried about.'

'I'm not sure I want to be an officer if I can't lead

from the front. I know that's what happens on your side of the army. I believe that to be an officer you should be able to do all the things that you ask those under your command to do. How can a girl who hasn't got the same specialised training be an effective officer on a mixed artillery site?'

'Her senior NCOs take care of that.' He drank his tea silently for a moment but she could see he was pondering whether to say something that was probably unwise.

'I honestly think you'd be better off becoming a warrant officer, we both know that it's sergeants and warrant officers who really run the army.'

'Thank you for being so frank, sir. I trained to be a kinetheodolite operator, then retrained to be a spotter, predictor or range finder and have changed tack again to come here. Surely being so indecisive and costing the army so much money will make my promotion any further than bombardier unlikely?'

'Good point. I'm going to suggest you complete your training, I'm sure you'll come out top in everything you do, then politely decline your commission and explain your reasons. That way you can always become an officer at a later date if things change. Have you actually considered the benefits?'

'I'll have a better uniform, better accommodation,

and an orderly to take care of me, and considerably more pay – but that means nothing if I'm not doing my best for the war effort.'

'Good girl, well said. Nobody knows you're here so you could leave at dawn and I'll say I had a telephone call saying that you changed your mind.'

'I can't do that, sir, as I'm presently unattached. My unit was at Binbrook and goodness knows where they are now.'

He nodded, drained his mug and put it down. 'Then continue as planned. This meeting and conversation didn't happen. Goodnight, Bombardier Cox.'

After putting everything back where she'd found it and removing every trace of their illegal occupation of the kitchen, Ruth collected her kitbag and went in search of the rec room. Tomorrow she would have to report to whoever was in charge and would offer to work in admin until her cohort arrived as she didn't want to be idle.

The rec room was large and well furnished. There was a sideboard which had dozens of boardgames, packs of cards and even two sets of darts, although there was no sign of a dartboard. There were a dozen wooden chairs around a long table at one end of the room and two dozen assorted armchairs and three sofas at the other. More than adequate to accommodate the forty or so girls who would be training here.

After the illuminating conversation with the one-armed officer, Ruth was wide awake. She got out her stationery folder and sat down to write a long apologetic letter to Sam.

* * *

Sam explained to his parents how he thought they could solve the problem of Nan not being able to manage the stairs and Grandpa not wanting to live with her.

'The front room's large enough to put a single bed, a wardrobe and dressing table as well as having a couple of armchairs and so on. As you have a downstairs WC, Nan could move into that room permanently. She's obviously happy there. By the way, Mum, she ate every mouthful and is now asleep.'

'That's the best news I've had in months, Sam,' she said as she carefully stirred the generous portion of stew for his grandfather's supper. 'I think moving her downstairs makes perfect sense.'

'I could do that tomorrow, son, I don't know why we didn't think of that ourselves. What about my dad?'

'Convert the workshop for him – in fact, why not

get him to do it with you? I reckon it would make the perfect home for him. He'd be independent and can come and go as he likes but still have his meals here if he wants to,' Sam replied.

His dad pursed his lips and then nodded. 'That might just work, son. Give the old man something useful to do and he might be less belligerent.' He grinned at Mum. 'Are you ready, love, shall I let him in?'

'Yes, hopefully he'll have calmed down by now.'

Sam heaved himself upright. 'I'm going to sit with Nan, don't want things to get heated again.'

He spent the remainder of the evening happily listening to the evening big band concert but was pleased when his mum arrived with a mug of cocoa at ten. Nan had slept throughout.

'Here you are, love, nice and hot. Your dad and I will get your nan sorted and put her to bed. You'll be pleased to know your grandfather was sweetness and light when he came in. He's eager to get the work-shop converted and agreed he'd live there when it's done.'

'That's the best possible news. I'll drink this quickly, Mum, and get on to bed.'

Sam left his parents with his nan and hopped to the stairs. Going up backwards on his arse was the safest option. He did this, carefully manoeuvring his crutches beside him.

When he got to the top, he wasn't sure how to negotiate the turning and having to stand in order to get safely onto the landing and wished he'd asked his dad to come up with him.

There was a sound behind him and his grandpa spoke. 'Here, let me give you a hand, son, you'll likely fall headfirst down the stairs and break your neck otherwise.'

He glanced over his shoulder and smiled. 'Ta, Grandad, that would be a great help.'

Who was this genial bloke? His grandfather had never smiled or spoken to him so nicely and Sam could hardly believe the apparent change in the old man.

It was easy to regain his feet with his grandfather hauling on his arms. 'There. Goodnight, Sam. Pity you can't help with the conversion as it would be done in a trice if you were. You've always been good at your trade. Being a first-class builder runs in your blood.'

'It certainly does. Goodnight, Grandpa.' He had been about to mention the knife incident but changed his mind. Let sleeping dogs lie. He chuckled as he entered the bedroom he'd once shared with his younger brother.

Using that silly saying reminded him of Ruth. To-morrow he'd write to her, try and put things right between them. Tonight was a night for miracles. His nan had held his hand and eaten her meal and his grandad had just been pleasant. Neither thing had ever happened before.

* * *

Sam had a decent night's kip and was woken the next morning with breakfast on a tray. 'Blimey, Mum, I told you I didn't want waiting on. But ta for doing it. I can't remember the last time I had breakfast in bed.'

'I expect it was when you had the measles when you were little. Your grandparents didn't hold with making a fuss but you were so poorly you couldn't get out of bed.'

'I'll be down soon and will keep Nan company.'

'There's no rush, love, that banging you can hear is your grandad and dad sorting out the front room. I'm leaving Nan where she is until all that's done. Whilst I'm getting her dressed in the bathroom, they'll take the bed down.'

'I've got to write a letter to someone, someone I hope you'll meet if I can put things right between us.'

Mum smiled but didn't ask any questions. She left

him to his boiled eggs, soldiers with Marmite and mug of tea. He needed to unpack his kitbag, find his wash bag and stationery, put everything away as it should be or his uniform would become creased.

He hopped out to the bathroom before it was needed by Nan and shaved quickly, then returned to his bedroom to write the most important letter he'd ever written. Not that he'd written many and the only ones to a girl had been to Ruth.

His fountain pen was empty and he didn't have the ink to refill it so he'd have to wait until he was downstairs and could use the bottle that was kept in the desk in the office for writing invoices and so on.

He heard his grandmother being escorted to the bathroom and thought this was a good time to emerge from his bedroom and bump his way down the stairs. He wouldn't need any help going this way to stand up.

The front room door was wide open and both his dad and grandpa were in there chatting away as if they hadn't been rowing last night.

'Morning, gents, this looks just the ticket. I'll make the bed up. I can do that on one leg – I reckon I could do it standing on my head. Every bloke in the army, apart from the officers, is a dab hand at bed making.' If Sam had suggested that he sang the national anthem, they couldn't have been more surprised.

'That's women's work, son, it doesn't seem right that you do it,' Dad said.

'Been doing it for the past three years like every other soldier. Why don't you two push off and let me get on with it? Nan will be down soon and I want it to look tidy for her.'

He issued the order without thinking, it was something he did every day as an NCO. His heart thumped heavily and he waited for the explosion.

'Right, son, Dad and I will leave you to it. We're going to have a look at the workshop and then your grandpa will start clearing it whilst I get off to work.'

The two of them left without another word – how things had changed. Sam was still wary of his grandfather – he might be friendly and polite this morning but last night he'd grabbed a kitchen knife and had wanted to gut him. Something he wouldn't forget in a hurry.

He was kept busy helping in the office all morning and didn't get the chance to even consider writing his letter until after lunch. The changes to the front room had been completed and his nan was content with the new arrangements. Or he thought she was, it was hard to tell. The fact that the old lady had walked over and climbed onto the bed for her afternoon nap had to be a good sign.

He left his grandmother to sleep and returned to the kitchen, where his mum was preparing the veg for the evening meal.

'Mum, I'm finally going to write that letter. Did I hear you telling Dad that the lady from the council houses will be starting tomorrow? How did Grandpa take the news?'

'He doesn't know. He'll have to get used to it. You coming, that scene last night, was just what was needed to push us into making the changes we should have done years ago.'

'About that, Mum, I'm still bothered by the knife. Has Grandpa been violent before?'

His mother looked away, didn't answer for moment. Then she sighed. 'Yes, it started when Nan got ill. He slapped her a few times but your dad put him straight. That's when the drinking started.'

'Then the sooner he's living elsewhere the better. None of you are safe when he's so unpredictable.'

* * *

Ruth had written her letter to Sam and then curled up on the sofa using her kitbag as a pillow and her great-coat as a blanket. Her sleep was fitful as she was determined not to be found where she was in the morning.

She was jerked fully awake by the sound of a bugle. She almost fell off the sofa. Why would reveille be sounded at an OCTU? Surely the girls training to be officers weren't expected to do the same things they'd done as privates?

She'd never moved so fast in her life. The bugle had hardly stopped playing by the time she'd repacked her kitbag, straightened her skirt and pinned up her hair. Thank God she'd had the foresight to change her collar, put on clean stockings and polish her shoes last night as there wouldn't be time to do it now.

After snatching up her uniform jacket from the back of a chair, she pulled it on, hastily buttoned it and adjusted the belt. All she had to do now was pin on her cap and she'd be ready for inspection.

She hid her kitbag behind the sofa, checked the room was as tidy as it had been when she'd come in last night, and was ready to emerge and pray that whoever was in charge wouldn't be annoyed at her early arrival.

Dozens of officer trainees were trooping down the central staircase, all immaculately dressed, many of them were looking rested and happy – but there were exceptions. A fair number of them had miserable faces, which wasn't something she'd expected to see.

They were presumably heading for breakfast, but none of them were carrying their irons. This was fortunate as she'd forgotten to get hers out of her bag. Cutlery and mugs must be provided here.

There were no bombardiers, no white lanyards to be seen on any shoulders which was a shame as she could have bonded with them. She'd expected to be spoken to but was ignored as they fell into groups and marched to the mess hall.

Ruth followed behind them and as each group peeled off, she noticed that one of them was missing a member. She followed them and slipped into a place at the same table. Only then did someone comment on her unexpected appearance.

'You must be replacing Penny, she left yesterday, compassionate grounds,' a tall dark-haired girl said without much enthusiasm. From her diction, she was definitely the sort of young woman the army wanted to promote to officer status. 'You are not a welcome replacement in our group.'

'I'm not replacing anyone as far as I know.'

The dark-haired girl raised her aristocratic eyebrows. 'No one arrives late for officer training. It just isn't done. I expect you will be in disgrace. Look at her, girls, she's not one of us, is she?'

A surge of irritation ran through Ruth. She knew

responding was a bad idea, but she was tired and un-happy and being sneered at wasn't on. This supercil-ious girl reminded her of the bullying she'd received when she first went to boarding school. She'd not al-lowed that to continue either.

'Is it not? Then I must be invisible.' She leaned for-ward so she could speak quietly. There was a nervous collective withdrawal of breath as she spoke. The others must be expecting an outburst from the bully.

Then something she'd noticed but not registered made her smile. She was the only one with any stripes. She outranked them.

'You privates must be both ignorant and blind. You are insubordinate and I intend to make a formal com-plaint. I do hope you enjoy scrubbing latrines.'

Finally, the penny dropped. The girls stared at her in horror. Ruth ignored them and smiled her thanks to the mess orderly who'd just put her breakfast in front of her. The shocked silence didn't bother her and Ruth tucked in, knowing she'd have no further trouble from anyone on this table.

22

Sam wrote the all-important letter to Ruth and it was waiting on the hall table for Mum to post next time she went into the village. The woman who was supposed to arrive to meet Nan had failed to appear.

'That's not a good start, Mum, you need someone reliable so you can organise your life without the worry,' Sam said.

'I don't understand why she isn't here, she's always on time for WI and WVS meetings. I hope she's not had an accident.'

'Nan's eating if I feed her and went to the WC on her own earlier. This new arrangement is going to make life easier for all of you.'

Grandad hadn't come in for his midday meal but Dad offered to take it out to him. 'He's a bit wary of you, son, and so he should be. He's already cleared the workshop and we're going to start the conversion tomorrow.'

His dad was working with two boys and an old bloke as the others had been conscripted. Sam wished he could help, he enjoyed the physical side of the trade and was feeling a bit useless sitting at the kitchen table drinking tea whilst everyone else was busy. Then his lips curved. If he was fit, he'd be with his section and not here.

Nan was asleep, Mum had dashed off to see why this Ada Brown had failed to come and he was reading the *News Chronicle* when he heard a letter fall through the letter box. He ignored it and continued to read.

Then he remembered who Ada Brown was. She was a big woman, jolly, with a house stuffed with kids, but kind hearted, generous with her time and with what little she had, and perfect for the job. Now he too was worried that she'd failed to come that morning.

He tossed aside the paper; there was no good news, things were going badly in Africa, and he didn't want to read any more. He might as well collect the mail and take it to the office.

There was only one letter and he recognised the

blue envelope and the handwriting. Ruth had written to him first. He snatched back his letter, knowing the one from her might mean he couldn't send his.

He held it between his teeth as he made his way back to the kitchen. He needed to be seated to read this. His hands were shaking as he carefully opened the envelope.

Dearest Sam,

You might well be surprised to receive this letter and I hope you won't throw it away without reading it.

I do sincerely apologise for my behaviour, for going behind your back and arranging for you to be taken by car, for saying that I didn't want to be engaged to you.

I hope you will have guessed from the way I started this letter that that my feelings haven't changed. I do love you and I do want to be your wife. I hope you haven't reconsidered.

I would love to come to St Albans and meet your parents and I think I might be free to do so before you've returned to duty. I'd better explain why this might be the case as we both know that training an officer takes twelve weeks.

He was clutching the letter so hard his fingers had scrunched the paper. He was dizzy with happiness; his eyes were wet and he couldn't read the rest until he'd recovered.

It didn't matter how long he had to wait until could hold her in his arms again, as long as he would do so eventually. Ruth loved him. Carefully he smoothed out the paper and with his smile wide he continued.

When he'd finished the three closely written pages, he read it again. It was as if she was actually in the room speaking to him. Thank God he hadn't posted his letter as now what he wrote would be quite different.

He wanted to share this amazing news with his mother but she was out. He'd agreed to keep an eye on Nan and it must be more than an hour since he'd done so.

The front room door – now her bedroom – was open and he heard movement. He was still some distance away when she came out and saw him approaching on his crutches.

'There you are, Sam, I was coming to find you.'

He almost dropped a crutch. 'Nan, I'm sorry, I'm here now. I can't make you a cup of tea but Mum will be back soon.'

She smiled. 'I'd make us one but I don't think I know how to do it any more. Are you coming to sit with me?'

'I certainly am. I've just had a letter from my fiancée. Would you like me to read it to you?'

She didn't answer but returned to her room. When he got there, she was back in her armchair by the fire. She looked at him blankly – the few moments of lucidity gone. Coming as they had just after what he considered to be his miraculous letter, he thought it was a good omen.

He read her the letter and she appeared to be listening but didn't speak again. 'Shall I put the wireless on for you? I think there should be something to listen to.'

She understood and looked at the table where the wireless sat. It took a while for the valves to warm up and then there was the crackling and hissing as he twiddled the knobs to find the programme.

Eventually the room was filled with the lovely voice of Vera Lynn singing the 'The White Cliffs of Dover' and he turned to say how much he liked this song, but Nan had fallen asleep. He turned it down and folded into the armchair opposite hers to read his letter for the umpteenth time. Ruth had put the address of the OCTU which was handy so he could write directly to her.

She'd said in her letter that she didn't want to be an officer but thought that she'd better keep that information to herself, then in a couple of weeks she'd inform those in charge that she wanted to be able to use her skills and not just be doing administrative work and looking after the welfare and discipline of those under her command.

He thought that with the invasion likely to take place next year or the year after they'd be desperate to have as many trained ATS girls behind the guns as possible so the men could be released to go abroad.

Things had been exciting during the Blitz but now the only bombing was of cities and not RAF bases. He agreed with Ruth – he also wanted to do something active, not be spending his time doing drills and keeping his section in fighting shape, even though they weren't going to be doing any actual fighting.

Obviously, gunners would be wanted on the front line eventually, but he wouldn't know whether his unit would be going until the invasion plans were completed. Before he'd met Ruth, he'd have been first in line volunteering but now things were different – he wasn't a coward but remaining in Blighty protecting the home front did seem the better option.

* * *

Sam fed his grandmother and didn't leave her until she was comfortably settled on her bed, before going to the kitchen to have his own dinner. Although there had been no further signs of mental clarity, she did seem happier and her skin was definitely brighter and healthier looking.

'She's sleeping, Mum, and I hope you've got plenty of the casserole I gave her as it smelt really tasty.'

'I'll dish it up now, love, sit yourself down. I expect you want to know what happened to Ada.' She didn't wait for his reply but continued as she scooped out a bowlful of the rabbit stew. 'Three of her children have gone down with the chickenpox so she couldn't leave them. She couldn't send a message as the older children had already left for school.'

'That's a shame. Is she still going to come when they're back on their feet?'

'She certainly is. She's going to pop along after tea to see what's what. Even if she doesn't do a lot with your nan then she'll still be doing the cleaning and that. It'll make my life so much easier. The business is ever so busy and it's a job to keep up with all the bills and invoices.'

'I've got some good news for you. I'm officially engaged to Bombardier Ruth Cox – I wasn't sure how things were between us until I got her letter this morning. She said she'll come and see you as soon as she gets sufficient leave.'

He deliberately didn't mention that Ruth was currently training to be an officer as he knew what his mum's reaction would be. She'd say that he shouldn't marry out of his class as it would never work, she'd also say that having a fiancée who was an officer when he was only a senior NCO would be a recipe for disaster.

Time enough to tell her all the details if Ruth actually completed the training, which seemed unlikely after reading the letter.

* * *

Ruth finished breakfast, nodded at the other girls at the table and left them to it. She needed to speak to the officer in charge and find out where she was going to be sleeping tonight.

She smiled as she hurried into the central hall where the offices were – her letter to Sam had gone from the table and would now be winging its way to him. Thank goodness he'd given her his home address so it could go directly and not meander around the country until it found him.

The clerks, telephonists and typists were already at their posts so she feared she was tardy announcing herself.

'Excuse me, I'm Bombardier Cox and I arrived at midnight last night so I'm not sure that I'm officially here,' she said to a smart young woman sitting at the desk nearest to the door.

Before the girl could answer, a plummy female voice called from an open door at the far end of the large room. 'Come in, Cox, I was beginning to think that you might be a figment of Captain McAllister's imagination.'

Ruth marched to the room and saluted in the doorway. Facing her behind the desk was a woman of middle years, short grey hair and a friendly smile, which was unexpected.

'Bombardier Cox reporting for duty, ma'am.'

'Yes, I can see that you are. Sit down and explain to me why you've arrived more than two days before we're expecting you.'

Ruth sat on the only chair, which was as far away from the desk as it could possibly be. As her bottom touched the seat, she realised she should have brought the chair to the desk. Now, in order to converse with her commanding officer, she'd have to raise her voice.

Which would be worse? Getting up again and moving the chair or remaining where she was? She rose smoothly to her feet and carried the chair across the room and placed it in front of the desk. This pantomime had been watched with amusement.

'Good girl, you made the right decision – eventually. I am Senior Commander Bartholomew.'

'The senior commander at Regent's Park sent me early as otherwise I would have had to find a bed and breakfast for three nights.' This information didn't go down well as the friendly smile had been replaced by a frown.

'I made it quite clear I was quite happy to do that, but the senior commander insisted and I couldn't disobey a direct order.'

'Hmm!' She looked a little less disapproving. 'I think it was remiss of her to not to have spoken to me first but there you are – or rather I should say, "here you are", as it's a fait accompli for both of us.'

Ruth wasn't sure if she was supposed to answer or remain silent so nodded enthusiastically and this seemed to be sufficient.

'Where did you sleep last night?'

'In the recreation room, ma'am, my kitbag's in there now behind the sofa.'

'Unacceptable. In fact, as this cadre started four days ago, you are already disgracefully late. Fortunately for you, one of the girls has been obliged to leave as her father is dangerously ill. You can take her place. If she hadn't left yesterday then I would have sent you away. This isn't a good start, Cox, and I don't understand why anybody would think it acceptable to send you here without checking that there was space for you.'

'I apologise for my unwanted arrival. If I'm not expected, not on your list, then I assume that I'm free to leave and return to my section?'

'You're here now, and despite your unorthodox arrival, you have shown resourcefulness and backbone. You will remain here. Lance Corporal Smith will take your details and show you to your billet.'

'Yes, ma'am. Thank you, ma'am.'

'You have a quarter of an hour to put away your kit correctly before the lecture starts. Make sure that you're not late for that.'

The last thing Ruth wanted was to be placed with the group of girls she'd already met but she feared that was where she was going. It was unlikely that more than one girl had left for compassionate reasons.

Sharing a dormitory with those girls wasn't going to be a pleasant experience but as she'd already established her authority, maybe it wouldn't be so bad.

She saluted, about turned, and marched out. The girl at the front desk swivelled in her chair and beckoned her over.

'Actually, Bombardier Cox, I've got your details. Captain McAllister left them with me. You do realise that you're joining the course late so will have missed several lectures? The officers must think a lot of you to have allowed you to stay.'

'I hope so as I've already got several black marks against my name.'

'I'm sure you'll soon erase them. You're with C group. I expect you'll find them.'

'Was the girl who left called Penny?'

'Yes, how on earth did you know that?'

'I've already met them – I had breakfast with them.'

* * *

Ruth was escorted to a room conveniently close to the bathroom and WC in which there were only two iron-framed beds. One was made up, the other not. There was an actual mattress on both of them, which was a relief as it meant she didn't have to stack the 'biscuits' every morning.

'You're sharing with Sergeant Ramsay, she's not in your group but I don't suppose that matters. NCOs don't have to share with the privates.'

'Thank you, I'll let you get back to your duties. I know where the lecture hall is.'

Ruth was used to unpacking speedily and was on her way downstairs with five minutes to spare. The chairs had been arranged in four groups of ten and she headed for the one with the empty seat.

When she arrived, the girls stood up as Captain McAllister strode in. Everybody saluted, he returned the gesture and then waved them back into their seats.

There then followed a lecture on the subject of dealing with any disciplinary matters that they might encounter. As she hadn't attended the corporal's cadre as most NCOs did, she was interested and listened closely. Most of it was common sense but McAllister had a dry sense of humour and was an excellent speaker and the two hours passed relatively quickly.

During the latter half of the lecture, the captain shot quickfire questions and most of the girls were able to answer immediately. They'd obviously been listening as closely as she had.

'Right, A and B groups, you will return here after

the break. C and D, you will report to the gym dressed appropriately. Dismissed.'

Ruth now had the tricky task of attempting to meld into her group. She'd no idea where the gym was so had to remain with at least one of them if she wasn't going to get lost.

As they trooped out, the unpleasant dark-haired girl and her five acolytes rushed off together, leaving her with the remaining three.

'I'm Ruth, I didn't tell you my first name earlier. I hope we don't refer to each other by our surnames here.'

'Some do, some don't,' a pleasant girl with frizzy brown hair said with a smile. 'I'm Maisie, welcome to C group. As you've no doubt realised, it's not a particularly harmonious one.'

'Never mind, as long as the three of you are happy to speak to me then that's a start. I was intending to change first and then if there's time grab a cuppa – is that what you usually do?'

The three exchanged a glance. 'No, this is the first time we've had to go there. We do have morning exercises but that's before breakfast, not in the middle of the day,' Maisie said.

They agreed getting changed first made sense. Ruth discovered that these three were sharing with the other six on the floor below her. It didn't take her long to put on the hideous pink top, divided skirt and plimsolls and she was waiting outside the dormitory when the others emerged.

'We've still got twelve minutes – time enough to gulp down a cup of tea,' Ruth said and they agreed. 'Is the gym far from the dining hall?'

'Five minutes – it's outside – so that gives us seven minutes,' Maisie said with a grin.

'Plenty of time, the tea's always tepid,' said Emma, a pretty girl with her hair in plaits around her head.

They gulped down their tea standing up and raced to the gym, where Ruth spotted a grim-faced male sergeant was waiting for them. There was no sign of the others but there was still three minutes to go – Ruth prayed they'd arrive in time as she really didn't want anybody, even them, to be put on a charge.

'Let's wait out here, girls, and go in together. It would be better if we didn't look as though we were early and the others are late.'

'I'm not getting put on fatigues for them,' Hannah said crossly.

'I don't think they'd put all ten of us on a charge, do you?' Ruth replied, hoping she was right.

She checked her watch – thirty seconds and they'd all be late. Then the missing six pounded up to them.

'In file, ladies, we'll march in,' Ruth snapped and they obeyed her. She led the girls into the gym, marched them to the front and stood at ease. One by one, the others followed suit so that they were standing facing the sergeant.

23

Sam avoided any contact with his grandfather. Not just because of the knife incident but because hitting Nan was unforgivable. Ada had duly appeared and recognised him at once.

'Why, bless my soul, if it ain't little Sam all grown up and handsome,' she exclaimed on seeing him in the kitchen.

'Good to see you, Mrs Brown. You're looking well.'

'Ta, love, I'm fighting fit. Can't say the same for you. Never mind, nice for your ma and pa to have you home for a bit. I ain't seen my George or my Sid since they went off to Africa last year.'

'I'm hoping to serve overseas when the invasion starts.'

'You stop in Blighty, son, your ma's already got two in the thick of it.'

Mum put the second-best cosy on the brown china tea pot and put it on the table. 'There's some nice broken biscuits I managed to get at the Co-op yesterday to go with it. They all taste the same and are half the price.'

Ada drank her tea and returned to the front room, where she was doing the ironing whilst keeping Nan company.

'Ada gets on famously with Nan, and she's going to be here every day apart from Sunday. This wouldn't have happened if you'd not come home, love, and things will be so much easier from now on.'

'Does Grandpa know about this yet?'

His mother smiled nervously. 'He's hardly in the house during the day and Ada goes at four o'clock so with any luck he won't even notice.'

Sam frowned. 'He'd better not kick up a fuss or he'll have me to answer to.'

'Your dad will take care of that, love, you don't have to be involved. By the way, you haven't given me your ration book and I need it. I'll just nip up and get it if you tell me where it is.'

'I'm sorry, Mum, I didn't get a chance to collect it when I left so I've written to ask them to send it. I've also got a letter for Ruth – do you think you could nip down the post office with them? I hate asking you, but it would take me all afternoon to get there and back at the speed I go on these crutches.'

'I've got a WVS meeting in the village hall later, so I'll do it then. Have you and your Ruth decided on a date?'

'Good God, not yet. We've only just got engaged and I haven't given her a ring yet.'

She smiled and lifted the lid of the silver-plated tea caddy that had belonged to her mother and re-moved something. 'Here you are, love, it was my mum's ring and she wanted you to have it for your girl.'

He flicked open the little leather box and his eyes widened. 'Blimey, is this a real diamond?'

'Yes, if your grandfather had known that I'd got it he would have insisted that I sold it. Even your dad hasn't seen it. My dad died young and my mum never really got over it. She died just after you were born. She gave it to me then and said to keep it for you.'

'This must be worth a fortune. Ruth will be over the moon to have it but I don't think she'll be able to wear it whilst she's in the army. I'll keep it safe for her.'

He couldn't wait to slip it on Ruth's finger, make

things really official and doing so with a family heir-loom made it even better.

* * *

Later Sam was reading the newspaper – Ada was in with Nan, Mum had gone down the village and Dad was out on a job – and he had the kitchen to himself. He'd make a pot of tea for the three of them – he reckoned he could manage that if he was careful – and then let Ada know it was done so she could collect it.

He was at the sink in the scullery filling the kettle, precariously balanced on one leg with his crutches resting on either side of him when the back door crashed open. His grandfather barrelled into the room, sending him flying.

The miserable old sod didn't apologise or stop to help him but stormed through the house yelling the odds. Sam heaved himself up and went after him. His grandfather had obviously just found out about Ada and wasn't happy about it.

He was haranguing the poor women and making the most god-awful threats. Sam almost went headfirst through the front room door he was in such a hurry. Ada was standing in front of Nan's armchair, protecting her.

'Get out of my way, you interfering old witch, or I'll make you.'

His grandfather was about to grab hold of Ada and Sam acted instinctively. He balanced on one crutch and his good leg, reversed the other and shoved it into the old bastard, sending him sprawling on the carpet.

'Ada, Mrs Brown, take Nan into the kitchen and block the door. I'll deal with this,' Sam said and placed himself in front of their abuser. He didn't recognise the man hauling himself to his feet, his cheeks scarlet with rage, his eyes almost popping out of his head and, more worryingly, his big fists were clenched.

'Get out of my way, what happens between a man and his wife is nobody's business but theirs,' his grandfather snarled.

'No, you're wrong. Nan's not well, she needs help and so do you. For God's sake, get a grip, man, you're supposed to be a pillar of the church. What do you think they'd say if they saw you now?'

Sam thought his words were working, that he was calming things down, but he was wrong. Without warning, his grandfather surged forward, fists flailing, and Sam barely had time to defend himself.

He received a crashing punch on the shoulder, which almost knocked him off his feet for a second time. He really didn't want to hurt his attacker, but the man was berserk. If he didn't stop him then he might well seriously injure the ladies hiding in the kitchen.

He acted on instinct. Desperately he swung the free crutch at the man's knees and it did the trick. His grandfather went down and this time he didn't get up, he lay on his back gasping and clutching his chest. Sam thought the old man was possibly having a heart attack.

* * *

Two hours later, the ambulance, the local bobby and Ada had gone, leaving just his parents and himself in the house.

'Do you think Nan will be all right?' Sam asked.

'Dr Wyndham said it was just precautionary, son, and my dad's as strong as an ox, he'll be back on his feet in no time,' Dad replied.

'You can't have him back, you know that, don't you? He's seriously unbalanced and dangerous. If I hadn't been here, he might have killed both Ada and Nan.'

His mum was crying quietly, wiping her eyes on her handkerchief, and he reached out and squeezed her hand. 'Neither of them can help what's happening to them, Mum, and it's certainly not your fault. Grandpa needs to be somewhere safe...'

'My dad's not going in a lunatic asylum, son, so don't suggest it. Dr Wyndham said he'll be in hospital for a week or two. I'm going to get the workshop finished so he can move in there. He won't need to come into the house at all – I'll change the locks and put a bolt on the doors as well.'

Mum sighed loudly. 'I'll pray that his heart attack will have changed him for the better. He's always been a domineering, bad-tempered man but as far as I know has never been violent until recently.'

'If he's prowling about outside, Mum and Mrs Brown won't be able to leave the house safely when you're at work. You can't take the risk, Dad.'

'I suppose you're right, son, but I don't have to make any decisions for a while. Do you think that Mrs Brown will come back after what happened today?'

'Yes, she's indomitable. A bit of argy-bargy won't put her off. Now, it will have to be egg and chips as I've not had time to do anything else,' Mum said as she tied her pinny round her waist.

Sam didn't have much appetite but as Mum had gone to the trouble to cook, he forced the meal down. His shoulder was sore where he'd been struck but the doctor had assured him it was just bruised. With his right arm out of action, he was unable to use his crutches. God knows how he was going to get to bed later.

'You sleep in Nan's bed tonight, son, you'll not be able to manage those stairs until your shoulder's better,' his dad said.

'Thanks, I'll sleep on top of the covers so no need to change the sheets, Mum.'

'Right, love, that'll be a help.'

Sam now had to hop on his good leg and balance against the wall with his uninjured arm. He made his way to the bog and as he emerged, he overheard his parents talking.

'I know I said it was good that Sam came home but now I'm thinking that if he hadn't then none of this would have happened,' Mum was saying and he leaned against the wall, shocked by her words but knowing they were probably true.

* * *

Ruth stared ahead, not directly at the fierce-looking sergeant standing with his hands behind his back and not a glimmer of welcome on his face. From the corner of her eye, she could see the other nine cadets doing as she was. Maybe this wasn't going to be as awful as she'd feared.

As the silence lengthened, she was tempted to introduce herself but something told her it was better to remain silent, let him speak first. This was obviously a test of some sort, but heaven knows what of.

She was thrilled that not one girl fidgeted; they all stood at ease as she was. When their instructor spoke, his voice was loud and she almost jumped.

'Good show, ladies. Punctual to the second, professional and disciplined. C group is the one to beat.'

The tension evaporated and when she glanced sideways, the others, like herself, were smiling. There followed a rigorous and exhausting hour of exercise but they performed the manoeuvres as instructed and at the end they lined up as they had at the start.

Sarge pointed at Ruth. 'You're new. Where have you appeared from?'

'I was sent to replace the private who left. Bombardier Cox, Sarge.' Not true, but it satisfied him.

Finally, he almost smiled. 'Mixed RA. Good show. Dismissed.'

Ruth was about to congratulate the group for doing so well but to her dismay the six who'd arrived late rushed off without a backward glance.

'Don't take any notice of Priscilla and her clique,

Ruth, we know what you did saved them from being put on a charge,' Maisie said cheerfully.

'I really didn't expect to meet such animosity here. We're training to be officers, for heaven's sake, we're not in the playground. If those six can't behave like leaders, they shouldn't be here.' Ruth shivered. 'Shall we get out of these hideous garments? It will be lunch time soon.'

* * *

Things didn't improve over the meal. Priscilla made sure none of those in her group spoke to Ruth but pointedly included Maisie, Emma and Joan. This made it difficult for the three she'd made friends with to talk to her. By the end of the meal, she was determined to sort this nonsense out.

There was no time before the next lecture, which all four groups were to attend. There was a fifteen-minute break after the two hours of lectures and Ruth headed for the CO's office. She was able to speak to the senior commander immediately.

'My arrival in group C has upset the dynamics. I fully understand, ma'am, that as officer cadets we must get on with everyone, behave correctly, but I wondered if I could possibly be moved to the other group, D, that appears to be missing a member.'

'Exactly what do you mean by dynamics, Cox?'

'I'm an NCO, am a kinetheodolite operator as well as being trained to use a predictor and range finder. The others have come straight from basic training.'

This didn't exactly answer the question but it made the point that she didn't fit.

'Sergeant Mather was impressed with your control of the group. Private Hadleigh is the one that I'll move. I don't suppose you're aware that she's the daughter of a senior government minister and this has given her the erroneous assumption that she's a natural leader.'

Ruth was shocked that this personal information had been revealed so readily. Surely personal details should be confidential.

'Thank you, ma'am, but...'

'No, Cox, the matter's settled. Dismissed.'

Ruth saluted and marched out, horrified that her impulsive rush to complain was just going to make things worse. Moving Priscilla would create problems elsewhere and then there would be two unhappy groups.

She'd only been in the office for a couple of minutes so had ample time to join the rest of the cadets in the rec room. She was immediately accosted by Maisie, Emma and Joan.

'I've just heard that it's our turn to clean the ablutions and latrines tomorrow. I don't understand why we have to do that sort of thing? Aren't we training to be officers?'

'I suppose they think we need to do the tasks those under our command are doing to understand the demands,' Ruth said.

This wasn't strictly true as she was well aware that once promoted, she wouldn't be doing anything more taxing than supervising the girls who did the real work.

'I've spoken to the senior commander and asked to be put in a different group.'

'Oh, no, that would be an absolute disaster,' Maisie interrupted. 'We've been so miserable since we arrived three days ago and all because of Priscilla. Today's the first time things have been all right.'

'Actually, my request was refused. They know about Priscilla and she's the one being transferred.' Ruth frowned. 'I'm not sure that will make any difference as the other five will continue to be difficult and not want to include me in the group.'

'If she has to move from our billet then those others will soon come round,' Emma said.

'I hope your optimism isn't misplaced,' Ruth said as they returned to the lecture hall for the remainder of the day.

* * *

That night, she met the sergeant she was sharing with and immediately liked Molly Fergerson.

'I'm delighted to meet you, Ruth, I'm in A group, and thank God for it. The private you had moved to D is already making life difficult for them. I admire your courage. I warn you there'll be repercussions. Her father and uncle are something big in the government and the War Office.'

'I asked to be moved but the CO insisted I stay and she go. To be honest, I'm not sure I want to be an officer, I'd rather become a warrant officer instead.' Ruth was regretting her decision to come to OCT and things had just got worse.

* * *

The next morning, after all the groups had competed a five-mile run, they had twenty minutes to shower and appear for breakfast. There were four NCOs in this cadre and they shared a separate two-shower unit and this meant they were on their way to eat before a lot of the privates had had their turn.

'Bombardier Cox, you're wanted immediately in the CO's office,' Ruth was told as she reached the dining hall.

As she marched through the building, she asked the clerk if she knew what it was about.

'There's been hell to pay since yesterday. I'm afraid you're going to be sent packing.'

Ruth shrugged. 'I shouldn't have interfered. Having me dismissed won't improve things for that girl, it will make her even more unpopular. To be honest, I hope she fails this cadre. She'll make the worst kind of officer.'

Ruth straightened her shoulders and marched, head high, into the senior commander's office. She'd expected to be greeted by a grim face, disapproval, but what she saw was sympathy.

'Come in, my dear, this is most unfortunate. I have no option but to dismiss you from the course. It's not what I want or what should be happening, but my hands are tied,' Senior Commander Bartholomew said.

'I understand, ma'am. Do I have to leave right now? Do you know where my section is now based?'

'Sit down, and I'll explain how things are going to

be.' She waited until Ruth was settled and then continued. 'You are to be promoted to sergeant as from now. You will be able to progress to WO2, but sadly no further.'

Ruth beamed. Her heart was pounding, she was overjoyed at this unexpected and very welcome news. 'That's the best news, ma'am. I had decided I'd rather be a warrant officer than a subaltern or commander. About my next posting?'

'You have a week's leave and then will join the mixed RA at Regent's Park.' Ruth could hardly believe how well things were turning out. She could go and see Sam and then have the perfect job in the perfect place.

'Thank you, I'll go to my fiancé in St Albans.'

'Run along, my dear, and get packed. Captain McAllister is travelling to London first thing. You can get a lift to the station with him, but it will be at seven.'

Ruth couldn't believe her luck. Getting a lift tomorrow would make things so much smoother.

* * *

The following morning, her new stripes proudly displayed on her sleeve, Ruth was standing in the hall waiting for the one-armed captain. He didn't seem pleased to see her, which surprised her as she'd thought they'd got on rather well in the kitchen the other night.

'It seems, Sergeant, that I am to give you a lift in my staff car.'

'Yes, sir. I'll sit in the front with the driver, of course.'

'Absolutely not. Come on, I have a train to catch.'

The short journey from the OCT centre to the station had been silent and awkward. It had been a relief to both of them when she was able to scuttle off to third class and leave him to travel in first with the officers and businesspeople.

She fought her way onto the train and was able to squash in a corner of the narrow corridor. At least there wouldn't be a problem knowing when to get off as the soldier she was next to told her he was alighting at St Albans. She hadn't realised that it stopped there until she'd enquired at the ticket office for the best way to get there.

She perched on her upturned kitbag, chatting to the friendly men travelling with her, and this made the journey seem short. She soon realised that as she was a sergeant, they'd had no option but to be polite.

Would Sam be as happy to see her as she would be to see him? What would he think about her being the same rank as him and the reason she'd been thrown out of the OCTU?

On enquiring from the guard at St Albans, she was told the street she wanted was about a fifteen-minute walk away. She hefted her bag onto her shoulder and marched away, her heart pounding, not from exertion, but from the excitement and anticipation of the forth-coming reunion with her beloved Sam.

24

Sam was tempted to retire without speaking to his
parents but he couldn't leave them thinking he was to
blame.

'Mum, Dad, we need to talk about this.'

Mum dropped a teaspoon on the quarry tiles and
the tinkle was loud in the silence. Dad was the first to
recover.

'You shouldn't have heard that, son, we don't really
blame you. My dad was a timebomb waiting to ex-
plode and God help us, it might have been so much
worse. Now we know what's what and can deal
with it.'

'What about you, Mum? Do you agree with Dad?'

She wiped her eyes on the corner of her pinny and

hurried across to embrace him. 'Of course I do, love. We're just shocked, that's all. You have to admit, you being here started things off...'

'That's enough, Alice, Sam being here's the best thing that's happened for years. Neither of us knew how bad things were with my dad, and Nan was slowly starving to death until Sam thought to feed her.'

His parents never argued and them doing so was down to him. He'd always thought his mum was bi-ased towards him, but he'd obviously got that wrong. Like a lot of things lately.

'Look, my being here has stirred things up. You'll be better off without me causing problems and making extra work. I'll find somewhere else to recu-perate. There are places for us soldiers, I'll make en-quiries tomorrow.'

He waited hopefully for one or other of them to disagree, to ask him to stay, but they didn't. Sadly, he hopped off to Nan's room and closed the door qui-etly behind him. He couldn't leave until he'd heard from Ruth, and it would almost certainly take a day or two to organise his transfer to a convalescent home.

Dispirited, he flopped onto the armchair and closed his eyes. He was jerked from his sombre thoughts when the door flew open and both his parents burst in.

'We're ever so sorry, love, we shouldn't have let you go off thinking we don't want you here,' Mum said, her eyes red. He hated that she'd been crying again.

Dad bundled in behind her and looked equally upset. 'We want you to stay, of course we do, son. It's been a difficult day, but none of it's your doing. We should have acted years ago, then things wouldn't have got so bad.'

'Thanks for telling me. I still think that I'll not stay for more than another week. I promise I'll not leave it so long to visit. I'm stationed on a base near Lincoln, bit of a trek, but I could be moved a bit closer, you never know.'

'You do as you think's right, son, this is your home, same as it is ours,' Dad said. 'Your ration book's going to be chasing you all over the shop if you don't wait for it to come.'

Sam was surprised that his dad even knew about the missing ration book. 'Good point, Dad, I'll definitely stay until I've heard from Ruth and I've got my ration book.'

They said their goodnights and left him to remove his one boot, his outer garments and then drop onto the vacant bed and pull over the candlewick bedspread and eiderdown. His mind was made up – he wasn't going to be here when his grandfather returned.

The next morning, an official-looking brown envelope dropped onto the mat just as he was making his way to the kitchen. He was getting better at balancing with his crutches and leaned down easily to pick it up. The letter was addressed to him.

'Was that the post, love?'

'Yes, Mum, it was – I think it's my ration book.'

She appeared in the door. 'I expect they'd already sent it and your letters crossed. Your dad's already busy in the workshop and Ada's two lads turned up ever so early and were very keen to work.'

'With any luck, Dad can show them what they have to do and leave them to it whilst he goes off to do his paying jobs.' Sam took his usual seat at the table. 'Do you mind if I open this before I have my porridge?'

'You go ahead, love, porridge will keep.'

Sam carefully opened the envelope and pulled out the contents. His ration book was in the envelope and he smiled and didn't immediately read the letter that accompanied it. 'Here you are, you were right, Mum. Don't hand it in as I won't be here that long, but you can use my coupons until I go.'

She took it from his hand and then nodded at the other papers. 'What's all that then? Seems a lot of official-looking writing just to send you a ration book.'

Sam frowned. She was right. He picked up the papers and his eyes widened. The letters danced in front of his eyes and it took him a few minutes to understand what he was seeing.

These were his discharge papers. With growing incredulity, he read the letter. He was now considered unfit for duty and was being medically discharged with a pension.

'What's wrong, love? You've gone white as a sheet.'

'I've been chucked out of the army, Mum, they say I'm no longer able to do my job, which is absolute bollocks...'

'Sam! Don't use language like that in my house.'

'I'm sorry, but I'm upset and angry and don't understand. I've got a cracked ankle, I've not had my leg amputated. There's something else going on here.'

He had a horrible suspicion this *something* was connected to that Arthur bloke, that one of his influential friends was involved. He slumped against the table, dropped his head in his hands, and closed his eyes.

What the hell was he going to do now? He didn't want to stay here and couldn't go to an army convalescent home. The pension was just enough to scrape by on and he had a few pounds in his post office book. Money wasn't the problem – being thrown on the scrapheap, being considered useless by the army, was.

Slowly his head cleared and he began to see a way forward. 'Don't look so worried, Mum, I'm all right now. It was just a bit of a shock. As soon as I'm out of this plaster, I'll re-enlist – I'm not keen on the sea, so I'll try the boys in blue.'

'Oh, love, don't do that. You've got a trade, you've done your bit, when you're better you can help your dad. After all, the business will be yours and your brother's eventually anyway.'

He was going to tell her that wasn't an option, that as long as his grandfather was alive he couldn't live here or work with his dad, but thought there'd been enough shocks for one day.

'I'm not rushing into anything, I'll just make a few enquiries. I don't have the education to be a pilot. As far as I know, it's only public-school and grammar-school boys but maybe they aren't so fussy now.'

'There's two families I know that have lost sons in the RAF. Mary Forrester has lost both her boys.'

'And I'm sure there were more families that lost sons and fathers at Dunkirk, Mum. Folk die in a war and a lot of them are civilians.'

Sam finished his breakfast and wanted time to himself. The sitting room was vacant but he thought he'd venture outside. He was a dab hand with his crutches and thought he could make his way through the neighbourhood without falling on his face.

He was pleasantly surprised that so many of his neighbours were pleased to see him – of course the boys he'd gone to school with were away fighting – but there were plenty of others ready to spend five minutes chatting about how his leg came to be in plaster.

By late morning, his leg ached and he was more than ready to return home. As he paused to open the front gate, he heard running footsteps and somebody calling his name.

He turned so fast he lost his balance and was about to fall into the hedge.

* * *

Ruth just managed to grab Sam's arm and keep him upright. 'I didn't mean to scare you to death, my love, but I can't tell you how pleased I am to see you.'

His smile was blinding. He reached out a tentative hand as if he couldn't quite believe she was real. 'I've had the most bloody awful news but now I don't care. You're here, we can work it out together.'

She stepped into his waiting arms and they kissed. They were both breathless and pink-cheeked when they finally drew apart.

'I'm sorry to arrive unannounced. I can find a B & B somewhere if there's no room here.'

'You're not going anywhere. I'm not letting you out of my sight. I've got so much to tell you but first there's something I've got to give you.'

He leaned against the gate and removed a small leather box from an inside pocket. 'This belonged to my grandmother on my mum's side. It was her dying wish that it be given to me for my fiancée.'

He flipped the lid back and she stared, scarcely able to believe what she was looking at. 'This is beautiful, but it's far too valuable for me to wear even around my neck on a chain.' She held out her hand. 'I'll wear it when we're together, but will you keep it safe for me when we're not?'

He slipped it over her knuckle and it fitted perfectly as if made for her. 'I love it and I love you. Don't you want to know what I'm doing here?'

'I do, but I've got other news that can't wait. There's a bench in the churchyard just up the road where we can sit and talk. I don't want to introduce you until we've talked as we won't get a word in edgeways once my mum sees you.'

'Would it be all right if I dumped my kitbag be-hind the hedge? Seems silly to keep carrying it if I don't have to.'

His answer was to pick it up and throw it over one-handed. She laughed and so did he.

* * *

They sat on the bench and she told him how she came to be in St Albans and why she wasn't still being trained to be an officer in Leicester. Then he told her about what had happened with his grandparents. This was bad enough, but the devastating news he'd just received was even worse.

'This is something to do with the two people you've upset recently. It could be linked to the traffic accident but I think it's more likely to be to do with Arthur.'

'The more I think about it, the surer I am that this is his revenge.' He took her hands and looked at her seriously. Her stomach clenched. Whatever he was about to tell her wasn't good news and she thought she'd had enough of the bad already.

'I'm going to see if I can be aircrew. If I can't be a pilot then I could be a navigator, bomb aimer or rear gunner.'

She couldn't hide her horror. 'Please don't, we both know how many aircrew are being killed every day. People need builders as much as they need pilots. You could be an air-raid warden, a firefighter, join the observation corps, there are plenty of ways you can do your bit for the war effort without joining the RAF.'

'I'll think about it, but it's not as simple as you think. After what's happened, there's no way I'm going to work with my dad whilst my grandfather's alive.'

'Then come to London with me. You'll find plenty of work there of one sort or another. It's just occurred to me that maybe you could join the police force? Does that appeal to you?'

He looked thoughtful. 'I don't fancy being a regular bobby, the sort that marches the streets, but I think I'd make a good detective.'

'Then that's settled. I'll stay here tonight and then we can go to London together. Do you have to return your uniform?'

'It didn't say anything about that in the letter, but I'm not entitled to wear it so it's no use to me. God knows if I've got any civilian clothes in the wardrobe at home that still fit me.'

'I don't care about your clothes, there's bound to be something you can wear, or something your mother can alter to fit.'

'Sod the clothes, I want to ask you a question. I haven't quite made up my mind what I'm going to do next, love, but if I decide not to re-enlist, would you consider getting married immediately?'

'No, but if you promise me now that you won't join the RAF then I'll absolutely marry you as soon as we can get a licence.'

He leaned across and lifted her easily so she was snuggled on his lap – highly unsuitable but she didn't care. 'Then it's no contest. Being your husband trumps being a Brylcreem boy any day of the week.'

'I don't have any family but I do have several really good friends. I'd like them to be at the wedding. What about your family?'

'I'd like them to be there, but my brother and sister are unlikely to get the leave. I'm not sure that my parents would come to anything but a church wedding. I'm assuming that we're talking about doing it at a registry office?'

'I don't want a white dress and all that nonsense. I'll be married in my uniform. Don't you think we'd better tell your parents that I'm here and that we're getting married in London in a few weeks?'

He grinned, kissed her again, and then she scrambled off his lap. 'It's all very well talking about getting married but maybe you won't get the time off.'

'I think if I'm married I'm allowed to live off site when I'm not on active duty. I don't suppose things will be any different at Regent's Park. Also, don't forget we get thirty-six hours every ten days and an evening off as well. I'm sure we can fit our wedding plans into my schedule.'

He could move smoothly on his crutches and although they couldn't hold hands, she walked close beside him. She was so lucky to have met this wonderful man and even luckier that she would soon be Mrs Johnson, have a legitimate name, and could finally move on from her unfortunate birth.

'I love you so much, my darling, and I'm going to be the best wife I possibly can.'

He pulled her close, remaining balanced whilst he did so. He looked down at her, his smile told her everything she needed to know. 'I love you more, Sergeant Ruth Cox, and whatever happens next, we'll face it together.'

BIBLIOGRAPHY

Girls in Khaki by Barbara Green
Sergeant Elsie by M. Crossley
Sisters in Arms by Vee Robinson
Army Girls by Tessa Dunlop
Farming, Fighting and Family by Miranda McCormick
The Girls Who Went to War by Duncan Barrett and Nuala Green
Wartime Women by Dorothy Sheridan
The Girls Behind the Guns by Dorothy Brewer Kent
The Women's Royal Army Corps by Shelford Bidwell
A to Z Atlas Guide to London by Alexander Gross FRGS
Wartime Britain 1939–1945 by Juliet Gardiner
How We Lived Then by Norman Longmate
The War Illustrated News edited by Sir John Hammerton
BBC History Archives
It's a Long Way to Tooting Broadway by Reginald Cambridge
The War Diaries of Colin Dunford Wood edited by James Dunford
    Wood
*An Englishman at War: The Wartime Diaries of Stanley Christopherson
    DSO, MC, TD, 1939–45* edited by James Holland
Oxford Dictionary of Slang by John Ayto

ACKNOWLEDGEMENTS

I'd like to thank my readers everywhere who take the time to leave a review of my books. It really means a lot to me.

ABOUT THE AUTHOR

Fenella J. Miller is a bestselling writer of historical sagas. She also has a passion for Regency romantic adventures and has published over fifty to great acclaim.

Sign up to Fenella J. Miller's mailing list for news, competitions and updates on future books.

Visit Fenella's website: www.fenellajmiller.co.uk

Follow Fenella on social media here:

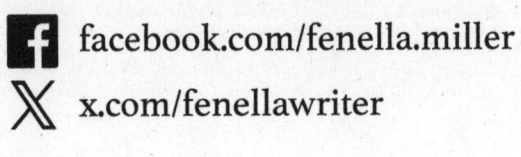

facebook.com/fenella.miller

x.com/fenellawriter

ALSO BY FENELLA J. MILLER

Goodwill House Series

The War Girls of Goodwill House

New Recruits at Goodwill House

Duty Calls at Goodwill House

The Land Girls of Goodwill House

A Wartime Reunion at Goodwill House

Wedding Bells at Goodwill House

A Christmas Baby at Goodwill House

The Army Girls Series

Army Girls Reporting For Duty

Army Girls: Heartbreak and Hope

Army Girls: Behind the Guns

The Pilot's Girl Series

The Pilot's Girl

A Wedding for the Pilot's Girl

A Dilemma for the Pilot's Girl

A Second Chance for the Pilot's Girl

Standalone

The Land Girl's Secret

Sixpence Stories

Introducing Sixpence Stories!

Discover page-turning historical novels from your favourite authors, meet new friends and be transported back in time.

Join our book club
Facebook group

https://bit.ly/SixpenceGroup

Sign up to our
newsletter

https://bit.ly/SixpenceNews

Boldwood

Boldwood Books is an award-winning fiction publishing company seeking out the best stories from around the world.

Find out more at www.boldwoodbooks.com

Join our reader community for brilliant books, competitions and offers!

Follow us
@BoldwoodBooks
@TheBoldBookClub

Sign up to our weekly
deals newsletter

https://bit.ly/BoldwoodBNewsletter

Milton Keynes UK
Ingram Content Group UK Ltd.
UKHW040650220424
441549UK00003B/37

9 781801 628945